The War Never Ends

by

Gary Ader

&

Tom Hooker

Escarpment Press
www.escarpmentpress.weebly.com
INDIAN LAND, SC

Dedication

The authors wish to dedicate this work to the brave Americans who served in uniform during the Vietnam conflict, and to those brave Americans who have fought and died in this country in the continuing battle for equal rights for all. For them, the war has not yet ended

1

Five-year-old Lastun Wicker knew right away that the thing he'd just picked up was not a stick. So he did three things; two of which probably saved his life. He blurted a word he'd heard his father use before, he dropped the thing, and he stumbled backward several steps. His charcoal skin broke out in goose bumps.

By dropping the snake, he deprived it of its chance to strike. With nothing to push against, it could only flail in the air until it hit the ground. By that time Lastun had moved out of the snake's striking range.

Lastun's sister, Daisy—older by two years—ambled over from where she'd been helping her brother collect deadfall to be used in the family woodstove. In Mississippi, the early March mornings were cool, another disadvantage for Lastun's snake.

"Mama hear you use words like that, you be spittin' soap bubbles for a week," Daisy said cradling her bundle of wood against her slim body.

"Sorry," Lastun said, though he wasn't.

"What was it?" Daisy continued.

"A snake."

"I know that, but what kind?"

"It didn't say."

Daisy made a farting sound with her mouth. "Probably a water moccasin. That's about all they is around here."

By around here, she meant the swampland that bordered the Yazoo River as it flowed past their home in Satartia on its way to merge with the Mississippi River in Vicksburg. Located about twelve miles southwest of Yazoo City and about fifteen miles northeast of Vicksburg, downtown Satartia consisted of a post office and Barney Kilgore's dry goods store. The Wicker home lay east of "town" on land owned by Al Connor.

"Good thing that snake didn't bite you," Daisy said. "If it didn't kill you, Papa would, after Mama got through with you first."

Lastun gave his sister a stern look. "I done picked up snakes before. If that snake hadda bit me, it woulda been sick for a week."

Daisy shrugged. "Can't argue with that." Leaving Lastun to wonder if she'd turned his jibe around on him.

They finished loading Lastun's hand-me-down Radio Flyer wagon with deadfall and pulled it back to the house. After they unloaded the wagon's contents into the wood bin, they called Mama to allow her to pass judgment.

Shandra Wicker inspected the results of their morning's work and made a show of assessing the weather.

"I reckon it'll do. Not much cold weather left," she opined. Her body had thickened and grown heavy as the result of birthing eight children. Lastun was the last one, hence his name.

"Lastun, time to collect them eggs," she ordered.

"Yessum."

Lastun was too young to do the field work his father and two older brothers did, sharecropping for Mr. Connor—so his job was to do chores around the house, like collecting firewood and eggs, and helping in the garden.

Egg-collecting duties included keeping track of where the hens made their nests. He grabbed a straw basket lined with grass from the back porch and set out on his tour of the yard.

There was no coop enclosing the fowl. They roamed the yard and outlying fields, feasting on grass seed and the

2

occasional insect. They had the good sense to watch out for hawks and strange dogs. At night, the chickens found roosting spots under the eaves of the tool shed, corn crib, or other high perches to ensure that foxes and skunks couldn't get them or their eggs.

Lastun roamed around the open area, fishing brown eggs from their roosts.

He gave them to Daisy, who washed them in soapy water and dried them with a dishtowel made from an empty flour sack. Once washed and dried, she held each egg to her ear and gently shook it. She couldn't have described exactly what she was listening for, but if one sounded "off" she would have discarded it as bad. She put the good ones in a cane basket.

"Okay, Mama," Daisy hollered. "They ready to go."

"Kissy, come here with paper and pencil!" Mama commanded. Kissy, aged ten, was the only one of them who could write. "I need some flour, sugar, and tobacco."

Kissy's tongue protruded between her teeth as she painstakingly wrote each word. Quantities weren't necessary. Mr. Kilgore would know to send the smallest package available.

"Oh, and coffee," Mama added. "Awright, Lastun, take these eggs to Mr. Kilgore and swap them for the stuff on this list." A twinkle sprouted in her eye. "Tell him if they's any left over, jus' credit it to my next purchase."

"Ain't you comin'?" Lastun asked.

"Not this time. You can go on by yo'self."

"Yessum," Lastun said. He swallowed the lump in his throat as he took the eggs from Daisy and the paper from Kissy. He also picked up a brown cloth tow sack. He'd often accompanied Mama to the store, but had never gone alone. *A test.* How would he behave in the presence of the white storekeeper, and how would the white storekeeper treat him?

3

He walked out the front door of the weather-worn, unpainted house and down the dusty road. He didn't hurry. Time held little sway over the colored people of Satartia. Twenty minutes later, he arrived at Kilgore's store. It was also unpainted and weathered. Two round-shouldered gasoline pumps guarded the entrance, and a barrel of kerosene lay on its side on two saw-horse supports alongside the building. Assorted colorful tin signs hawking Winston cigarettes, Martha White flour, and Coca-Cola plastered the front and sides of the structure.

Lastun passed from the sunny outdoors into the darkened interior. A couple of bare light bulbs tried unsuccessfully to brighten things a bit. Dust motes floated in the pale rays of sunlight which passed through a pair of dingy windows.

Mr. Kilgore had the wide butt and saggy paunch of a man who worked too little and sat too much. He wore khaki pants and a long-sleeve khaki shirt, with the sleeves rolled up to expose his hairy forearms.

"Ain't you Abraham and Shandra Wicker's boy?" he asked.

"Yessuh," Lastun said, bobbing his head. He offered the basket of eggs and the shopping list. "Mama ast you to swap these eggs for the things on this paper. She say if they's any left over, jus' put it on her next purchase."

The same twinkle Lastun had seen in his Mama's eye now shone in Kilgore's. "She did, did she? Well, tell her if there's any left over, I'll put in on what she already owes."

From the twinkles he seen in the eyes of the one sending the message and the one receiving it, Lastun figured this was a running joke between the two. Mama would never have enough eggs to come out ahead on one of these transactions. Mr. Kilgore would add any deficit to the running tab he kept for the Wicker family—just as he did on every trustworthy poor family in Satartia, black or white. When Papa brought in his cotton crop and, after he'd paid his shares to Mr. Conner, the landowner, as well as the gin owner, the rest would go to settle his debt at the store. In a good year, Abraham Wicker might be able to square the debt, but he would never come out ahead.

Mr. Kilgore held the list up to the puny light. "Who wrote out this list? I can't hardly read it."

"Kissy, she wrote it. It say flour, sugar, tobacco . . . and coffee."

Mr. Kilgore gave Lastun an appraising look. "How old are you?"

"Five, suh."

"And you can read already?"

"Nossuh, I jus' heered Mama tell Kissy what to write." Kissy had been working with him on his letters, but he hadn't gotten very far yet.

"Hmmm . . ." Kilgore fished a cigarette from a pack in his shirt pocket and lit it. He began to transfer the eggs into a cardboard egg tray.

A cloud of dust accompanied the arrival of a black Chevy pickup outside. A grizzle-faced white man in bib overalls and a thin white woman in a flower-print house dress walked in. Mr. Kilgore immediately put aside Lastun's eggs and list.

"Good morning, Lee. Good morning, Mrs. Barr. How're y'all doing today?"

Following the example his mother had set in the many times Lastun had accompanied her on these trips, he silently faded toward the back of the store, where he stood in a dark corner, waiting.

Lee Barr ignored Kilgore and headed for the soda cooler, where he retrieved and de-capped a Pepsi-Cola. His eyes flicked over Lastun's small body before turning back to the storekeeper.

For the next fifteen minutes, Mr. Kilgore tended to the Barrs — answering questions, quoting prices, fetching merchandise, making small talk.

Lastun didn't exist, and wouldn't until the store was again empty of white customers.

When the Barrs were gone, Lastun stepped back up to the counter and Mr. Kilgore resumed counting the eggs. Once finished, he wrote a number down in a book and stored the eggs in a big refrigerated display case. Lastun didn't know what number had been recorded, nor did he think it mattered. Mama took the price Mr. Kilgore gave for the eggs and paid the price, in credit, that he charged for the goods. As long as they got the staples they needed to live on, nothing else mattered.

Mr. Kilgore loaded the goods in the tow sack Lastun brought. The little boy swung the bag over his shoulder. Since nothing breakable was there he didn't have to be careful.

As he walked, his bare feet kicked up dust from the road. The only time he wore shoes was when it was too cold not to.

"Was anybody else at the store?" Mama asked when he returned.

"Mr. and Miz Barr come in while I was there," he answered.

"They say anything?"

"No'm, not to me. I stayed in the back until Mr. Kilgore finished up with them."

Mama gave a satisfied nod. "Mr. Kilgore say anything?"

"He say if they's any extra on the trade, he put it on what we owe. I don't think they was any extra."

Mama smiled. "Get you some water, then go help Kissy in the garden."

When the Tennessee Valley Authority dammed up the Arkabutla River, electricity came to the Mississippi delta. For the rich folks, this opened worlds of possibilities. The best the

6

Wicker family could do was a single light bulb in each of the house's three rooms, a third-hand chatter-box of a refrigerator, and a radio. For these few luxuries, they gave thanks.

Lastun grabbed an empty pint Mason jar from the cabinet and pulled a half-gallon jug of water from the Frigidaire. He poured the cold water into the jar, returned the jug to the refrigerator, and drank the cool liquid.

The garden plot stood on the opposite side of a small grass yard, away from the back door. Kissy pushed a tiller across the garden's cloddy dirt. The odd-shaped piece of equipment had a single iron-rimmed wheel attached to plow handles. Three curved tines hung behind the wheel and below the handles. Kissy buried the tines in the ground and pushed the handles. The wheel rolled, easing the work of moving the tiller and tearing the soil. Even under the best conditions, this was hard work for any adult—let alone a child—but the Wicker children grew used to hard work at an early age.

Lastun got a long leather strap from the barn. Kissy stopped to watch his approach.

"What you doin'?" Kissy asked. "You too little to push this thing."

"Watch."

The two plow handles converged to connect with the tiller wheel and form a fork—much like that which held the front wheel of a bicycle. Lastun tied each end of the strap to the arms of the plow handles, making sure nothing impeded the wheel's ability to roll. Now he had a loop, which he put his arms through so the strap rode across the back of his neck and under his armpits. He gave Kissy a grin, turned, and leaned into the harness.

Kissy smiled back. "Giddup, mule," she said.

"Hee haw," answered Lastun.

Out in the cotton patch, Papa, David, and Russom stopped their work to marvel and laugh at Lastun's ingenuity.

Momma was so pleased with how quickly they tilled the small plot that she gave each a leftover breakfast biscuit slathered with honey.

The Wicker's house sat on a corner of the small plot of land Abraham rented by shares from Mr. Conner. Lastun, his Mama, and his sisters had watched Papa and his two oldest sons as they prepared the field to receive its cotton seed in a few weeks.

Papa harnessed old Tinker, the mule, to the turning plow. He now urged the animal up and down the cropland, raising dust like a low-hanging brown cloud around them. The plow, a single blade that looked like a curved trowel, cut through the dry soil that had become packed by winter rains. Before long, the plow exposed the softer, moister underbelly of dirt, leaving behind soil that curled like slivers of wood behind a plane. It was the first step in rendering the dirt into the powdery texture suitable for planting. Birds flocked behind the plow, feeding on the worms exposed in the soft, moist soil.

Papa Abraham partnered with five other shareholders in a harrow, a device designed to break the turned soil into fist-sized clods. Cletus Pickens had use of the harrow today. Papa would probably get it next Monday, if the weather held.

Lacking the harrow, and not one to allow a family member to sit idle, Papa set his two oldest boys to doing the harrow's work with hoes. Twenty-year old Russom and twelve-year old David followed in the path of the turning plow, chopping the ropy coils of dirt, their hoes rhythmically rising and falling like hens pecking corn off the ground.

Lastun knew that, before long, Papa would let Russom take the plow handles, while Papa would swing the hoe. Later,

David would relieve Russom, and so on. That way, each person got a little rest, if following the mule could be called rest.

"Lastun," Mama called, "tell Papa and yo' brothers that dinner's ready."

Lastun walked twenty feet or so closer to the cotton patch. He cupped his hands around his mouth. "Papa! Russom! David!" he shouted at the top of his lungs. "Come eat!"

Mama shook her head. "Shoot, I coulda done that."

Papa unharnessed Tinker and walked him toward the house, followed by his two sons. While they came in, Lastun pumped the water handle to fill a bucket, which he and the girls used to wash their faces and hands. Then he pumped another bucket full for Papa, Russom and David.

While the older men washed up, Lastun took Tinker's reins and led him over to the corner of the grassy part of the yard. He tied the mule there, went back and filled a third bucket of water, putting it on the ground in easy reach for Tinker.

Once inside, Papa sat at the head of the dining table, with Russom, David, Lastun and Safara filling the other seats. Kissy and Daisy would load their plates and eat on the back porch because there weren't enough seats at the table. Mama hovered near the stove to keep the dishes on the table filled. Even though he was the youngest, Lastun sat at the table because he was male.

Papa scanned the table, laden with black-eyed peas, cornbread, stewed tomatoes and boiled potatoes. All but the cornbread and potatoes were canned produce from last year's garden, while the potatoes came from the root cellar, which doubled as a storm cellar when tornado weather hit.

"No meat?" Papa asked, without really expecting an answer.

Mama looked embarrassed, as if it was her fault, though Lastun knew it wasn't.

"Ah, well," Papa continued, "one of these days, we'll get us a electric freezer. Then we won't have to count on fresh meat all the time."

The lack of meat didn't seem to slow anyone down. By the time the steady clink of forks and spoons on plates faded away, the serving bowls had been pretty much cleaned out. The cornbread plate held only a few crumbs.

Papa leaned back in his chair. "Good dinner, Mama."

Mama smiled, seemingly recovered from the no meat slight.

"Well, you boys ready to get back to the field?" Papa asked Russom and David.

"I reckon," Russom said, "though I don't see why you don't wait until next week when you get use of that harrow to break up them clods. Trying to use a hoe on 'em is just too slow."

Lastun leaned forward. "Me'n Kissy finished tillin' the garden this mornin'. You could use that tiller 'stead o' them hoes."

Papa studied him quizzically.

"You'd still have to harrow next week, but you'd have to do that anyway, even with Russom and David usin' the hoes," Lastun continued.

"You aiming to harness up and pull like you did this mornin'" Russom said, and smiled, a twinkle in his eye.

Lastun's chest swelled. "I could."

Papa reached over and circled Lastun's skinny bicep with his thumb and forefinger. "Maybe you could. But I think we need somebody with more muscle." He took a deep breath. "But usin' that tiller might do. What do you boys think?" he asked, turning to Russom and David.

"Cant' be worse than swinging a hoe," David reasoned.

With no further conversation, Papa and the two older boys rose and marched out the back door, while the women began stacking dishes.

Lastun went to the back yard and pumped a bucketful of water, which he used to fill the dishpan. He refilled the bucket for a second dishpan – one for washing and one for rinsing.

All the chores were done. Lastun was now free for the afternoon. He fetched his BB gun and headed for a piece of wooded marshland south of Papa's sharehold. Just about all the land that didn't stay too wet to plow was in cultivation. Each patch operated by a different sharecropper was separated by a fence line that harbored some scrub brush and maybe a scraggly pine or two.

Lastun knew any rabbit or squirrel—or mouse or chipmunk, for that matter—that ventured into an open field would quickly become a meal for one of the hawks that constantly rode the air currents above the delta farmland. If he was going to find table meat, it would be hiding in the scrub along the fencerows or in the woody marshland. Mice and chipmunks, by the way, were not table meat.

He wanted a rabbit or a squirrel, something to make Papa happy, which in turn would make Mama happy, but he didn't hold out much hope—not with the BB gun he held in his hands. It just wasn't powerful enough, and it didn't shoot straight enough.

Papa had a .22 caliber single shot rifle, but Lastun was deemed too young to use it. Only Papa, Russom or David had that privilege. *One of these days, though . . .*

When Lastun arrived at the wooded area, he cocked his gun and found a quiet spot in the shade of a cypress tree. He was dressed in ratty jeans and wore no shirt. The dapple effect of the early afternoon sun shining through the leaves served to camouflage his dark skin. He allowed his breathing to become slow and regular. He stood very still. He would make no sudden movements that might startle his prey. He had no watch and didn't need one. He waited as long as it took. At first, only a few birds showed themselves; blue jays and robins. There were some crows feeding on the grubs in the field where Papa and Lastun's brothers plowed. But it would take a mess of birds to feed six mouths.

Eventually, Lastun spotted the outline of a rabbit at the base of a holly bush a short distance away. When a rabbit sensed danger, its natural response was to freeze, hoping to blend into its surroundings and become invisible to the predator. It had almost worked. Very slowly, Lastun lifted his BB gun, resting the butt against his shoulder and his cheek against the stock, so he could sight down the short barrel.

Papa called the BB gun a "little man's musket." According to him, the smooth interior of the barrel and the round shot made the gun just as inaccurate as an old-timey musket. But it was all Lastun had. The young boy had shot it often enough to know that it had one quirk; it consistently shot low and to the left. So he aimed high and to the right.

He drew in a breath, letting half of it back out. When he was satisfied with his aim, he squeezed the trigger.

Dust flew from the ground in front of the rabbit, which disappeared in a flash of brown fur.

Lastun suppressed the urge to repeat one of Papa's cuss words. He worked the lever to cock the air rifle and resumed his vigil.

A short time later, a squirrel scampered along a low branch in a pine on the tree line. Again, Lastun slowly raised his gun, and he waited for the squirrel to pose. This smaller animal would be harder to hit, but Lastun refused to be faulted for not trying.

The squirrel sensed his presence and wouldn't settle down. Lastun felt a slight breeze on his face and knew he was downwind. The squirrel didn't smell him. But he knew squirrels had good eyesight, and they were a lot smarter than people gave them credit for.

He took careful aim, uttered a low whistle, freezing the animal as it tried to assess the danger.

The BB gun made a metallic cough in response to Lastun's trigger pull. The squirrel fell eight feet from tree limb to ground.

Lastun rushed over. The animal was yet alive, struggling to get to its feet and scurry away. Lastun pinned its body down with the heel of the air gun's stock, while he fished his jackknife from his pocket. He knew better than to grab it with his bare hands. Squirrels had sharp teeth.

Once he had the knife out of his pocket, he opened the blade with his teeth and cut the squirrel's throat. He then field dressed the animal and marched back to the house.

When Mama saw the kill, she smiled. "What do you think, Lastun? Squirrel stew or squirrel an' dumplins?"

"Dumplins," Lastun answered.

That night at supper, Papa was in a very good mood.

2

July 4th was the day most of the country celebrated its independence from the British. July 3, 1863 was the date the city of Vicksburg surrendered to Grant. Coupled with the Yankee victory at Gettysburg, also on July 3, 1863, these events made white citizens of the Vicksburg area disinclined to feel patriotic. If the members of the colored community felt differently, they wisely chose to remain silent.

On the Monday after that non-holiday, Lastun Wicker stood on the roadside with Daisy, Kissy, David and Safara, waiting for the big yellow and black bus to pick them up and take them to the first day of school.

Noisy children, all with various shades of brown skin, filled the bus. The white kids rode another bus to a different school.

Yazoo County Colored School was housed in a white lapboard wooden building, constructed in the 1930s by the Civilian Conservation Corps. It was formed in the shape of an **H**, with the elementary classrooms located on the left side, the high school and junior high classrooms on the right, and the shared auditorium forming the crossbar in the middle. Since few colored kids stayed in school beyond junior high, the right side was lightly populated.

Daisy took Lastun by the hand and walked him to his classroom in the elementary wing. He would share this room with the other first and second graders.

"Here you go," Daisy said, standing at the door and pointing inside. "You behave or Papa will tan your ginhouse, an' if he don't Mama will."

Lastun scowled at his sister and walked into the room. He could easily tell the first graders from the second graders. The younger kids all had "scared rabbit" expressions on their faces, while the older kids seemed comfortable, accustomed to their surroundings, quickly selecting desks and settling into a routine that was familiar to them.

A matronly woman in a blue gingham dress and a black patent leather belt left her desk at the front of the room and walked toward him. *Mrs. Frost.* Lastun knew her from church.

"Good Morning, Lastun," she said. "How are your mother and father doing?" she said her words almost like a white woman.

"Good, Miz Frost. Thanks for astin'."

Though it was not yet eight in the morning, a sheen of sweat already coated the teacher's face. July got hot in the Mississippi Delta. The school had been built with high ceilings to allow the heat to rise above the students' heads, and the outside wall had many tall windows, now open, to entice an occasional breeze to pass through. Still, it was hot.

Lastun knew why school started in July. Colored and white, the kids would get in six weeks of schooling while the cotton crop matured. In late August, school would dismiss for six weeks, while the students joined their parents in harvesting the crop.

The white farmers paid three cents a pound for picked cotton. This was an important source of cash income for the coloreds and poor whites.

Papa had heard about a mechanical cotton picker. International Harvester started making them when the war ended. He and the other farm laborers feared that hand-picking cotton as a source of income would soon come to an end. But not this year.

All this was beyond Lastun's concern. At the moment, his worry involved finding out what it took to keep Mrs. Frost happy.

"Why don't you sit at this desk right here?" Lastun's teacher said, indicating a spot on the right side of the classroom about a third of the way back. Lastun sat.

All Lastun had in the way of school supplies was a pencil painted the same color as the bus he'd ridden that morning, and a lined Big Chief writing tablet. His papa had sharpened the pencil with his pocketknife the night before.

Mrs. Frost took a stack of thin books from the corner of her worn brown desk and distributed them to the first graders. "These are copy books. They contain the letters of the alphabet. You will use these to learn to read and write." Her face grew solemn, and she spoke almost to herself. "A hundred years ago, you would have been flogged, or maybe even killed, for what you are about to learn."

Lastun didn't know what to make of her words. He only knew they seemed important to her.

"I want a second grader to pair up with a first grader," Mrs. Frost added. "Do it now, please."

The older students knew what to do. They rose from their desks and moved to the right side of the classroom. They'd been the new students in this exercise last year.

A lanky, dusty boy stood beside Lastun's desk. "I'm Carl," he said. He must have lived on the other side of the county because Lastun didn't know him.

"I'm Lastun." He scooted over. There was barely enough room for both to sit on the seat.

"Second graders, using the copy books, I want you to teach your partners the first six letters of the alphabet and how to draw them in their writing tablets," Mrs. Frost instructed. She paused. "Begin."

Carl opened Lastun's copy book. "Thass a A," he said, pointing to the first page. "It look like the roof of a house, only with a line through it." He gestured toward Lastun's writing tablet. "Less see can you draw one."

Mrs. Frost had returned to her desk and sat. She made notes, occasionally glancing up at her students. The combined classes generated a low burble of sound.

Lastun found Carl's comparison to a rooftop helpful. He pictured the gabled angles of his roof at home and drew two diverging diagonals, then connected them with a crossbar. "How's that?"

Carl nodded. "Looks fine ta me. Miz Frost will look at 'm later and say what she think."

That frightened Lastun a bit, but he didn't let on. He had no reason to be afraid of his teacher.

For the next hour, Carl named the assigned alphabetic characters and guided Lastun through drawing them on paper. Lastun was accustomed to hard physical work, but he was surprised at how the concentration required for this exercise drained his energy. Carl had Lastun repeat the characters a number of times.

Lastun had begun to grow bored and restless when a young girl knocked on the classroom door. Mrs. Frost let her come in. She whispered in the teacher's ear before disappearing back into the hall.

Mrs. Frost stood and clapped her hands. All activity stopped.

"Mr. Hardy, our principal, has summoned everyone to the auditorium for an assembly. No doubt he wants to welcome the student body back for the new school year. Second graders, please return to your desks." When she was satisfied with the arrangement, she continued. "Melissa." This appeared to be the second grader at the head of the row nearest the door. "You

17

will lead your row to the auditorium. You know where to sit. The second row will follow the first, and so on. Quietly. I will follow the last row to make sure no one gets lost." She smiled as she said it, as if she thought someone might "get lost" on purpose. She nodded at Melissa. "Begin."

The seats in the auditorium were unlike the pews at church. The rows were made of individual seats, separated by armrests. A raised stage spanned the front of the large room.

Within a few minutes, the auditorium was two-thirds full. Lastun had never seen so many people in one place.

After a quarter of an hour, a large-bellied man walked onto the stage. Like Mrs. Frost, sweat beaded his brown face. He wore black pants, and a white shirt with large circular sweat stains under each armpit. A black tie seemed to choke his thick neck like a noose.

He stood at the center of the stage until everyone noticed him and quieted down.

"Good morning." His voice had a booming baritone quality that matched his body. "I am Mr. Hardy. Welcome to Yazoo County Colored School. For those of you who are new here, your teachers will explain about restroom locations, recesses, lunch breaks, and so on."

He paused and took a deep breath. "I want to discuss something that you may have heard of, or that you soon will hear of." He pulled a handkerchief out of his back pocket and mopped his forehead. "Some time ago a colored girl tried to enroll in a white school in Little Rock, Arkansas."

A rumble of whispers rolled through the auditorium.

"They didn't let her in, o'course," Hardy continued, "but a bunch a lawyers filed in court to make 'em." He had given up his effort at white folks talk. He began to pace back and forth across the stage, like a preacher at church.

"Them lawyers took it to the Supreme Court. Well, about two months ago, in May, them Supreme Court judges said they hadda let her in."

The rumble increased in volume.

Mr. Hardy stretched his hand and swept it across in front of him, as if trying to point at everybody at the same time. "Some a you teachers, and some a your mommas and papas will wonder what that means for us here in Yazoo County." He put his hands on his hips. "The answer is not a damn thing!"

He stopped, seeming to await an answer, but the rumble had died and the great room was silent.

"The white folks'll keep going to their school. We coloreds will keep going to our school . . . Nothing will change. Nothing ever does . . . They won't let us vote . . ." He wiped his hand across his mouth, like he was trying to make himself shut up. "We'll still use the colored bathrooms at the courthouse . . . and the colored drinkin' fountains. We'll still take our food at the back doors of the restaurants, if we can afford to buy a meal there. Nothing will change."

He seemed to come to his senses, as if he'd been in a trance. "Well, forget about that. If your parents say somethin' about it, don't let on that I said anything. Like I said, it won't change anything here. You're dismissed."

Back in the classroom, Mrs. Frost seemed as rattled as the principal had been. "You all pray for Mr. Hardy. Ask your parents to pray, too. He over spoke himself today."

Lastun didn't know what he was supposed to be praying about. Mr. Hardy hadn't made much sense. Still he did resolve to pray.

After supper that night, fourteen-year-old Safara, the oldest child still in school, tried to explain Mr. Hardy's rant to

19

Momma and Papa. Lastun listened. Being an eighth grader, she understood more about the issue. The family sat on the front porch of their house in the fading light. Trying to find some place that had cooled a little from the hot day. Everybody but Momma and Papa sat on the plank floor.

"According to the Supreme Court, that colored girl can go to the white school in Little Rock," Safara explained. "But Miz Barnes, my teacher, said none of the Mississippi schools will have to go along right away, 'cause we're not in the same." She paused, trying to remember the phrase her teacher had used. "Judicial district." She held up her hand as if to forestall an argument nobody had yet made. "I know, the Supreme Court judges the whole country, but Miz Barnes says the schools in Mississippi still won't go along until the law makes 'em. But some day, that'll probly change and white folks and coloreds will haveta go to school together."

She also went on to recount Mr. Hardy's rant that morning. Even though he'd warned the students not to repeat what he'd said. Loyalty to parents trumped loyalty to teachers.

Papa sat in his long-armed rocker, his head shrouded in pipe smoke. "Hmmm, they ain't nothin' good can come from this. White folks won't abide it."

"Miz Frost ast us all to pray for Mr. Hardy," Lastun added, surprised at himself because he hadn't planned to say anything.

"That's right, son," Momma said from her smaller rocking chair, where she stitched a quilt piece. "Pray his neck don't get stretched."

Momma's remark puzzled Lastun, but he stayed quiet because the tension was so thick.

Papa looked over his crop of children. "Y'all don't need to say no more 'bout this. Anybody start tryin' ta do anythin' . . . I mean anythin' . . . the white sheets'll come' outta the closets, and tha crosses'll start burnin', and tha Klan'll bring hellacious pain upon all our heads. So shut up. Hear me?"

Six heads nodded.

The next day at school. Mrs. Frost called the class to attention first thing. "Mr. Hardy suffered an accident last night. He's alive, but he's hurt pretty bad. He'll be in the hospital for a while. Mr. Wells will take over his duties for the time being. He was lucky." This last seemed an aside.

Later, at recess, Lastun overheard Mrs. Frost and Mr. Wells talking.

"Don't know who told on him." Wells said. "Wasn't nobody but us coloreds in that auditorium. You know Mr. Hardy grew up in Atlanta before comin' out here to teach. Maybe things was different, better somehow, in the big city, but he always did strain against the yoke us coloreds have to bear here in the Mississippi Delta."

"Doesn't matter," Mrs. Frost said. "They find out. They always find out. There's always somebody trying to get in good with them."

Over the next six weeks, Lastun struggled through the laborious process of learning how to put alphabetic characters together to make words. Later, Mrs. Frost assured him and his classmates that the words would be put together into sentences.

He also learned to count numbers, with similar promises about such things as addition and subtraction.

All this quickly became tedious. Lastun's favorite part of the day was recess when he was thrown together with more boys than he could count, and allowed to play baseball, tag and kick-the-can.

After a while, Mr. Hardy returned to his duties. He said nothing more about Brown v. Board of Education, or any other issues related to race relations.

3

By the end of Lastun's first six weeks of school, the cotton crop had matured and was ready to be picked. School dismissed for harvest break and Lastun and the other students felt as if they'd been paroled from prison.

Mr. Conner hired Papa and his three oldest unmarried children—Russom, Safara, and David—to help pick his crop at three cents a pound.

This left Mama, Kissy, Daisy and Lastun to pick Papa's small patch. The family would receive market price for their remaining cotton after Mr. Conner and the gin owner received their shares.

The family woke before daybreak. Mama and Safara cooked breakfast and fed everyone. While Kissy and Daisy washed the dishes, Lastun fed and watered the chickens and collected the eggs, and David fed and watered Tinker. By sun up, everybody had gathered by the road, waiting for Mr. Conner's driver to come by in his flatbed truck. The men and boys wore long-sleeve khaki work shirts under denim bib overalls and wide-brim straw hats. The women and girls wore khaki shirts, denim skirts, and straw hats.

"Look at that!" Lastun said, pointing up the road.

A huge monster of a machine approached. The red color of International Harvester. It stood higher than the basketball hoop at school. At the top, an overall-clad white man sat in a glass enclosed cab, his large hands gripping a steering wheel. Behind the cab, a large basket perched atop the rest of the machine. Near the ground, four finger-like prongs protruded in front. The rear of the machine looked like a tractor turned around backward. Dust followed like a rooster-tail.

"Thass a cotton-picker," Papa said. He fingered the pipe in his pocket, as if he wanted to pull it out and light it up. "'Member the story about Big John and his contest diggin' a tunnel against a steam drilling machine?"

"Yeah," Lastun answered.

"Well, we're Big John, and thass the machine that will put us out of the cotton-pickin' business."

Lastun didn't know what to say. He'd never seen anything that big before.

As the cotton-picker rolled by, the driver in the cab gave everybody a big wave. He knew the spectacle he presented.

"Is he goin' to Mistah Conners'?" Safara asked.

"Not this year, thank God," Papa answered.

Mr. Conner's truck came a few minutes later. The flatbed already had a half-dozen men and women that had been collected from other sharecroppers' farms.

"Here's dinner," Mama said, handing a paper bag to each of the four who would pick in Mr. Conner's fields that day. Lastun knew each bag contained a can of Vienna sausages, a nickel pack of saltine crackers, and an apple. Mr. Conner would provide the water to drink.

When the truck had disappeared in a cloud of dust, Mama clapped her hands. "Well, let's get to work, then"

The remaining four grabbed their canvas cotton sacks and headed to the field behind the Wicker's house, where six acres of cotton plants awaited. Each plant looked as if it was loaded with snowballs. Each sack had a strap that looped over the picker's head and one shoulder.

When a cotton boll matures, it opens like a popcorn kernel, revealing a handful of pure, fluffy white cotton. The pickers walked between two rows, plucking the cotton out of the bolls and stuffing it in the sack they pulled along behind. The vexing part was that the leftover part of the outer boll had sharp ends similar to thorns. The pickers wore cotton gloves to protect their palms, but the fingers of the gloves had to be cut off to allow the bare human fingers the dexterity to grab and pull the cotton. Until their hands toughened up, there would be plenty of cuts and scratches.

Within a couple of hours, Lastun's fingers were sore and puffy, as if they'd been pricked by a hundred needles. Yet he knew stopping was not an option.

About halfway to lunch time, Mama stood, stretched her back and announced, "Okay, let's weigh."

Everybody breathed a sigh of relief and trudged back to the barn, dragging their cotton sacks behind them.

The Wickers had no wagon big enough to hold a full bale of unginned cotton, so the crop would be stored in a stall in the barn. When they had a bale, about fifteen hundred pounds, Papa would borrow a wagon to haul it to the gin.

Lastun pumped a bucket full of water from the well. They took turns filling a dipper with water and drinking.

Mama operated the scale, which looked like a steel walking cane with a crescent shaped head. It hung in the passageway that ran through the middle of the barn. The building provided shade from the oppressive heat, and a small breeze helped evaporate the sweat from everyone's body. Mama hung her sack—full of cotton—on a hook that descended below the scale. She put a bell-shaped weight on the long shaft of the scale opposite the side where the cotton hung. She slid the weight until the shaft became horizontal.

"Kissy?" she asked.

Lastun's literate sister stepped up to read the number. "Fifty-three pounds." She wrote the amount in a notebook she held in her hands. "Pick that much three more times today, and you'll have two hunnert and twelve pounds."

"Yore Papa will have 'bout seventy-five by now. How much would that be for the day?"

"'Bout three hunnert. That'd come to nine dollahs for the day. Russom and Safara would get, maybe, same as you, so they'd earn a little over six dollahs each. David, maybe five."

Mama looked satisfied. "Not bad." She looked at Lastun. "Time was I could match yore Papa, though he wouldn't own up to it. Not anymore, though."

None of the children could pick like Mama. Everybody else except Lastun got about thirty-five pounds, while Lastun produced twenty-five. Kissy recorded all the numbers in her notebook.

By the time all the weighing was done, everybody had a drink of water and were as cool as they were going to get. "Okay, let's get back to the field," Mama sighed.

At mid-day, they weighed again, then ate Vienna sausages and crackers, just like Papa and the others.

At the end of the day, Mr. Conner's driver brought the rest of the family back for supper and a night's sleep. The routine would be repeated the next day and every day until everyone in Satartia had brought their crop in.

When, by Kissy's count, they had collected fifteen-hundred pounds of unginned cotton in the barn's storage room, Papa borrowed a wagon from Leroy Harmon, one of Satartia's more successful sharecroppers. The wagon was a flatbed with six-foot-tall sideboards and a single tongue, so two animals could be hitched to it. Mr. Harmon also provided his mule so it could be teamed up with Tinker.

Cash money was too valuable to give in trade, so Mama and the younger children were obliged to give a day's labor in Mr. Harmon's patch in payment. That would be done as soon

26

as Mr. Harmon asked for them—probably one day the next week.

Papa rode Tinker to pick up the wagon at daybreak. An hour later, he came back with his mule and Harmon's pulling the wagon. Papa guided it into the wide passageway that ran through the middle of the barn. Lastun unhitched the animals and set them out to graze, while Papa, Mama, Daisy and Kissy used pitchforks to move the cotton to the wagon.

Mama led the family in a song to make the work go easier.

Onward, Christian soldiers,
    marching as to war,
with the cross of Jesus
    going on before!

Christ, the royal master,
    leads against the foe,
forward into battle
    see his banner go!

The family used the rhythm of the song to set the pace of the work. As pitchfork loads of cotton flew, fibers floated free and covered everyone in a white dust storm.

Once the wagon was loaded, Lastun re-hitched the mules. Mama went to make a peanut butter and blackberry jam sandwich for Papa.

Lastun sidled up beside Papa, who fed carrot bites to the two animals. "Can I come, Papa? To the gin? With you?"

Papa gave Lastun a skeptical look. "Reckon you can behave yoself?"

Lastun swelled his chest in a show of confidence. "Yes, suh."

"You got to do what I say. You got to stay out of the white folks way. If somebody says somepin' to you, you got to say suh, and say it quick."

"I can do that."

Papa turned to Daisy. "Go tell Mama to fix another sandwich for Lastun."

"But Papa," Daisy complained, "how come Lastun gits to go with you and I hafta stay and pick more cotton?"

Papa cocked his head to one side. "Seems like you rode to the gin once with me last year."

Daisy conceded defeat. "Yes, sir."

Lastun gave her a triumphant look.

Papa saw it. "Besides, Lastun can shovel the mule shit when the animals move their bowels."

Now Daisy looked triumphant.

Mama came back with the sandwiches and a half-gallon jug of tea. "Now you behave Lastun. Do what yo Papa –"

"I done got that speech," Lastun interrupted.

Mama sniffed, seemingly disgruntled at getting cut off.

The mules shifted in their traces. Tinker nuzzled Papa's hands, looking for another carrot.

"Time ta go," Papa announced. "Else the animals will start without us."

The man and boy climbed up on the wagon's bench seat. Papa grabbed the reins and released the brake. "Giddap, you two," he called, snapping the reins over the mules backs.

The wagon lurched to a start. Lastun waved. Mama returned the gesture, but Daisy and Kissy just gave sullen looks.

The trip took half an hour. The gin was a tall, high-peaked building with tin siding. It, too, had a wide passageway running through its center. A line of wagons — these pulled by pickups or tractors — extended from one end of the opening, with White farmers waiting for their turn. As Papa and Lastun pulled up, a green and yellow John Deere tractor pulled an empty wagon out of the passageway exit at the opposite end of the building.

The gin roared like a sound Lastun had never heard before. It was loud enough to make his ears ring. Papa pulled two tufts of cotton from the back and stuffed these into his ears. Lastun did the same.

A cluster of wagons, with mules or horses hitched to them, were parked in the shade under a grove of trees off to one side. Colored sharecroppers would wait until all the white customers' loads were ginned.

Papa pulled his wagon over to join them.

Lastun had pictured his day as an eventful one, but he quickly discovered just how boring a trip to the gin could be. An afternoon of waiting faced him. The grownups told stories and swapped gossip. *At least I'm not picking cotton.* He was also thankful for the shade. After a while, most of the men-folk picked a soft patch of grass, lay down and went to sleep.

Lastun waited until Papa was asleep before he wandered over toward the gin. A door marked "*Office*" stood on one side of the central passageway. White men walked in and out of the door, giving Lastun dismissive looks.

The air was filled with so much cotton lint that Lastun might have thought it was snowing if the temperature hadn't been a hundred degrees.

Large signs adorned the exterior wall on each side of the passage—two words, one short and one long. Lastun could read both words, which he did silently. "*N-O. No. S-M-O-K-I-N-G. Smoking.*"

A white man saw him looking and said, "Can you read that sign, boy?"

Lastun remembered his father's instruction. "No, suh."

The man looked satisfied at his answer. "It says 'No Smoking.' Do you see all this cotton lint?"

Lastun nodded.

"If somebody lit a match, this place would go up like a bomb. It would burn to the ground in minutes. Do you smoke?"

Lastun figured the man was funnin' him, since he was only five, but he didn't get sassy. "No, suh."

"Good." The white man walked off.

After a few minutes, Lastun returned to the colored group. White folks made him nervous. He discovered that Carl, the second grader from school who'd helped him with his letters, had arrived with his papa.

"Hey," Lastun said.

"Hey," Carl answered, "you wanna play marbles?"

"I ain't got none."

Carl pulled a small cotton pouch, the kind that held loose tobacco, from his pants pocket. Lastun guessed Carl's Papa had smoked up the tobacco and then had given Carl the empty bag. It had a drawstring closure.

"I kin lend you somma mine," Carl said. He knelt and dumped a dozen cat's eye marbles onto the ground.

"'Kay," Lastun said, and knelt, too.

For the rest of the afternoon, the two competed to see who could knock his opponent's marbles out of a hand-drawn circle on the ground first. A year older and more experienced at the game, Carl won almost every time.

Late in the afternoon, all the shareholders broke out their bags of sandwiches and tea, and had an impromptu picnic.

As the sun neared the western horizon, the last of the white farmers finished up, and the colored sharecroppers lined up in the order in which they'd arrived.

Dusk was falling when Papa pulled his borrowed wagon into the gin's passageway. Lastun looked up to see a big black tube that looked exactly like a stovepipe hanging from the ceiling. Papa climbed up into the cotton and immediately sank up to his knees. Lastun made as if to follow, but Papa said, "Unh-unh, you stand on the seat. You can see everythin' from there."

Papa grabbed a handle on the side of the hanging pipe. It must have been attached to a spring because it slid down and Papa held it just above the cotton, then signaled a colored gin employee who stood off to the side. The man threw a switch.

The pipe made a *whooshing* sound and began to suck cotton up its tube like milk being sucked up a straw. Papa swung the pipe from one side to another. The pile of cotton shrank steadily. In a matter of minutes the wagon was empty. Papa nodded and the colored man turned the suction off.

Papa climbed onto the seat and snapped the reins. The mules pulled the wagon out the back of the building and Papa parked the wagon off to one side. He looked at Lastun.

"Wow," Lastun exclaimed, "That was somethin'!"

Papa grinned. "C'mon,' he said.

The two walked across to the side of the building away from the office. The din was even louder there. Rows of green-painted machines filled the space. Each machine had rows of spindles which moved up and down, as rivers of cotton moved through.

Papa leaned over so Lastun could read his lips. "The cotton gets sucked up that tube you saw and comes through here. Them machines separate the seed from the cotton fibers. The gin owner keeps the seed as part of his payment for the ginnin'. We brought about fifteen hunnert pounds of unginned cotton. After the seed is ginned out, it'll weigh about five hunnert pounds."

He stood and led Lastun to a loading platform on the back side of the building. "Once the seed comes out, a machine packs the pure cotton into bales like this." He gestured toward stacks of bales about half the size of Mama's chest of drawers in her bedroom at home.

Lastun followed Papa back to the door that read "*Office*," and the two went inside.

A fat-bellied, balding white man in khaki pants and shirt sat in a wooden chair that looked too feeble to hold his weight. He had an unlit stub of a cigar in his mouth.

"Wicker," the man said. He picked up a piece of paper from his desk. "Five hundred and thirty two pounds. That's good output."

"Thanky, suh." Papa treated the man with the same exaggerated courtesy he'd required of Lastun.

He spotted Lastun. "This your boy?"

"Yes, suh."

The man nodded and moved on to business. "I guess you want to sell at market price?"

"This my first'un," Papa explained. "Mr. Conner get it. You'll hafta ast him what he wont to do." Mr. Conner, the land owner, would get one-fourth of Papa's cotton crop as rent.

"Right." He wrote out a receipt and handed it to Papa, who folded it and put it in his pocket without looking at it. "Thanky, suh." He and Lastun left without another word from the gin owner.

Now that he was away from the gin, Papa removed the cotton from his ears, filled and lit his pipe.

Lastun removed the cotton from his ears, too.

On the way home, their way now lit by moonlight, Lastun asked, "Papa, what does that man do with the cotton seed?"

"He sell it to this company that crushes most of it to get the cottonseed oil," Papa said around his pipe stem. "The leftover husks go to make feed for cows. What don't get crushed go to make seed to plant fo' next year."

"What do they do with the cottonseed oil?" Lastun persisted.

"Heck if I know, son."

4

1966

Once teeming with children, the Wicker household had now become quiet. Only Papa, Mama, and Lastun remained. All the older kids had grown, married and moved out to start their own families. Lastun truly was the last one.

Despite the perpetually tight purse strings, Mama had been unable to adjust to the reality of having fewer mouths to feed.

"Lawd, woman," Papa said, looking at plates filled with biscuits, sausage, eggs and grits. "We'll never eat all this."

Mama wiped her hands on her apron, made from an empty flour sack. "Well," she said, nodding toward Lastun, "that one done got to be a eatin' machine. You watch, he'll make this disappear like he a magician."

It was true. Like many teenage boys, Lastun ate continuously, and he was still skinny and muscled. And he wasn't even tall.

"Besides, if they any left, I'll just heat it up for breakfast tomorrow."

Lastun spooned a dollop of apple jelly onto his plate, beside his open biscuit. "That'll work," he said. "Save you from havin' to cook then."

Papa chuckled. "Don't worry, she'll have another batch just like this."

Mama snapped the end of a dish towel at her husband.

"It's early yet, Lastun," Papa said. "Reckon you can help run the turnin' plow a while before school lets in?"

Lastun leaned back in his chair and frowned. "I was aimin' to hunt until time for school. Maybe get a rabbit or squirrel. But if you druther I plow, I'll hunt tomorrow."

Papa scratched his chin. The family had scraped enough money together to buy a freezer. This allowed Mama to freeze some of her garden produce, while canning the rest. And it also allowed them to store a supply of meat. "Go ahead, then. Jus' be careful. Ain't nothin' in season. If the game warden catch you, you'll get a fine we can't pay."

"I see a warden, I'll take off runnin'. He won't catch me."

Papa grinned and resumed eating, scooping a spoonful of grits and honey into his mouth. "The boy is fast."

"Don't dawdle around and wind up late for school," Mama warned.

Lastun sighed, thinking, *Mama always has to worry about something*. "Mistuh Saunders won't mind," Lastun said, and smiled. "I'm close enough to graduatin', he won't say nothin'."

The teaching staff at the colored school had always been lax about enforcing attendance policies. They understood that in the colored community, responsibilities around the house and farm came first. So when a student failed to show up, no penalty was applied. Lastun wasn't above taking advantage of that leniency. Even so, he'd excelled in his schoolwork. He would graduate in two months, and not many graduated from the colored school.

Mr. Saunders was the principal now. Mr. Hardy had understood too well the disparity between life in the white community and in the colored one. After the serious beating he took in Lastun's first year of school, he'd toned his behavior down some. But when the Freedom Riders had come into Yazoo County on their mission to register colored voters, Mr. Hardy had been unable to hide his enthusiasm.

35

That was in 1964, two years before. Lastun remembered when Papa, Mama, Daisy and he were sitting on the porch, trying to catch the cool evening air, when a 1962 Ford Fairlane drove up. Before the dust stirred up by the car could settle, Papa said, "Y'all get inside, now."

Papa also went inside, but only long enough to get and load his double-barreled, twelve gauge scattergun.

Two college-age white boys they'd never seen before got out of the car and began to stroll up to the house. Both had dark brown hair and slender, youthful bodies. Papa walked out onto the porch, shotgun in hand. The boys stopped when they saw the gun pointed at them. The older, the leader, seemed shocked by the threat. Lastun watched from behind the screen door.

"Why don't you men just mosey on down the road? Y'all don't have no business here," Papa said.

That was the first time Lastun had ever heard Papa speak sternly to a white man.

The leader held out his hands, palms up. "We mean no harm, sir," he said with a Yankee accent. "We'd like to talk to you about registering to vote."

I know who you are and what you're up to. Y'all linger here for a while, talk some, then men in white sheets will show up 'fore long. By that time, y'all be long gone. Me and my family don't need that."

"But, sir," the man began, and stopped when Papa pulled back the hammers on the gun.

Undeterred, the younger man stepped forward and said, "Are you saying you want to let the whites continue to deny your right to vote?"

Without saying a word, Papa swung the shotgun up and fired a shot over the young men's heads. The boom echoed across the hollow.

"We're going. We're going," the older boy said. They hustled back to their car. The Fairlane's rear wheels spun as the car pulled away.

Lastun walked out onto the porch. "Wouldn't it be good for us to get to vote?"

"You too young yet. I reckon it would be good for me and Mama to vote, but the Klan would never let that happen." Papa gave a sad smile. "Votin' is good, but breathin' is better."

No one was surprised when a burning cross showed up in Mr. Hardy's front yard. Once it burned out, he said, "Leave it be." The charred cross became a perverse badge of honor.

That wouldn't do. The ones who'd put it there surely didn't want the principal to feel any pride about being singled out for his stand in the conflict that had become known as *The Civil Rights Movement.* So Mr. Hardy disappeared. The white folks said he must've gone off up north, as the coloreds are prone to do. But Lastun knew better.

Unlike the three Yankees who'd disappeared over in Philadelphia, Mississippi, Mr. Hardy's sudden absence didn't cause a stir. Nobody went looking for a missing black man.

After breakfast, Lastun pulled out the family's rifle, a .22 caliber Remington single-shot bolt action. Lastun's many hours with that old BB air rifle had left him with a sharp eye and a steady hand. He could kill small game with the .22 almost as good as Papa could with the shotgun. Only thing was, he couldn't hit a rabbit at full gallop—*yet.*

Woodland around Satartia was still scarce. Just some acres too low and wet to plow, and some rows along property lines to prevent the kind of wind erosion Papa had told about in the depression-era dust bowl. He knew of one copse of trees about a half-mile behind Mr. Kilgore's store. If he was patient, and if he made sure not to shoot in the direction of the store, he might find a squirrel on a limb, or a rabbit trying to hide beneath a bush.

Lastun picked a spot where the trunks of two small pines and a bush formed a passable blind. He plucked a twig from the bush, put it between his teeth and hunkered down to wait for the birds and small animals to forget he was there.

He really did want to bag something. It always helped to get some food for nothing more than the cost of a bullet. But he also wanted a little time to be alone and think. As he'd said at the breakfast table, he'd finish school in two months. *Then what?*

He'd seen the life his parents lived. The life his older brothers and sisters lived. Slavery might not exist anymore in law, but his family and the colored community lived at the pleasure of the white landowners and the white businessmen. They had many reminders of the differences between the races. White customers got waited on first in the stores and at the cotton gin. Lastun and other "darkies" could only use the colored water cooler and the colored restroom at the courthouse. If a colored man acted out of turn, people in white sheets would come and put the colored man in his place, and that place might be a six-foot-deep hole.

Then again, more and more young men were being drafted by the Army once they turned eighteen.

He'd known Bizzy Polk just about all his life. Her family had gone to church with his family. On Sundays after the evening service, he, Bizzy, and the other kids had played games in the church yard while their parents stood around and talked about who knows what.

Lastun remembered the gangly girl running amid the fireflies under the starry sky, trying to avoid his tag.

They grew older. Lastun began to feel the stirrings of young manhood. Bizzy's slender body grew soft round curves. Lastun noticed.

One Autumn night, along about Halloween, the preacher had put together a hayride for the young people. Lastun climbed into the wagon and sat on a padding of straw beside Bizzy. She didn't object.

As the wagon trundled along the narrow back-country roads of Yazoo County, the kids sang songs the white folks called "Negro Spirituals." After a while, the songs faded away and the teenagers grew mostly quiet. Only soft conversations between couples remained.

"How come you got to be called Bizzy?" Lastun asked, just to have something to say.

"Don't you be judgin' names, *Lastun*," Bizzy said, putting emphasis on his name. Moonlight revealed the twinkle in her eye, so Lastun knew she wasn't insulted.

"I'm serious," he responded. What he really wanted was to hear her voice.

"My real name is Bessy," she said, relenting. "Only when I was first learning to talk, I couldn't say it right, so it came out Bizzy."

"I figured you were on the go so much, everybody said you were busy. You know B-U-S-Y."

Although she slapped him on the shoulder, she smiled. "That too."

They studied each other silently for a moment, before Lastun had leaned in to see if their lips would fit together. They did.

Along the edge of the tree line, about thirty yards away, a squirrel darted into view, followed closely by another. They scampered along the ground to the base of a tree. The second squirrel chased the first up the trunk in a climbing spiral. *Frisky.*

Lastun realized he'd forgotten to load his rifle. He slowly drew back the bolt, fished a cartridge from his pocket, slid it into the open chamber, and gently pushed the bolt home. The mechanism made only the slightest of clicks, but it was enough. The squirrels froze. Lastun debated about bringing his rifle up to his shoulder and trying to get off a snapshot, but he had no confidence in it. And he didn't want to waste a shell. The squirrels broke and ran.

The sun rose higher, moving the shadows a bit. Lastun shifted to keep himself in his shady spot and maintain his camouflage. He'd have to wait for another opportunity, even though it probably meant missing school completely. He checked the breeze, making sure he was downwind from his shooting zone.

His thoughts returned to his romance with Bizzy. They began to spend more and more time together. Although it took most of his spending money, he took her to the theater every time they changed movies. They sat in the colored section in the balcony and held hands. That was about all they could do without getting thrown out by the white manager.

One summer night after a movie, the two strolled along the sidewalk. Moths and mosquitoes flitted around the streetlights. A white man approached, accompanied by two others.

"Hey, Nigger, that's a fine-looking chick you got there. How about sharing some of that stuff with me?" The unshaven man stank of beer. He looked to be about thirty-five.

Bizzy looked at Lastun, her eyes big and white.

"Come on, Bizzy, let's go," Lastun whispered.

They turned to walk away.

"Hey, Nigger, I'm talking to you!" The man tried to follow on unsteady legs.

Lastun turned back to face him. "Look, Mistuh, I don't want no trouble. We're just tryin' to get home." Fighting would probably get him killed, but while he was alive he wouldn't let this man hurt Bizzy.

"Ellis," one of the other white men said, "let's go. I'm tired of you picking fights. Besides, it's too hot."

"Aw, shit. I'm just tryin; to have a little fun."

Lastun slowly backed away, keeping Bizzy behind him.

Ellis suddenly clutched his belly, a sick expression on his face. He leaned over and began to vomit. The other man made a shooing gesture. Lastun took the hint. He spun, grabbed Bizzy's arm and they split.

Sex between a white man and a colored woman was all too common — often uninvited by the woman. But it wasn't something to be acknowledged in public. Ellis Barber — Lastun made it a point to learn his name — had embarrassed everybody by showing his lust for a black woman to the moviegoers who'd seen his drunken behavior that night.

Lastun had fallen in love. He knew he would propose, probably on graduation night. He knew Bizzy would say yes. What he didn't know was whether he'd be able to keep his wife safe in this boiling pot that was Yazoo County, Mississippi.

Years ago, whites and blacks lived together peacefully; whites made the rules and blacks followed them, or else.

Now the Civil Rights Movement was causing rifts in the fabric of their communities.

Sometimes, blacks spoke out, like Mr. Hardy had, or the way Lastun had spoken to Ellis Barber.

Incidents like that often provoked retribution by the whites, and the blacks suffered. Which invoked a repetition of the cycle.

A flicker of movement caught Lastun's eye. A doe. About fifty yards away—looking right at him, it seemed.

It would take a precise shot to take down a deer with a .22, but it could be done. He could shoot the heart, but the bullet wouldn't easily penetrate the thickness of flesh there, and it could be deflected by a rib. If he didn't get the heart, the animal could run quite a distance before blood loss caused it to fall.

He could shoot the spine, right at the withers. That would cause paralysis, but it would require Lastun's most accurate skill. If he failed to cut the spine, the deer could still get away.

Then there was the head shot. He knew a .22 to the brain probably wouldn't kill the animal right away, but it would knock the deer down long enough for Lastun to run over and use his Barlow knife to cut its throat.

The deer was still looking in his direction. Lastun didn't move. He wouldn't be able to get off a snapshot before the deer saw him and bolted. Finally, the deer looked away toward something across the cotton field along the copse of trees where hunter and prey stood. In one smooth motion, Lastun brought the rifle to his shoulder, aimed at a spot just behind its eye, and fired.

The small caliber .22 sounded like a firecracker. It lacked the deeper percussive boom of a larger caliber weapon. The deer dropped as if its legs had been cut from under it.

Lastun was moving before the doe hit the ground. His long fingers plucked the knife from his jeans pocket. He flicked the blade open and knelt beside the fallen deer.

Its eyes were closed. Blood oozed from a small hole the size of a pencil eraser behind its eye. A clump of grass under its nose fluttered as it exhaled. Lastun slashed the doe's throat and stepped back to allow it to bleed out before field dressing it.

Won't Mama be surprised?

5

Old Tinker passed on a few years before. Afterwards, Papa made a trip to Yazoo City to look for a used tractor, but the cost was just too high. He talked with a few other colored sharecroppers about pooling their money to buy one, just as they had with the harrow and planter. But they couldn't swing the deal.

Papa wound up buying a yearling filly from Wade Nash. The animal was too young to put to the plow yet, so Papa traded off labor for the use of Leroy Harmon's mule. The labor Papa gave in trade was Lastun's. Mr. Harmon put him to work draining a bog on his property and then cleaning stumps from it so it could be cultivated. Yes, Mr. Harmon was a landowner now.

Lastun managed to free up a few hours each week to walk over and help Silas Polk with some of his field work. He did this so he could spend more time with Bizzy. Plus, it didn't hurt to cultivate a little good will with his future father-in-law, even though he hadn't popped the question yet.

Turnabout being fair play, Bizzy always seemed to find a little time to come to the Wicker's place and help Mama with her housework or her garden.

Graduation for all schools was scheduled for mid-May. Yazoo County Colored School would have three graduates in 1966; Beulah Jackson, Bizzy Polk, and Lastun Wicker. Everybody else had already dropped out to get on with their lives. Lastun might have done the same, but he realized that Mama had high hopes that her youngest son would become the first Wicker to receive a high school diploma. Lastun planned to propose to Bizzy that same night.

"If I was to ast somebody in this room to marry me, reckon what they might say?" Lastun said one night in early May. He and Bizzy were in the Wicker's kitchen making popcorn balls. He had popped a dishpan full of popcorn, while Bizzy mixed butter and peanuts into a gooey syrup of molasses. They would eventually stir everything together and shape the concoction into baseball-sized spheres. Half the fun was in seeing just how messy they could get.

"Are you askin'?" Bizzy said with a smile.

Lastun smiled back. "I'm astin' what you might say if I did ast."

Bizzy swung her hips, making her pleated dress swirl around her legs. "Well, how would I know what I might say until somebody really asks me?"

Lastun paused, stuck. *What if she say no?*

Bizzy grinned. "But I do know that the church is available the last Satiday in June, if somebody wanted to hold a wedding then."

Lastun would've turned a flip, if he hadn't been afraid he'd break some of Mama's dishes. He settled for putting his arms around Bizzy's slim waist.

She placed her sticky hands on his cheeks and gave him a deep kiss.

All his worries about how he would take care of this beautiful woman fled from his mind, at least for a while.

Once the popcorn balls were made, the couple brought them out to the front porch where Mama and Papa sat, along with Silas and Mary Polk, Bizzy's parents. Lastun passed the treats around, while Bizzy went back to get glasses of iced sweet tea for everybody.

"I heard tell Iowa got a big rain yestiday," Mr. Polk said. Ice clinked in his glass, as he took a sip of tea.

"Oh, Lawd. They ain't talking about floodin', are they?" Mama asked.

"May be. It's been wet all spring, and you know how rains up north often bring high water down our way. Only good thing about it, we always get good crops in years after a flood."

"The delta is God's mixin' bowl. The floods come, as much dirt as it is water. Mud. Then God stirs it all up, and when the water goes down, they's new soil everywhere," Mama said.

The group was silent for a while, only cricket-and-bullfrog song filled the night.

"I 'member the high water of '27," Mama said. "I wasn't' no more than eleven, I'd say. Papa was long gone. Me and Mama and my sister Rose lived with Mama's parents over in Tinsley.

"When the Mississippi River floods, it causes the Yazoo and all the other rivers to back up. It's bothersome. The sun is shinin' and here comes the water, quiet as a snake, coverin' the low ground, then movin' on up. Water had reached the porch and started in the house, maybe ankle-deep.

"Along come a couple a angels. Two men in a little row boat. They wasn't room for everybody, so me and Mama and Rose got in. Grandma and Grandpa stayed behind."

She grew quiet again. So was everybody else, waiting for her to finish the story.

"That's the way it is, I reckon. It's the old ones that sacrifice when it has to be done. They know they's lived their lives. Grandpa said he'd get out the ladder and they'd climb up on the roof, if they had to. I guess thass what they did 'cause the water just kept on risin'.

"They mighta made it, but the water cut the foundation out from under the house. It musta just floated on down with the current. When the high water went down, we come back. But they was gone, house and all. I never seen 'em again."

"Oh, Shandra," Mary Polk said, "what a pity."

"Yes, indeed,' Mama replied, "yes, it was."

High water came, but not like '27. Water covered the fields and roads. All farming and gardening work stopped. The only movement between houses and stores was by boat. The cow and the filly found a hillock that stayed dry. Lastun made a barge from one-by-four timbers, with empty five-gallon jerry cans as pontoons, and used it to float bales of hay out to them. He had to wade in thigh-high water to do it. The hens roosted in the higher levels of the barn.

The water lapped at the top step of the porch, but got no higher. It had begun to recede by the time graduation day came. Lastun didn't have to ask about the commencement ceremony. He knew it had been cancelled.

"It was a bit too much to have a ceremony for three people anyway," Mama said, but she couldn't hide the disappointment in her voice.

A week later, the water was gone, leaving muddy roads and fields behind. Lastun slogged his way over to the Polk home. He found Bizzy picking up branches and twigs that had washed into her family's yard from up-river. She stacked the wood in piles by size over beside the barn. When it dried out, it would be used for kindling or firewood.

Lastun helped. It didn't take long to finish the job, and the two took off their muddy shoes and rolled up the hems of their jeans. Bizzy got glasses of iced tea and honey cakes from the kitchen. They sat on the small back porch, beside Mrs. Polk's wash tub.

"Mr. Kilgore over at the store they's havin' a graduation ceremony at the white school next week, after the roads dry up some more," Lastun said, squinting out at the boggy field behind the house. "But they ain't gonna do one for the coloreds 'cause it's too much trouble."

Bizzy shrugged. "It don't matter to me. They's only three of us."

"Me, neither, but Mama's feelin's are hurt. She surely wanted to see me walk that stage."

"Well, if it means that much to her, I bet Mama could invite y'all and Beulah Jackson and her family over here. We could have a covered dish supper. Invite Mr. Saunders, too. We could have our own little ceremony." Bizzy took a bite of honey cake and waited for Lastun to think it over.

He fingered the item in his pocket. "You know, I think she'd like that."

So while the white school had its big ceremony, the graduates of the colored school and their families met at the Polks' home.

There were too many people to fit in their small house, but the weather turned warm and clear. The men-folk set up sawhorses under a shady oak between the garden and the barn and laid sheets of plywood on them. The ladies spread tablecloths and covered the improvised picnic tables with dishes that each family had brought; fried chicken, mashed potatoes, cornbread, black-eyed peas and butterbeans, corn, and peach cobbler for dessert. The vegetables and fruit had come from last year's stock, since the wet spring and flood had prevented any spring garden crops.

The picnic atmosphere buoyed everyone's spirits, and the breeze carried snatches of laughter and conversation between bites of food.

After the cobbler was served, and before Mr. Saunders began his little ceremony, Lastun pulled Bizzy aside, so the house stood between them and the rest of the group. He pulled a shiny object from his pocket. It was a steel bushing, a quarter-inch wide and the diameter of Bizzy's ring finger. He'd polished it so it glistened.

"You know I can't afford no ring," he said. "This is the best I can do. But it means all the same. Bizzy, I want to spend the rest of my days with you. Marry me." He slipped the improvised ring on her finger.

Bizzy's eyes glistened as she studied the ring. "You're right. It does mean the same. Yes, I'll marry you."

They kissed.

Mr. Saunder's voice carried from the back yard. "Lastun, Bizzy, I hope y'all ain't up to somethin', 'cause it's time to start this here ceremony."

The two returned to the picnic and announced their news. Mr. Saunder's speech was delayed, while everyone shook Lastun's hand and whispered bawdy jokes in his ear before hugging Bizzy.

Mr. Saunders spoke a while, but Lastun heard nothing. He received his diploma and shook the principal's hand. Mama hugged him and beamed like she was the graduate.

As the party began to break up, Mr. Saunders called Lastun back around the side of the house to where he'd proposed to Bizzy.

"They's somethin' you oughta know, Lastun," he said, a somber crease between his brows. "When you turn eighteen this December, the Army'll probly draft you. There's a place called Vietnam, over on the other side o' the Pacific Ocean, and President Johnson's aimin' to send a lot more of our soldiers there."

He'd heard men-folk gossiping about 'Nam, as they called it, but he hadn't really thought about how that war might apply to him. "Reckon is that good news or bad?" he asked.

"Both, I'd say. They draft you, you'll have to spend two years in the Army. You'd have to leave Bizzy and your family for a while. That's the bad news. As I see it, the good news is it pays money." Saunders frowned. "It'll be your money to do with as you see fit. And some boys wastes it on whiskey and women and worse. But if you're the man I think you are, you'll be sending most of it back home to Bizzy and your parents."

"Of course I will, Mistah Saunders."

The principal slapped Lastun's shoulder. "Well, I just wanted to let you know. I'm aware of how proud your mama is of that diploma."

That night, the Wickers and the Polks gathered on the Polk's front porch. Lastun related Mr. Saunders' news.

"I never had to go to war," Papa said. "Those colored that did in World War number two and Korea usually worked in the kitchens, or cleaned the barracks and other such stuff."

"I heerd the same," Mr. Polk said, "though I never wore a uniform neither."

"To hear Mr. Saunders tell it, they put colored in fightin' units now," Lastun explained.

The rocking chair Mama occupied had a squeak that showed up when she rocked backward. Usually, her motion was slow and rhythmic, making the sound melodic and soothing. Now it sped up, like the heartbeat of a frightened person. "Mebbe they won't call you up, Lastun," she said, "or mebbe you won't have to go where the fightin' is."

Lastun looked over at Bizzy, who sat on the wooden floor and leaned against one of the support posts. "Might be, we should wait about getting' married until after we get this sorted out," he said to her.

Bizzy flashed a smile that didn't carry to her eyes. "Oh, no. You ain't getting' outta your promise that easy. Besides, I done told the preacher we'd be needin' the church the last Satiday in June."

49

"But I didn't ast you 'til this afternoon."

"So what? I knowed what was comin'."

Lastun and Bizzy's parents laughed at the exchange.

"Well, looks like I got a weddin' cake to bake," Mary Polk said.

"I kin help," Mama Wicker said.

"You got yoreself a deal," Mrs. Polk responded.

The wedding took place as planned. Ruthie Lamp, Bizzy's best friend for all her high school years, served as maid of honor, while Carl Trees, Lastun's friend since first grade, acted as best man. Lastun stood with Bizzy, as the preacher said his marrying words. Bizzy wore a knee-length white dress. Her family couldn't afford anything fancy. Lastun wore his black Sunday suit. Bizzy already had the only ring Lastun had to give her, and Bizzy added a matching one to Lastun's hand.

In the days before emancipation, slaves often weren't allowed to marry, so a tradition developed in which the couple jumped over a broom lying on the ground to signify their intention to be married.

While Lastun and Bizzy stood before the preacher, Shandra Wicker and Mary Polk placed a broom on the floor behind them. The preacher declared them husband and wife, and once they kissed, they turned around and "jumped the broom" to honor their ancestral tradition.

Mrs. Polk had the wedding cake she'd promised. Mr. Polk supplied apple juice punch for the young folk, and Abraham Wicker had a hidden jug of applejack which he used to fortify the punch for the adults. Five of Lastun's siblings made it to the ceremony: Russum, Safara, David, Kissy, and Daisy. Lastun's sister Falana and her husband had moved up north to Chicago a few years ago. Georgia and her husband were living in Detroit.

The newlyweds didn't have a place of their own yet, so the Polks stayed with the Wickers. Lastun and Bizzy would have the Polk household to themselves for their wedding night.

The Polk house was of shotgun design, the same as the Wicker's. Bizzy retreated to the kitchen to get ready, while Lastun waited in the bedroom. Lastun had taken a substantial dose of applejack to prepare himself, and his heart galloped like a runaway horse. He took off his shoes, belt and shirt, leaving only his pants and undershorts to shuck.

Somebody had given Bizzy a lace nightgown that hid absolutely nothing. When she walked into the bedroom, Lastun thought he might faint.

"Baby, are you all right?" Bizzy asked, a concerned look on her face.

"I'm okay. I just need to sit on the bed here. Come sit beside me."

They kissed. She removed his remaining clothes. When he took off her lacy gown, he thought for a moment it was a lace doily and felt a sudden urge to laugh.

Her lips found his and he quickly sobered up.

A clamor of pots banging against pans resounded from outside. A dozen voices rose in ribald song. Lastun recognized Russum's and David's voices among the others.

"What the devil?" Lastun said with a frown. He knew what was going on, but their friends had incredibly bad timing.

"They's just givin' us a shivaree," Bizzy said with a small laugh. She wrapped a sheet around her bare body. "We'd better go out on the porch and let 'em have their fun. They won't shut up 'til we do."

Lastun looked at his crotch. "They coulda waited a while longer."

Lastun noticed that Bizzy made sure that some of her shoulder and one of her legs — but not too much — was showing when she went onto the porch. Lastun put on his undershorts and didn't try to hide the tent-pole effect his erection produced. This just made their friends all the more joyful.

Later, after they'd been serenaded, the newlyweds returned to their bed.

Later still, a sweaty Bizzy lay in the arms of an equally sweaty Lastun and whispered, "Do that again."

That summer and fall, Lastun and Bizzy lived with the Wickers, sleeping on a roll-away bed in the living room. Lastun spent his time helping his father and father-in-law bring in their cotton crops. He also worked at various farm labor jobs in the community—anything that came available. He hauled hay for a penny a bale, helping those with livestock prepare for the winter.

On December tenth, he celebrated his eighteenth birthday, and, following the legal requirements, registered at the Yazoo County Draft Board. Shortly after the new year in January 1967, he received a letter from the US Government which began, *"Greetings."*

6

The Yazoo City bus depot operated out of a gas station at the intersection of the city's two main streets. In fact, the owner sold tickets for Greyhound and Trailways buses as a side business to supplement his gas and car repair business.

The white folks' waiting area sat in the station's main lobby, which also housed the counter where patrons paid for gasoline, oil changes, and automobile repairs. While coloreds could enter to transact business, only whites could actually stay in the waiting area.

Lastun walked in with the usual trepidation of a colored entering a whites-only area. The room smelled of gasoline and motor oil wafting in from the mechanics' bays each time the door opened.

Calendars from past years, featuring photos of skimpily clad models holding auto parts, covered the walls. A Coca-Cola vending machine stood in one corner, accompanied by a rack filled with packages of Lance's salted peanuts and potato chips.

A white man in black pants and a white shirt sat on a bench and watched Lastun with sleepy eyes. Another white man in oil-stained khaki pants and shirt stood behind the counter. A lit cigarette drooped from his lips. "Help you?" he asked. The cigarette danced when he spoke.

"Ticket to Hattiesburg, suh," Lastun said. After a pause, he continued. "Do the bus stop at Camp Shelby?"

"Army got ya, huh?" the clerk asked, one eye half-closed against the cigarette smoke.

"Yes, suh."

"I'll sell you a Greyhound ticket from here to Gulfport. You'll change buses at Jackson. The bus from Jackson to

Gulfport will stop at Hattiesburg. Just stay with the bus. Tell the driver you want to get off at Camp Shelby. It's on Highway Forty-Nine between Hattiesburg and Gulfport. He'll stop at the gate and let you off. Got that?"

"Yes, suh. Thank ye, suh."

Lastun bought his ticket and went to the colored waiting area — a bench outside the station, beside the service bay doors. Mama, Papa and Bizzy waited for him there, bundled against the January cold.

"Bus'll be here in half a hour," Lastun said, taking a seat on the bench.

Bizzy sat with him. Mama and Papa stood nervously beside them. They made small talk until the behemoth of a bus pulled up with a gusty *whoosh* of brakes and the stink of diesel exhaust.

Lastun stood and picked up the burlap sack that held a change of clothes, a bar of soap, and a ham sandwich.

"You know what to do," Mama said, touching his cheek with her fingertips. "Always—"

"I know, Mama," Lastun interrupted. His smile belied the anxiety he felt. "Always say suh or ma'am to white folks or older coloreds, and sit in the back of the bus. You taught me that at Mistuh Kilgore's store, except for sittin' in the back of the bus."

Mama wiped a tear from her eye. "You a good boy, Lastun. I'm so proud a you."

Lastun couldn't speak because of the lump in his throat. He gave his mama a hug, shook Papa's hand, and gave Bizzy a big hug and kiss on the lips.

"You come back ta me, you hear?" Bizzy whispered. Her eyes glistened with unshed tears.

"I will."

"Promise me."

"I promise." Lastun's voice quivered. "Promise you'll be here when I get back."

"I promise."

Lastun walked to the bus driver, who stood by the vehicle's door and handed him his ticket.

The driver tore off his portion of the stub and handed the rest back to Lastun. "Sit on the back row."

"Yes, suh."

In the Jackson bus depot, Lastun hovered in the colored waiting room, watching the clock and checking every bus that came and went, afraid he'd miss his connection. His antics drew amused looks from the other, more experienced travelers, who were dressed in clothes finer than Lastun's faded jeans and denim jacket.

Finally, a matronly woman said, "Just set down, son. I'll let you know when yo bus get here."

She looked enough like Mama that Lastun decided to trust her. He sat. Once he settled down, the fatigue brought on by his anxiety made him drowsy. He'd dropped off into a light doze when the old woman nudged him. "Yo bus is here."

"Thank ye," Lastun said, as he jumped up. "Thank ye, Ma'am."

During the short drive from Yazoo City to Jackson, the landscape changed from flat, plowed fields to suburban and then urban surroundings. On the trip to Hattiesburg, the landscape changed yet again to seemingly endless miles of pine forest. He thought of Bizzy and his parents, who'd be home by now. *I wonder what they're doing?* A lump rose in his throat. *Are they missing me yet?*

Lastun waited until the bus stopped in Hattiesburg before eating his ham sandwich. Forty-five minutes later, he stepped off at the entrance to Camp Shelby, fearing that he'd arrived at the Gates of Hell.

Camp Shelby had served as the Army induction center for all Mississippi draftees at least since World War II. It had no fire or brimstone, and it didn't smell of Sulphur, but it teemed with an orderly chaos of uniformed men rushing about.

Lastun showed his letter to a guard wearing a green coat over a khaki uniform. The guard directed him to a bench where a non-uniformed man sat. Lastun shivered in the cool January air — or maybe it was fear.

The other man sitting on the bench looked just as overwhelmed as Lastun felt, but he was white, so neither spoke.

A short while later, a tan Chevy Impala pulled up to the gate and another white man got out carrying a plaid cloth suitcase. He showed a letter to the guard, who pointed to the bench where Lastun sat. The new arrival waved to the driver of the Impala. The car pulled away. Lastun shifted over as far as he could to allow the man to sit. He felt uncomfortable sitting on a bench with two white men.

The guard picked up a phone. Five minutes later an open-topped Jeep screeched to a stop in front of the bench. "Okay, boots, hop on," the driver said.

The other two men clambered into the vehicle, so Lastun followed. He pulled the collar of his jacket closer around his neck as the Jeep blasted through the maze of streets, finally stopping at a long metal building that looked like a half-buried pipe.

"Welcome to the Army, boys," the driver said. When the trio hesitated, he said, "C'mon, don't waste my time. Here's your stop."

They jumped out and watched the Jeep speed away.

Another man in khaki approached. He wore a green jacket with three stripes on the upper arms. "Okay, recruits, follow me," he ordered, and walked through the door of the metal building.

So far, Lastun had been called a boot and a recruit. His head swimming, he followed the man, carefully allowing the two whites to go first.

Inside the building, a center aisle separated two rows of cots. Almost all had a bag or suitcase resting on them, signifying that somebody had already claimed it. The man with stripes on his sleeves said, "You'll sleep here tonight." He looked at Lastun. "You should take that empty one over there." He pointed toward a spot where several other colored boys were congregated.

Lastun started in that direction when the man spoke again, but to everyone in the room this time. "Mess is at eighteen-hundred hours. That's half an hour from now. The latrine is at the back of the building."

Lastun dropped his burlap sack on the cot he'd been directed to. The other coloreds introduced themselves, but Lastun was too nervous to remember any names. He looked at the member of the group who seemed the friendliest—David Martin. Lastun remembered his name. "That man said mess is in half an hour. What's a mess?"

Martin grinned. "That's Sergeant Booker. Them three stripes on his shirt means sergeant. Mess is what they call eatin'. What he meant is we eat supper in half a hour." His grin widened. "I hope that means we get a mess of food."

Lastun smiled in response to his joke. "Okay. What's a latrine?"

"That's a bathroom." He pointed to the same spot Sergeant Booker had pointed. 'It's right there."

"What about for coloreds?"

57

"Son, your life is about to change. In the Army, coloreds and whites use the same mess hall and the same latrine."

Lastun goggled.

Martin laughed. "Yep, but still, watch out. Stay away from the white folk. Black skin don't mean much to most of them northern boys. But the southern boys, they won't appreciate you getting' too close." He laughed again at Lastun's confused expression, and looked around so his gaze took in the group of coloreds. "We just need to stay together. We eat together, we shower together. Everything together. That way, some white bastard won't likely try to pick on one of us."

That made sense. "How come you know so much?"

"My older brother got drafted last year. He told me what to expect."

Sergeant Booker appeared at the building door. "Listen up, recruits, form up in two lines . . . now!"

Everyone hustled to comply.

"Follow me to the mess hall," he ordered.

The building where the sergeant said Lastun was to sleep was called a barracks, and there were a lot of them in the camp. By the time Lastun's group got to the mess hall, a long line had already formed, but it moved quickly.

They entered a large, flat, square building. The line proceeded down a center hallway. To one side was a recreational area where ping pong and card tables were arrayed around a couple of sofas and a television. The other side contained the mess hall, which turned out to be a lunch room, much like the one at Lastun's school—only bigger.

Lastun watched the people in front of him in order to learn what to do. The man ahead of him picked a tray from a large stack and began walking down a cafeteria-style serving line. Lastun followed. Men in white T-shirts and aprons piled food on plates: green peas, corn, mashed potatoes and gravy, and a meat patty of some kind — plus a roll. The last man in the white apron line dropped the plate on Lastun's tray. He didn't seem to care if the gravy sloshed. Lastun grabbed a spoon, knife and fork. He placed a glass of iced tea on his tray and followed David Martin to a table in the corner of a large room of tables.

"How'm I s'posed to pay for this food?" Lastun asked Martin.

"You don't," Martin answered, without further explanation.

Lastun didn't pursue the subject. He just tucked in. It wasn't as good as Mama's or Bizzy's cooking, but it was good enough. And Martin was right. There was a mess of it.

He wasn't the only one who followed Martin around like a puppy dog. Every colored man in Lastun's barracks did the same. Having established himself as the expert, Martin didn't seem to mind. After all, he'd warned them to stick together.

They showered after mess. Naked men didn't bother Lastun; he'd played sports in high school. But he was unaccustomed to seeing naked white bodies. Martin's group stayed at one end of the shower area, and the whites stayed at the other.

"We'll have breakfast tomorrow just like we did supper this evening. Then we'll go to a big building where they'll run all kinds of tests. You know, medical stuff." He grinned. "When the doctor tells you to turn your head and cough, don't mind where he puts his hand. He's just doing his job. If you pass the physical, you'll have to fill out some papers . . . and bingo, you're in the Army!"

"What if you don't pass the physical?" another man asked.

"Well, they just send you back home," Martin answered.

The next day went just as David Martin had predicted, and Lastun passed his physical. Late in the afternoon, he and a group of others were ushered into a classroom with rows of tables and chairs—like at school. He sat when ordered to do so.

A sergeant stood at the front of the room. "Congratulations, soldiers, you are now the property of the United States Army."

A chill ran down Lastun's spine. He knew the sergeant was only making a point, and he probably repeated those same words to every group he inducted. But did he know how those words affected the coloreds who heard him? He would do what the sergeant told him. He would do what the Army required him to do. *But nobody owns me.*

"You're being given a packet of forms." As he spoke several men with two stripes on their sleeves—corporals, Lastun had learned—passed out the papers the sergeant had referred to.

"Do not. Repeat. Do not begin to complete these forms. I will guide you through that process."

Lastun spent the rest of the afternoon completing the paperwork. He wordlessly thanked Kissy and all his teachers for the hard work they'd put in teaching him how to read and write. Even some white folks seemed to struggle, but Lastun had an advantage; he'd spent his life learning how to follow instructions, literally and exactly.

He filled out tax forms, insurance forms, next-of-kin forms, and allotment forms for Bizzy and for Mama.

Back at the barracks, Lastun learned that two of the coloreds and four of the whites had failed their physicals.

"We've had it easy so far," Martin warned them. "Tomorrow, we'll go to boot camp."

"Where will that be?" Lastun asked.

"Different places, I expect."

"What will it be like there?"

Martin grinned. "I'll let you find that out for yourself."

The next morning after breakfast, Sergeant Booker ordered the recruits to stand in front of their cots. "When I call your name, you will announce, 'Present.' I will then tell you your bus number. You will immediately depart, find that bus, and board it. Anderson, Charles."

"Present."

"Bus number four."

A young white man jogged out the door.

"Arnott, William."

"Present."

And so it went until Lastun was the only person left in the barracks. The sergeant acted as if the building was still full.

"Wicker, Lastun."

"Present."

"Bus number eight."

Lastun grabbed his burlap sack of clothing and hustled out the door. Lines of school buses—painted Army green—were parked along the street between the rows of barracks. Recruits also piled out of the other buildings. Lastun found the bus which had a placard with an "8" posted in the windshield.

He climbed aboard. It was almost full.

Several colored were already sitting in their usual place. Lastun joined them.

A soldier boarded the bus, sat in the driver's seat, and placed a satchel on the floor beside him. He removed the numbered placard from the windshield and closed the door. All the buses began to roll out in unison.

Lastun leaned over and whispered to another of the colored recruits. "Do you know where we're goin'?"

"Nuh-unh, I don't think anybody does 'cept the driver."

When the buses passed out of the Camp Shelby gate, some turned north toward Jackson and some turned south toward

Gulfport. Bus number eight turned south. The southbound buses stayed in a convoy until they reached Highway Ninety, which ran parallel to the Gulf of Mexico beaches. Some turned east toward Alabama and Florida. Lastun's bus was among those that turned west. The soldier/driver had a supply of sandwiches and Coca-Cola on board, which he handed out at lunch time. He stopped at gas stations every couple of hours for bathroom breaks. Since these were privately owned, Lastun and the other coloreds had to look for a *"Coloreds Only"* bathroom. If there was none, they trudged off into the bushes or lurked behind the building to do their business.

The bus crossed the Louisiana line, then turned off Highway Ninety onto a smaller road. Later, it crossed the Mississippi River at Baton Rouge. The sun had long since set when the bus pulled into an Army base with a sign that read, *"Fort Polk, Louisiana."*

7

The bus entered through a gate to a checkerboard of streets lined with buildings similar to those at Camp Shelby. It stopped along the edge of an area that reminded Lastun of a football field. Banks of lights lined the space, turning night into day. Another bus stopped a few yards ahead of Lastun's.

The driver opened the doors and grabbed the satchel of folders. "Wait here," he said. He joined the other driver and two sergeants wearing Smokey the Bear hats. Lastun was surprised to see that one of the sergeants was black. He watched them shuffle the files as if they were a deck of cards. After a few minutes, the group broke up.

The white sergeant approached Lastun's bus, climbed up and stood next to the driver's seat. "Okay, listen up," he announced, "when I call your name, you are to exit the vehicle and stand behind the bus. Atwood, Bruce!"

When they were through, each sergeant had a group of thirty people. Each sergeant took his group to a corner of the field.

"All right, boots," Lastun's sergeant yelled, "form up in six lines, five to a line. Make sure you are an arm's length from the man beside you and from the man in front of you."

The group scrambled to obey. Lastun tried for the back row, but so did everybody else. He wound up in the middle.

When the group was formed to the sergeant's satisfaction, he stood in the center front and announced, "I've never had the misfortune of welcoming such a sorry-assed bunch of recruits before, but I have to follow orders, so welcome to the Yewnited States Army!" He seemed to think the group was hard of hearing because he shouted everything at the top of his lungs.

"You are Charlie Platoon of Alpha Company! Is that clear? Repeat after me."

And the entire platoon chanted the words in unison.

"Over the next nine weeks, you will undergo basic training here at Fort Polk, also known as Tigerland. You are fortunate. Why? Because the climate and geographic conditions in the Fort Polk area are very similar to that of a little place called Vietnam, which will be your next duty station after Tigerland."

Moving only his eyes, because he didn't want to draw attention to himself, Lastun tried to take in his surroundings. Even though it was January, the weather was warm enough for a few flying insects to hover around the lights. Occasionally a dark blur flashed through the sparse swarm. Bats.

"Now," the sergeant rubbed his hands together in a gleeful fashion, "let's get to know each other, shall we?"

It was the middle of the night. Lastun thought there would be plenty of time to get to know each other in the morning— *after a good night's sleep.*

The sergeant approached the first man in the front line and stood nose to nose. The recruit was a handsome fellow, and he knew it.

"What's your name, Boot?" The sergeant asked.

"Lamp, sir."

The sergeant did a double-take. "What did you call me?"

Lamp flinched under his gaze. "Sir."

"Well, Lamp, I am no sir. Do you see these stripes?" He pointed to the sleeve of his jacket.

"Yes, s—yes."

"That means I'm a sergeant. I work for a living. I am not a sir."

Lamp wisely said nothing.

The sergeant bounced on his toes. "Lamp, that won't do." He rubbed his chin. "I see you're a pretty boy. I think I'll call you Casanova."

Lamp still didn't say anything.

The sergeant moved down the line to stand before the second man. He pointed to a name tag above his breast pocket. "What does that name tag say, Boot?"

"Carter, S—Sergeant."

The sergeant flung his arms out and looked up into the night sky. "Good God in Heaven above! I've got pretty boys and illiterates! You see that tag?" He pointed at it again. "It says Drill Sergeant! That's my name . . . Drill Sergeant." He paused and allowed his gaze to flow over everyone in the platoon. "When you speak to me, you will address me as Drill Sergeant. Now, what's my name?" This to the man he'd originally asked.

"Drill Sergeant."

"Drill Sergeant, what?"

The man looked confused and miserable. "Drill Sergeant Carter?"

The drill sergeant snatched his hat off his head and seemed to be about to thrash the man. "No, no, no! When you answer a question, you always end your answer with my name. Now, what's my name?"

The man looked sick. "Drill Sergeant . . . Drill Sergeant."

"Yes, there's hope for you after all!"

And so it went. Each recruit got a cut from the drill sergeant's sharp tongue. Finally, he came to Lastun. He stood so close Lastun could tell he'd had onions with his hamburger at supper. "Well, who in the world would send me a runt like you?"

"I don't know, suh." Lastun had heard the drill sergeant tell the platoon not to call him sir, but his mother's training won out.

"What did you call me?"

"I called you suh. I'm sorry, Drill Sergeant."

He studied Lastun closely. "What's your name?"

"Wicker . . . Drill Sergeant."

"Not any more. From now on, your name is Runt. What's your name?"

"Runt, Drill Sergeant."

The drill sergeant wasn't through with him yet. "And what color is your skin, Runt?"

It was brown, but usually coloreds were said to be black.

"Black, Drill Sergeant."

Again, the sergeant looked up into the night sky. "I've got a pretty boy, an illiterate, and now I've got a blind man! No, for your information, Runt, your skin color is Army green. What color is your skin?"

"Army green, Drill Sergeant."

Just to make his point, the sergeant went to a recruit, an Indian whose skin was the color of red clay. "What color is your skin, Boot?"

"Army green, Drill Sergeant."

He stopped in front of a white recruit.

"Army green, Drill Sergeant," the boot said before he could be asked.

The sergeant only grunted.

Lastun understood the point the sergeant tried to make, but he chose to wait and see how his fellow recruits treated him and the others whose skin the sergeant might call Army green, but who were definitely not white. After all, he knew how people like Ellis Barber back home treated Bizzy and other coloreds. And he knew what would happen if he tried to drink from the white water fountain, or use the white restroom at the Yazoo County Courthouse.

Having tired of his game, the sergeant marched his platoon to a building about two blocks from the parade ground.

With no sun in the sky to help, Lastun could only guess at the time. *After midnight.* That was the best he could do. *Maybe they'll finally let us get some sleep.*

The drill sergeant assembled the platoon in front of the building. "This is the quartermaster's depot. The men inside will issue uniforms and linens for you. Enter single file."

Four sleepy-looking clerks stood behind a service counter in the front room of the building. They looked about as happy to be there as the recruits did. Another sergeant supervised the operation.

Each recruit was given a duffel bag—guess what color. The clerks questioned the recruits about clothing and shoe sizes, then gave each the standard issue of pants, shirts, shoes, socks, skivvies and linens.

When Lastun approached the counter, the clerk said, "We don't carry kids' sizes, boy."

Lastun had nothing to say.

The clerk eyed him more closely. "I'll give you the smallest sizes I've got. I think they'll work for you."

"Thank you, suh," Lastun said.

"Don't call me sir," the clerk responded with an uneasy glance at the sergeant. "Nobody gets called sir except officers."

"What's a officer?" Lastun asked.

"Next."

Lastun stepped away from the counter to pack his duffel with the items while another recruit had his order filled.

The next step involved changing into a set of khakis; GI issue pants, shirt, underwear, shoes and socks. They were given boxes and instructed to pack all their civilian clothes and personal belongings in the box, tape it up, and address it to their next of kin back home. Lastun had been too harried to think of Bizzy, but writing her name on the box sent a pang through his heart.

At last the task was completed and the drill sergeant marched them to their barracks. The set-up was much like Camp Shelby. A row of cots lined each long wall. This time an upright locker stood beside each cot. Lastun and the three other colored recruits chose spots together in a far corner of the room. A shower and latrine was located at the back of the building along with an office and separate sleeping quarters for the drill sergeant.

"Okay, listen up! You will now make your beds." At this point, Lastun was ready to sleep on the bare mattress. "You have two sheets . . ." The drill sergeant went through a step-by-step procedure for applying sheets, blankets, and pillow cases. Although Bizzy usually did this job, Lastun knew how—or thought he did.

"Do you call that making a bed, Runt? A polecat wouldn't sleep in that bed!" the drill sergeant shouted. "Pull the sheets tight. Make the corners square!" He stripped the bedclothes off the cot, leaving them in a pile on the floor. "Now try it again."

Lastun drew comfort from the fact that nobody else got it right, either. He guessed that the drill sergeant's goal was to make everyone's life miserable, to reveal just how incompetent all the recruits really were. He had no idea how correct his guess was.

Finally, the drill sergeant was satisfied, or maybe had just given up. Lastun went to bed, hoping he'd get to sleep late in the morning, since they'd been up most of the night.

It seemed his head no more than touched his pillow before the loudspeakers began playing some God-awful trumpet music. It was still dark outside.

The drill sergeant switched on the lights and stood at the head of the room, already fully dressed. "Awright, get your lazy asses out of bed! What do you think this is, a vacation? You've got five minutes to shower, dress in fatigues, and form up outside the barracks. Move!"

Before Lastun could enter the shower area, a big, white recruit whom the drill sergeant had named Goliath stopped him. "You Niggers can wait until the white guys shower. That goes for you, too, Injun." This last comment was directed to the Indian, who was also headed for the shower.

So much for everybody in the Army being the same color. Lastun knew he'd never be able to shower in the time allowed, if he waited for the whites to finish. So he skipped it. He'd been on the bus all day yesterday, and he knew he smelled rank. He could only hope the drill sergeant didn't stand too close to him this morning.

Lastun was one of the last to join the formation. He didn't know why the drill sergeant gave them impossible timeframes to do their jobs. He could only do his best. *But I'll have to get a shower soon.*

"Okay, Grunts!" the drill sergeant shouted when everyone was gathered in a ragged formation outside the barracks. "We're gonna take a leisurely three-mile jog, just to get our appetites up before breakfast. Right face!"

The drill sergeant executed a crisp right-face maneuver. Lastun did his best to copy it. As a whole, the platoon managed a listless shuffle which resulted in everybody facing right.

"Double-time, harch!" The drill sergeant started out in a brisk jog.

The occupants of every other barracks building had come out to do the same thing. Some seemed to have been here longer because their group movements were more polished.

This ain't what you call leisurely, Lastun thought.

The drill sergeant limited their route to streets within the camp, itself. The layout seemed like a small town. The streets were lined with buildings of various sizes. There was also plenty of woods around. Lastun figured many trails wound through them, but apparently travelling those would occur some other day.

He was used to hard physical labor, so the only discomfort Lastun felt was from his ill-fitting shoes. *I'll hafta find some rags to stuff in them*, he thought.

Not everyone was in good shape, though, and the drill sergeant seemed to exhaust himself trying to harass a half-dozen of the slower, fatter recruits into keeping up. Goliath was one of those who struggled with the run. This pleased Lastun greatly.

The drill sergeant ended their jog at the mess hall, where the platoon finished plates full of eggs, bacon, grits and biscuits, along with a few gallons of coffee and fruit juice. That was one good thing, the food was plentiful and boosted Lastun's energy, although he still felt bushed from lack of sleep.

Their next stop was the camp barber shop, a building with six chairs in a row, each with man in a white tunic. Lastun had barely settled into one of the chairs than he felt a cool breeze on his scalp and he heard the barber yell, "Next!" Someone had put a mirror on the wall. Lastun peeked and discovered he'd been sheared like a sheep.

Now we'll get a break, Lastun thought, *so we can rest awhile.*

8

The drill sergeant marched them to the parade ground and ordered them to form up. "I never saw such a ragged-ass buncha boots this morning on your three-mile run, and believe me, I've seen my share. You are a unit. You're going to learn to stand in formation as a unit, and march in formation as a unit. When you run, you will run in formation. Hell, I'll even have you shit in formation. Are we clear?"

"Yes, drill sergeant," the platoon shouted in unison.

The remainder of the morning was devoted to the drill sergeant's instruction on how to do everything—in formation. He taught them how to stand at attention. He taught left face, right face and about face.

"No! No! No, you dumbass!" he shouted at Casanova. "Start with your left foot! No! Your other left! Now, drop and give me fifty!"

Every mistake was punished with an order to do pushups, as a unit.

By lunch, Lastun's arms felt like rubber, and his brain felt as if it was made of mush.

At least he wasn't the worst of the bunch, and intentionally not the best.

The afternoon began with a five-mile run, followed by more marching drills. Even in January, every platoon member was sweaty and smelly.

After dinner, the platoon was given a few precious minutes of downtime. Everyone crashed, but not on their cots. Nobody wanted to muss the bed linen and incur the drill sergeant's wrath. They discovered that sleeping on the floor was not difficult at all, given the level of their fatigue.

Lastun checked to make sure that Goliath was lying down and decided to use this time to grab a shower. He took a clean pair of skivvies from his locker and started toward the rear of the barracks.

"You ain't plannin' to use my shower, are you?" Goliath leaned on one elbow.

"Mistah Goliath, I got to get cleaned up. The drill sergeant will hang me if I don't. Besides, you said I could shower if no whites was usin' it."

Goliath climbed to his feet. The yellow incandescent light reflected off his scalp and taut muscles.

"I changed my mind. No niggers are going to use my shower."

From the corner of his eye, Lastun saw the other colored recruits exchange glances. *Maybe they'll join up with me to stand against this man.*

Nope. They stayed still and silent. Lastun would have to resolve this problem on his own. He tried to hide his dismay. He knew the drill sergeant wouldn't let him get by. He'd been lucky that he hadn't already been called out for poor hygiene. *Maybe I could sneak over to another barracks and use their shower. No. I won't have time, plus there'd almost certainly be some white bully to hassle me wherever I go.*

"I'm sorry, Mistuh Goliath, I got to clean up."

"Are you challengin' me, boy?" Goliath slowly advanced on Lastun. "Look at you, Runt. Do you really think you can take me?" The big man threw a roundhouse hook, but Lastun saw it coming and easily side-stepped it.

"Come on, Mistuh Goliath, suh. I don't want to fight you."

"What's this?" The drill sergeant stood at the door to his quarters. "Fighting? If you two still have this much energy after today's training, I can see we'll have to do some more strenuous activities tomorrow."

The platoon groaned as one.

"In the meantime, if you two have a beef, you should know my solution for conflict resolution is in the boxing ring. Platoon, form up in the gymnasium in five minutes. Move!" The drill sergeant executed a crisp left face and marched out the door.

Despair flooded Lastun's spirit. His instincts told him he was among wolves, and showing weakness would be dangerous.

He hadn't slept more than an hour or two in the last thirty-six, and he'd spent the day doing push-ups, running, and marching. Not to mention, there was a reason the drill sergeant had named him Runt and the white man Goliath. The wind from one of the giant's punches would likely knock him down.

Still, Lastun had been in a few fist-fights and had done okay. Goliath might have him in size, but Lastun was a small and nimble target. He began to form a strategy.

The boxing thing—settling disputes in the ring—must have been a regular practice. The drill sergeant corralled a couple of other sergeants to put gloves on the combatants. Sergeant May, the black sergeant Lastun had seen upon arrival at Fort Polk, put Lastun's gloves on. The two were left in their olive drab T-shirts, fatigue pants, and drill boots. Recruits from other platoons joined Lastun's group around the boxing ring. Immediately, the group started placing bets. Lastun didn't have to guess which way the odds were going.

The two met the drill sergeant in the center of the ring. "Sergeants Towne and May," he indicated the noncoms who'd taken positions in opposite corners of the ring, "will serve as your seconds. You'll fight three minute rounds until somebody goes down for a ten count or throws in a towel. There'll be no rabbit punches, no kidney punches, no punches below the belt." He looked at their footwear. "Anybody who kicks the other guy will spend a week in the stockade. Now go to your corners. When the bell rings, come out fighting."

Back in his corner, Sergeant May said, "I don't know what kind of boxer you are, kid, but I wouldn't let him land a haymaker. As big as he is, there won't be much of you left."

Lastun nodded.

The bell rang and both men lumbered into the center of the ring. Lastun didn't know how juiced Goliath might be at the prospect of beating up a scrawny colored guy, but he knew the adrenaline kick his survival instinct gave him might keep him going for a round or two.

Based on the punch Goliath had thrown in the barracks, Lastun judged that the big man's experience came from drunken brawls where two men stood toe-to-toe and threw punches until somebody went down.

If he'd had the energy, Lastun would have bounced around on his toes like that Muhammad Ali guy, teasing Goliath into throwing punches he couldn't land, tiring him out even more. Instead, Lastun plodded around, trying to stay out of the big man's reach. Goliath cooperated, eagerly throwing punches which Lastun easily slipped. The first round ended without Lastun ever throwing a punch. The crowd let him know its displeasure.

Halfway through the second round, Leroy Stockard, a colored recruit from his platoon, shouted at Lastun, "You gonna hafta hit him, Wicker. Else you ain't gonna beat him."

Lastun knew this, but he wanted Goliath to punch until his arms were too heavy to lift.

In the third round, Lastun sneaked inside to pepper Goliath's face with a couple of jabs. The only thing this did was make the giant mad. He increased his pursuit of the runt.

Lastun dropped back into a corner, and when Goliath lumbered after him, tried to slide past along the ropes. Fatigue made him too slow. Goliath wrapped his massive left arm around him and shoved him back into the corner. He hit Lastun with a right hook that made his vision gray out. All he could do was cover up as the giant launched a barrage of blows. Lastun ducked and twisted, trying to slip the punches. But even the grazing strikes felt like hammer blows. Lastun knew he wouldn't last long.

The bell rang.

The late flurry had aroused the crowd. The gym resounded with shouts and foot stomps. Someone hit Lastun with a paper wad. Even that hurt. The place smelled of sweat, testosterone and savagery.

Smelling blood, Goliath didn't stop.

The drill sergeant and Sergeant Towne, Goliath's corner man, had to pull him off.

Sergeant May wiped Lastun's face with a towel. "Your left eye is swelling up some, and you've got a bloody lip. If I was you, son, I'd just go down on the next punch and get this thing over with."

Lastun was too tired to respond.

The bell rang and Lastun met Goliath in the center of the ring. Both men staggered in a circle around each other, swaying on their feet.

The muscles in the big man's right shoulder bunched, and Lastun realized Goliath was about to throw a right hook. He always led with his right. Lastun, still quicker despite his exhaustion, threw a right of his own, so hard his feet left the ground.

Goliath's head rocked back and his knees almost buckled — almost.

Lastun stepped back and ducked, allowing Goliath's flailing punch to sail over his head.

75

The crowd sensed the change in the flow of the contest and the yelling increased. The match was about to end one way or another. Still low, he jabbed to Goliath's solar plexus. He moved in even closer so Goliath had no room to counterpunch, and launched an uppercut into the point of the giant's chin.

Goliath toppled like a felled tree.

Lastun stood over the vanquished. He couldn't believe he had done it.

"Not bad," the drill sergeant said after he'd counted out the loser. "You just learned what you can do when you have to."

Sergeant Towne walked up with a bucket of water and dashed its contents into Goliath's face. The big man woke and sputtered, but it took two of his buddies to get him to his feet.

"Okay, my platoon, listen up!" the drill sergeant shouted. "Everybody will have access to the showers, the latrines, and any other Army facilities at any time I say. If anyone is to be denied access to these services, it will be on my order only. Is that clear?"

"Yes, Drill Sergeant!"

"Dismissed." He turned to Lastun. "Runt, go get a shower." As Lastun staggered back to his barracks, Sergeant May walked beside him. "Don't get any ideas about everything being hunky-dory now," he said. "If you think you just created equality, you're wrong. A lot of those white guys are going to hold this against you and the other blacks. Things may not be easy, but show the same guts you did in the ring and you will get through it."

"Yes, Drill Sergeant," Lastun said.

After showering, Lastun planned to write a letter to Bizzy, but he was too tired. He hit the sack and immediately blacked out.

It seemed that he'd no sooner gone to sleep than the bugler sounded Reveille.

When they issue me a gun, Lastun thought, *the first thing I'm gonna do is shoot that damn bugler.*

9

Dear Bizzy,

I'm fine and hope you are, too. I think about you every day.

The drill sergeant says we have nine weeks of basic training, or "boot camp," as everybody calls it. The first three weeks are mostly PT. That's what they call physical training. That means we run, or march, or exercise all the time. Some of my platoon must have been pretty lazy before they got here because they're having a hard time. I never thought I'd be happy that I had to do all that farm work, but it sure has helped me keep up with all the PT.

Everything we do is in formation. We even have to march in step. To help with that, the drill sergeant counts time. Sometimes, he just shouts, "Hup, two, three, four." But he's also taught us some songs to sing as we run or march. I'm not going to tell you the words to the songs, though.

Yesterday, the drill sergeant added an obstacle course to our PT. We have to crawl through mud, go under and over barb wire, walk on a four-by-four rail, and climb a wall that's ten or twelve feet high. Sounds easy, right?

The middle three weeks will be weapons training. We'll have guns to shoot at targets, and throw hand grenades. I don't think it'll be anything dangerous, though. The drill sergeant watches out for us pretty good.

The last three weeks will be what they call field maneuvers. We're supposed to learn how to move around in the woods, and not get lost, and stuff like that. Sounds like a hunting trip in Yazoo County.

The food is good, and there's plenty of it. I was surprised about that.

Oh, and I bet I can make a bed better than you can. I got to go. I hope you're doing well. Have you and Mama got an allotment check yet?

I Love You,

Lastun

Lastun decided not to say anything about the throwdown with Goliath, or about how harsh the drill sergeant really was. He knew Bizzy would read every letter to Mama, and he thought it was best if they didn't know about such things.

When he sealed the letter in the envelope, he gently kissed Bizzy's name before he dropped it in the mail slot.

Since the boxing match, and what the drill sergeant had said afterward, the whites and the coloreds stayed clear of each other as much as possible. Both sides were careful not to start anything. Charley Greyfeather, a half-blood Comanche from Texas, was accepted in the colored group and was given the nickname, "Comanche." The stringent schedule meant that the groups couldn't shower at different times, so the non-whites got the back corner of the shower space.

The drill sergeants kept all the platoons in constant motion; run, march, hike, obstacle course. Even the flabbiest of the recruits dropped pounds and gained muscle.

The platoon did get a little personal time, although much of it had to be devoted to such things as spit-shining boots and polishing brass belt buckles. At least they could sit on the cots or on the floor in a group and socialize.

Jimmy Pennington, a tall, muscular colored from Dyersburg, Tennessee, loved to tell 'Nam stories — whether they were true or not. "The VC, that's what they call the Viet Cong, like to make a homemade mine called a Bouncing Betty. They use a C ration can and explosive from a dud mortar shell or some other weapon that they've found or stolen. When you step on the trigger, a spring throws it up to about balls' height before it goes off. Then you get castrated."

Lastun's groin clenched. He kept his head down and paid close attention to the brass belt buckle he was polishing. The problem with Jimmy was that half of his tales were true — only you didn't know which half.

"And they send whores with the clap out to service American GIs. That's why you always wear a rubber." Jimmy paused, a glint in his eye. "And don't let the whore give you one, 'cause she'll stick a pinhole in it."

Donnie Horton, a light-skinned colored man, tried to change the subject. "Comanche, why don't you tell us what it's like on the Indian reservation?"

Greyfeather looked just like all the Indian pictures Lastun had seen, right down to the stone-faced expression. "Why don't you tell us what it's like on the slave plantation?"

"Well," Donnie said, "I never lived on no slave plantation."

"I never lived on an Indian reservation, either. I grew up in downtown Houston."

Not long after boot camp started, mail call included a letter for Lastun with *"Mrs. Bizzy Wicker"* in the return address.

Jimmy Pennington saw it. "You mean there's a Mrs. Runt? How in hell did you get lucky enough to catch a wife?"

Lastun just grinned.

Lastun was the only married recruit of the non-white clique, so he was called on to relate his experiences in that area. He knew they wanted lurid details. *Not that anyone of them are virgins.* At least he didn't think so.

"If I was to tell you what you want to know, Bizzy would probly come and skin me alive."

"A real ball-breaker is she?" Leroy Stockard asked.

Lastun flinched. That wasn't the impression he wanted his friends to get. "Naw, she just likes her privacy. And I respect her enough to give it to her."

"Yeah, and I'll bet you give it to her all the time," Leroy crowed.

Lastun glowered at him. "Son, you need to take a cold shower."

February 1967

My Dearest Lastun,

It was so good to receive your letter and to hear that you're doing fine. I worried that Army life wouldn't suit you.

Your Mama and I both received our first allotment checks. We'd rather have you at home with us, but that money will be a big help.

Some people have been saying that the courts are going to make them integrate the county schools. Papa Wicker says it's a good thing you and me are graduated. He worries that people are going to cause trouble.

It being winter, there's not much to do right now. Mama Wicker, Mama Polk, and I have decided to make a quilt to keep us busy. Do you reckon they'll let us send it to you? I'm also knitting a bunch of socks. Didn't your sergeant friend say you'd need lots of dry socks, if you went to that Vetnam place?

Well, I better go and let you get back to your business. Don't forget me, cause I ain't gonna forget you.

Love Always,

Bizzy

Bizzy wrote often and Lastun kept her letters within easy reach in his locker, so he could reread them any time.

At the beginning of the fourth week of basic, the drill sergeant took the platoon to the quartermaster clerk, who issued each boot a M16A1 rifle. He recorded the serial number of the weapon in each recruit's file.

As he examined the strange-looking weapon, Lastun said, "This don't look nothin' like Papa's gun at home, Drill Sergeant."

The drill sergeant overheard his remark. "What did you say, Runt?"

Lastun knew he was in trouble, but he didn't know why. "I just said this don't look nothin' like Papa's gun at home."

During his personal time after evening chow, the drill sergeant had Lastun strip his weapon on a blanket spread on the floor beside his cot. As he did so, he had to hold up each part and proclaim in a loud voice, "This is the trigger guard of my M16A1 *rifle*, serial number 1091725." He continued with the trigger, firing pin, and so on.

At lights out, the drill sergeant took Lastun to the parade ground, where he was required to march around the perimeter of the field as he chanted, "This is my rifle (touch weapon on shoulder). This is my gun (grab crotch). This is for fighting (touch rifle), this is for fun (grab crotch)."

Lastun had to do this for an hour before he was allowed to return to his barracks and to sleep.

The drill sergeant introduced them to a variety of weapons in addition to the M16 rifle. They worked on learning how to throw hand grenades, and how to use a grenade launcher, which looked like a shotgun with a muzzle as big around as a soup can. Then there was the M60 machine gun, also known as a "Hog." The drill sergeant explained that the platoon would be split up after boot camp and be sent to different locations for AIT, which stood for Advanced Individual Training. But everyone knew that Goliath would become a machine gunner and would carry the M60. It took a big, strong guy to do that job. It was designed to be used from a tripod, but in a pinch it could be hand-held while it was fired.

Lastun fully expected his military occupation specialty, or MOS, to be that of riflemen, as did most of his platoon. When they'd qualified on the M16, Lastun discovered his experience hunting with Papa's .22 had prepared him well.

He'd been firing practice rounds at a target four hundred yards away. Donnie Horton had been beside him on the range. After watching him for a few minutes, Horton whistled. "You keep shootin' like that, Runt, and you'll get an expert's badge. They might even send you to sniper's school. Then you'll get the chance to kill a lot of VC."

Lastun remembered how his parents had always cautioned him, "Don't stand out. Don't draw attention to yourself. Can't nothin' good come from that." He'd also begun to think about what the Army was trying to do. He was being trained to kill people. The thought prompted mixed emotions. After all, the Bible said, *"Thou shalt not kill."* On the other hand, according to the drill sergeant, the Viet Cong would be out to kill him and all the other Americans. Lastun decided he'd just have to deal with that issue when he got to Nam. When qualifying began, Lastun made sure to miss a few shots. He qualified as a sharpshooter, the middle of the three accuracy ratings.

The final three weeks were devoted to learning how to work as a team in the field. The platoon roamed through what seemed like every acre of Fort Polk's expansive grounds. They marched through forest, waded through bayous, and slogged through mocked-up rice paddies. On one training maneuver, Casanova, the platoon's point man for the day, found a dusty knapsack which appeared to have been left by an earlier platoon. The curious soldier picked it up to see what was inside. A blinding flash, followed by an ear-splitting bang, rendered the platoon senseless for several long seconds.

The drill sergeant had hung back, anticipating the incident. "That was a booby trap armed with a flash-bang grenade." He shouted louder than usual because he knew everyone's ears were ringing. "In Nam, it would be a real grenade or a mine, and you'd be dead."

Having spent much of his life outdoors, Lastun developed a knack early on for recognizing anything that wasn't "natural." Once, when he was on point, he saw a cluster of rocks that looked funny. He motioned Comanche up to his side. "I think they's a booby trap yonder where those rocks are piled up. Whyn't you ask the drill sergeant about it?"

Comanche pointed this out to the drill sergeant and got praised for the find, as Lastun intended. That way, Lastun did his job, and someone else got the credit.

"If you see a dead body, or a knapsack, or anything lying on or beside a trail that doesn't look like it was put there by Mother Nature," the drill sergeant warned, "don't touch it. Charlie likes to hide grenades with the pin pulled under shit like that. If you pick it up or turn it over, boom!"

Lastun encouraged Bizzy and his parents to skip boot camp graduation. In his opinion, bus tickets were an unnecessary expense. So he was surprised when, dressed in his Class A uniform, he walked to the parade ground before the ceremony and found the five of them waiting for him, big smiles on their faces. He hugged Bizzy so hard she begged him to turn loose before he broke a rib.

Mama Wicker and Mama Polk got hugs, too. The men got firm handshakes.

"I'm mighty proud to see you," Lastun said, "but you shouldn't a come. I know how much them bus tickets costs."

"That allotment money the Army sends has helped a lot," Bizzy said. She wrapped her hand around his bicep. "Hoo, you done got some muscles."

Lastun had trouble keeping his eyes forward, as his platoon marched during the graduation ceremony. He kept wanting to look for Bizzy in the grandstand.

Lastun got a two-day pass after the ceremonies, which he and Bizzy spent in a local motel room, leaving their parents to fend for themselves during the evenings.

10

"Awright, you maggots, Kindergarten is over! You're in the real army now." Sergeant Piscopo faced his new platoon, including Lastun, which had formed on Fort Polk's parade grounds.

Five of Lastun's platoon had been given other Military Occupation Specialties, and had been assigned to different AIT programs. Eagleton had been sent to radio operator's school. Parker would become a medic. Saine was shipped to helicopter flight training. Harris failed to qualify as a marksman, the lowest weapons rating, and went to quartermaster AIT. Dickerson went AWOL. When the MPs found him, he went to the stockade. Eventually, he'd wind up at Fort Leavenworth Prison, or be sent home with a dishonorable discharge.

The remaining platoon members received an infantryman MOS, code 11B, and remained at Fort Polk—although in a different section of the base. Five men from another platoon were added to restore their thirty-man complement. Drill Sergeant Piscopo became their new platoon leader.

"Most people think the term AIT means advanced individual training. But you and I know better. We know it means advanced infantry tactics, at least for us." Piscopo paced to and fro in front of the men as he recited the speech he'd obviously given many times before.

"Our group will combine with four others to form a company. Over the next eight weeks, this company will learn to carry out two objectives." He held up one finger. "To adapt and prevail in the hostile tropical environment known as Vietnam and . . ." He held up a second finger. "To kill Charlie. This is what you must learn if you are to survive in Nam."

Sergeant Piscopo was true to his word. Over the next two months, Lastun and his platoon learned to mount a Bell UH-1 helicopter, better known as a Huey, travel to a landing zone — LZ — and dismount. The first time Lastun saw a Huey in flight, approaching from a distance, he thought it looked like a big dragonfly, with its bulbous body and long tail.

The mounting and dismounting part wasn't as easy as it sounded. The Huey never stopped. It would descend, hover a few inches above ground while eleven soldiers dove through its open doors, and then take off.

The first few times Lastun bruised his ribs as he did belly flops. His confidence grew and he learned to step first on the chopper's runner, then up into the cargo bay.

His first flights also grew some hairy butterflies in his stomach. He'd never been higher than the upper limbs of Mr. Kincade's oak tree. The Huey took him hundreds of feet up and swooped around as it maneuvered through the sky. Lastun grabbed a webbed canvas strap and hung on for dear life.

This, Lastun learned, was because Charlie just loved to shoot Hueys.

The company learned to set up camp and establish perimeters, and to maneuver at platoon and company strength. They also learned to navigate by map and compass.

By the end of AIT, the open hostility between the whites and blacks had subsided, which is not to say they spent their nights in the barracks singing *Kumbaya*. They were all going to Vietnam to meet a new enemy.

To a man, they knew what the drill sergeant meant about functioning as a unit. They were now dependent on each other for survival and, in the jungle, the skin color of the soldier that had your back didn't matter.

That was simple reality. The guys that didn't get it had a lower probability of returning home in one piece.

"You think you're a soldier now, don't you?" Piscopo asked on their last day. "Wait until you get to Nam. You'll find out just how green you are." He grew pensive. "I hope you've learned the skills to stay alive long enough to become a real soldier.

"A couple of reminders in closing. Listen to your platoon sergeant and do what he says, and always keep a pair of dry socks handy. Good luck."

Lastun's company received a thirty-day leave with orders to report back for deployment to Vietnam. He made a beeline for the bus stop.

While Lastun was at boot camp and AIT, Bizzy stayed with her parents. After dismounting the bus—Lastun chuckled at the military jargon that had now become second nature to him—at Yazoo City, he hitched a ride to the Polk household. The dust hadn't even begun to settle behind the car he'd just stepped out of when Bizzy barreled through the door, leaving it to slam behind her.

Lastun dropped his duffel in time to catch her flying leap into his arms.

When he finally put Bizzy down, she stepped back and said, "Look at you! They ain't a ounce of fat on you. I thought you said they fed you good."

Lastun wore his Class A uniform: green dress pants, khaki shirt with black tie, green uniform jacket with a single PFC stripe, and a dress uniform cap adorned with the U.S. Army insignia.

"You look pretty fine yourself, Bizzy Wicker," Lastun responded. "Yeah, they fed us good, but then they worked it off of us. Besides, it's only been two months since we saw each other. I ain't changed that much."

Bizzy sighed. "Husband, two months is a long time, let me tell you."

Lastun grinned at her before turning to Bizzy's mom waiting on the porch. "You lookin' good, too, Mama Polk."

She waved her hand, as if swatting a fly. "Aw, go on wit you, Lastun Wicker. Did they teach you that smooth talk in the army?"

"No, ma'am, that just comes natural."

"Well, come on in. We got some tea cakes and iced tea." Bizzy hooked her arm through Lastun's, while he picked up his duffel with his free hand and they began a slow walk to the house.

"I guess Papa Polk is in the field?" Lastun asked.

"You know he is," Mama Polk replied.

"How long you get to be home?" Bizzy asked.

"Thirty days. Then I report back to Fort Polk. From there they sendin' me to Vietnam."

"Oh, Lawd," Bizzy said, "and how long you got to stay there?"

"A year."

Bizzy stopped, her bare feet kicked up a small cloud of dust. She faced her husband. "A year? How'm I gone live a year without you?"

"The question is, how'm I gone live a year without *you*?"

The two looked into each other's eyes for a long moment.

Finally, Lastun sighed. "Well, we'll just have to make do. We can write each other every day, or near 'bout."

Bizzy smiled. "Yeah." She sighed. "We gotta do a year's worth of livin' in the next thirty days."

"Amen to that."

Lastun stayed at the Polks with Bizzy. Mama Wicker seemed to struggle with that, but Lastun and Bizzy made sure to spend part of every day with her. Lastun split his time between helping Papa Wicker and Papa Polk with planting the cotton crop and other farm work. The labor kept him in good physical shape.

After one such day, Lastun, Bizzy and both sets of parents gathered on the Wickers' front porch to rest and enjoy the cool air that followed the sunset. Fireflies danced across the yard, while crickets—nature's static—provided background noise. An occasional bullfrog added a "*Rum, rum, rum*" bass rhythm.

"If it wasn't for that integration, you probly wouldn't have to go off and fight this war, Lastun," Papa Polk said.

"How's that?" Lastun asked.

The tip of Papa Polk's hand-rolled cigarette glowed red as he took a draw on it. "I knew some folks who went to Korea, and I reckon they was a few coloreds who fought there. But not many. Most of them did what they called 'non-combatant' work. Cooks. Janitors. Body men for generals and such."

"Body men? What's that?" Lastun asked.

"I've heard 'em called butlers and valets. A body man did what household slaves used to do before the Civil War. They did it after, too, only they was called servants then. A body man would help the general get dressed, as if he couldn't do it hisself. Bring his coffee and his food. See that his clothes got washed and ironed. He'd even shave him. I wonder if the general ever got nervous 'cause a colored man was wavin' a straight razor around his neck."

That drew a laugh from everyone.

"Well, like that Dylan feller says in his song, 'The times they are a'changin'.'" Lastun observed.

"Yeah, but for good or bad?' Papa Wicker asked.

"The way I figgered it," Papa Polk continued to pursue his train of thought, "they put the coloreds in non-combatant jobs 'cause they didn't want 'em to carry guns."

Lastun winced. "The Army calls them rifles. I learned that the hard way."

"We got guns now, at home," Papa Wicker said. "What difference does that make?"

"Not a whit, in the long run," Papa Polk said. "It goes to show just how nonsensical them white folks is." Which put an end to that conversation.

Occasionally Lastun ran errands to Kilgore's store to get supplies for Mama, just as he had for the previous thirteen years. On one trip, a counter display caught his attention. He grabbed the whole box and carried it to the cash register.

Kilgore looked at his purchase. "Plannin' on doin' a little celebratin', are you?"

"You might say that, suh," Lastun replied.

The store owner frowned. "You ain't aimin' to cause no trouble, I hope."

Lastun met his eye, something he would have never done to a white man before he entered the Army. "Mistuh Kilgore, suh, you've known me all my life. I ain't never done nothin' like that, and I ain't gonna start now."

Kilgore nodded. "Okay," he said, and rang up the sale.

As the time for Lastun's departure drew nearer, he and Bizzy clung to each other more and more. But time could not be denied. Showing the depth of her understanding and restraint, Mama Wicker said goodbye at the Polk house, along with Papa Wicker and Bizzy's parents. Only Bizzy accompanied Lastun to the bus station. She handed him a brown, letter-sized envelope.

"What's this?"

"A present."

He opened it to find a calendar.

"That's for you to keep track of the days 'til you come home," Bizzy said. "I got one, too."

"Oh, honey, I won't need a calendar to keep up with how many days 'til I see you again." He held his gift up. "But I'll keep it, and I'll mark an X on every day that goes by."

"You take care of yo'self, y'hear?"

"I promise. Just wait for me. Be here when I get back."

"I will."

11

Until he travelled to Fort Polk, Lastun had never ventured more than forty miles from his home in Satartia. After saying goodbye to Bizzy at the Yazoo City bus depot, he returned to the Army base. The next part of his journey would take him nine thousand miles away.

At Fort Polk, his duty officer gave him orders directing him to report to II Corps at Pleiku, South Vietnam. After changing into khaki fatigues, he was dispatched to the base airfield, where he boarded an old beater of a twin-engine airplane along with a dozen other soldiers. The inside of the plane was nothing more than a hollow tube designed to haul cargo. Their seating consisted of webbing formed into chairs attached to the interior sides. Once airborne, the aircraft shimmied like one of the heavy duty washing machines at base.

"This is a C-47 cargo plane," the man beside him, a corporal, had to shout to be heard above the engines' deafening roar. He seemed to just want to make conversation, or maybe he wanted to show off his knowledge of all things military. "It dates from World War II. Commercially, it's a Douglas DC-3, but nobody outside the military uses it any more, except to fight forest fires or smuggle drugs."

Although Lastun nodded, none of what the corporal said made sense. He wouldn't have bet on being able to sleep in such an uncomfortable chair, and such a loud and rattly airplane, but he did.

After refueling at Fort Carson, Colorado, they traveled to Travis Air Force Base, near San Francisco, where they were put in a barracks used for soldiers in transit.

Lastun approached the duty sergeant assigned to the barracks. "Please, Sergeant, may I have a pass? I'd like to look around a bit."

The sergeant removed a thick cigar from between his teeth and looked Lastun up and down. "Not a chance. You're a soldier, not a tourist. The last thing I'm going to do is give you a chance to go AWOL."

Lastun's ingrained training kept him from arguing with the noncom. He spent his time until lights out in the enlisted men's club watching "I Love Lucy" and "The Dick Van Dyke Show" on TV. The Wicker family had never owned a television at home, and he found the shows fascinating.

Early the next day, Lastun joined a hundred other GIs aboard a McDonnell-Douglas DC-8 jet operated by MAC, the Military Airlift Command, a private company that contracted to ferry soldiers across the oceans. The flight offered more amenities than the previous one, including a couple of pre-cooked in-flight meals.

Lastun sacrificed embarrassment for an opportunity to sightsee, and he bounced around the cabin trying to get a look out the windows at the vast, cloud-spotted ocean below. Finally, a stewardess insisted that he take a seat and stay there.

"Don't worry, bud," a guy with sergeant's chevrons said. He was trying to act cool, but Lastun could see he was a bit nervous, too. "You're not the only one rubbernecking. I'll bet half of these guys have never flown this high or this far. Switch places with me and sit by the window. That way, you can look as much as you want. It's okay."

Lastun later discovered that this was the sergeant's first overseas flight, and the man was afraid of heights. Having a window seat made him uncomfortable.

"Thank you, sergeant," Lastun said.

"'s okay."

Lastun smiled his gratitude. He couldn't recall having been treated with such respect by a white man. Usually, the treatment came in the form of indifference or aggression.

The sergeant was slender with dark hair and brown eyes. He extended his hand. "I'm Howard Fishman."

Lastun shook hands. "Lastun Wicker. 'Scuse me for sayin', but you shore do talk funny." Fishman laughed aloud. "I could say the same about you." He slipped into an exaggerated nasal twang. "Fageddaboutit. Us guys from Brooklyn has our own ways of saying tings."

Lastun smiled. "I'm from Yazoo County, Mississippi. I reckon I talk funny, too."

"Youse can say that again," Fishman said, still in Brooklynese.

The plane flew over the Pacific Ocean, stopping to refuel in Alaska and again in Okinawa. The two new friends exchanged histories. Lastun told about his experiences as the son of a sharecropper in the Mississippi Delta and Howard told of his youth in Brooklyn, the son of a disabled World War II veteran who worked his way into a partnership in a men's clothing store and a mother who clerked in a woman's fashion shop.

"My papa wasn't never in the war," Lastun said. "He cut his foot on a plow when he was a boy and he's limped ever since. His name's Abraham."

Fishman brightened. "So's mine. He was a navigator on a B-24 bomber." He went on to relate accounts of his days as a kid, drinking egg creams — which had neither egg nor cream in it — and playing stickball and ringolevio in the streets.

"What's stickball?'

"It's like baseball, only we used a broom handle as a bat and a Spaldeen — "

"What's—"

Fishman held up his hand. "It's a little pink ball made by the Spalding Company. Only we didn't say 'Spalding,' we said 'Spaldeen.'"

"We played with a broom handle, too. Or sometimes with a piece of scrap wood. We used a rubber ball, but it didn't have a name. We played tag, and kick-the-can, and—"

"Kick-the-can," Howard interrupted. "Yeah, we played that."

The two grew quiet, thinking about those days, as the miles passed by under the jet's wings.

Lastun stirred, breaking the moment. "How did you get to be a sergeant?"

"I've got a degree from NYU—New York University—in sociology and poly sci." Seeing Lastun's question forming on his lips, he said, "I'll explain later. When I finished my AIT, I was offered the chance to enter NCOCC. That's the Non-Commissioned Officer Candidate Course. It's like officer candidate school for sergeants. Some people call it the "shake and bake" school. They're so short of NCOs for service in Nam, they cooked this up," Fishman smiled at his pun, "to get sergeants ready faster." He shrugged. "It's more pay. And it has a few perks, so they tell me."

What's a—"

"Oh, give it a rest," Fishman said. Then seeing Lastun's downcast look, he added, "We'll talk more later."

Lastun's ears popped, and he realized the airplane was descending. He craned his neck to look out the window and saw the plane's wing plunge into a bank of pure white clouds, as white as ginned cotton.

They continued to descend. As the clouds blocked the sun, everything turned gray and foggy. Raindrops speckled the outside of the clear Plexiglas window. The plane jounced in the rough air, and Lastun realized these were storm clouds.

Howard watched his new friend. "This is monsoon season, or so they say. We can expect to see a lot of rain over the next couple of months," he said.

The plane dropped below the cloud ceiling. Lastun saw a seashore. A large bald spot nestled against the beach. A long, ruler-straight ribbon of pavement split the barren, muddy scar. *A runway*. The plane banked to make its landing approach.

Da Nang Military Base looked like the scalped head of a giant. The construction battalion assigned to establish the base had taken a dozen or so bulldozers and scraped the area clear of everything green — grass, bushes, trees — leaving an expanse of splotchy red and tan clay and sand. Then they'd constructed rows of buildings for barracks, administration, mess halls, infirmaries and stockades. And that didn't include the paved airstrip and the hangars for planes and maintenance crews.

With the monsoon season in full swing, all the area that would be dusty clay during the dry months was now boggy mud. Only plywood strips spread over the morass allowed them to walk without sinking up to their ankles.

Howard and Lastun found themselves unhappily downwind of a row of latrines after they climbed down the rolling stairway the ground crew had pushed up to the jet's exit door. Not even the steady rain could wash the terrible stench out of the air.

A staff sergeant met them and asked for their orders. "The indoctrination center is over that way," he said, pointing. "Report in and they'll get you some housing and tell you where to get chow."

The two new arrivals grabbed their duffels and turned in the direction the sergeant had indicated.

"Oh, by the way," the staff sergeant yelled after them, "welcome to Vietnam."

Their reception wasn't over. A row of grizzled-looking soldiers, obviously veterans, stood nearby. As the two headed for their destination, the old-timers razzed them.

"Hey, look, cherries," one guy said.

"Fresh meat," another crowed. "How long do you think they'll last?"

"Hey, what size are those shoes? How about letting me have them when they put you in the body bag?"

Lastun knew they were trying to have fun. His anxiety level, already high, ticked up another couple of notches.

12

Howard and Lastun were assigned to the 4th Infantry Division, known as the Ivy Division. They were issued a tan, diamond-shaped shoulder patch with a green four-leaf clover in each corner of the diamond.

"I don't want you to go out there and die for your country. I want you to go out there and make the other son-of-a-bitch die for his," said Lieutenant Colonel Michael Erickson. The regimental commanding officer stood at the head of the new arrivals orientation class, which included Lastun and Howard. He was tall with sandy hair, and had not yet developed the paunch that was characteristic of so many desk jockeys.

The classroom reminded Lastun of the ones in his high school. They sat in individual chairs with metal arms that curled around to support a flat writing surface. Chalk boards, cork boards, bulletin boards and maps decorated the walls.

"I didn't say that, of course," Erickson continued, "though I wish I had. General George Patton did. But it makes my point. I want you to stay alive. That being said, we do have a mission. We are tasked with driving the North Vietnamese Army — the NVA — out of this country, and with suppressing the Viet Cong insurgency."

Somewhere in the distance, a series of *crump, crump, crump* sounds resounded — explosions. Erickson smiled. "Artillery. Ours. There's some NVA activity north of here. Once you get in the bush, you won't have to worry about enemy arty. Their cannons are too heavy to transport along the Ho Chi Minh trail. But you will have quite a bit of enemy mortar fire and small arms fire to deal with."

Erickson clasped his hands behind his back and paced across the front of the classroom. "Where was I? Oh, yes. Our mission. Carrying out that mission will involve casualties. It's inevitable." He stopped and faced the group. "If you're diligent in following the training you've already received, and if you obey the instructions of your platoon leader and sergeant, you'll have a better chance of making it home alive and in one piece. Good luck." With that Erickson left without offering to answer questions.

Over the next week, Fishman and Wicker continued their orientation: receiving instruction on regimental organization, hygiene, access to a chaplain, and first aid. They received refresher training on guerilla warfare, booby traps, leeches and jungle rot. The training instructor repeated a phrase they'd heard before, "If it doesn't look like God put it there, don't touch it." This represented the corps command's effort to prepare them for their upcoming year in hell.

In the evenings, the new arrivals were on their own. Lost in spirit in yet another strange place, Lastun wanted nothing more than to stick close to the more world-savvy Fishman. But it wasn't that easy. In the more structured regular army environment of Da Nang Military Base, NCOs and privates didn't mix socially. Howard Fishman found himself welcomed into the NCO Club, invited to drink and play cards with the other three-stripers. Lastun was relegated to the enlisted men's club and barracks.

Like all military facilities around the world, however, myriad private businesses flourished just outside the boundaries of the base. Here, adventurous souls could find access to alcohol and other temptations of the flesh, and the businesses didn't separate its patrons by rank.

One day after evening mess, Howard and Lastun wandered off base to investigate these establishments. They entered a bar, which was little more than a shack with an assortment of tables and chairs. The lighting was bad, the floor was dirt, and a light fog of dust hovered around knee-level. The place smelled of sweat and puke. Each ordered a beer. The beverages were brought by an old Vietnamese woman, a mama-san with a withered, prune-like face. Her clothes looked like black pajamas, what the locals called an *"ao dai."*

Lastun was more familiar with the various flavors of berry wine his father made, but he'd had beer before. This particular beer, whatever brand it was, tasted like fermented grass. Howard's expression indicated he shared that opinion. *Oh, well, beer is beer.*

"What do you think of Da Nang?" Howard asked.

Lastun frowned. "I think they made a mess of it. Reckon why they scraped all the grass off?" He looked at his glass of beer. "Maybe they used it to make this here stuff."

Howard laughed aloud. "Roger that. This is lousy. But I don't think it's made of grass. Improperly stored hops can give beer a grassy flavor. About the way they bulldozed the ground here, that's military efficiency for you. Now they don't have to mow or landscape anything. Plus, there's no cover for any VC that might get through the perimeter."

"Hmm, I don't like it."

"Neither do I. Just be patient, Lastun. When we get in the field, we'll get all the greenery we want, and then some."

Lastun noticed a couple of local ARVN troops at another table. They were chewing something. It reminded Lastun of the men at home who chewed tobacco, only the juice they spit was red instead of brown.

Lastun waved the old woman over. "Mama-san, what's that those men are chewin' on?"

The woman looked. "Oh, that betel nuts. It give you *oomph*. Lotta energy. Want some? It grow hair on your chest. Wanna see?" She made as if to unbutton her top, and laughed when the two GIs demurred.

"Also got hash, bennies, heroin, opium," she whispered as she looked furtively around—checking for MPs, Lastun assumed. "Anything you want, ask for Mei Li."

Even among the enlisted men, Lastun noticed the division between the whites and non-whites still existed, even in Nam. Most of the colored soldiers, even those from the north, were conscious of the invisible barrier and were complicit in keeping the races separate.

After Lastun's shower, a black guy named Terry pulled him aside. He had broad shoulders and blue-black skin. A poorly-healed scar flowed like a pink river from his left ear down to his collarbone. "Wicker, I seen you hangin' around with that Jewboy sergeant. You need to stick with your own kind."

Lastun frowned. "Sergeant Fishman? He's all right. He's not like the others."

"I'm just sayin'," Terry responded, "the time come when bullets start flyin', you need to know who's got your back."

"Is that a threat?"

"It's a fact," Terry said, and walked away.

The next day, Lastun saw Howard heading to the mess hall and decided to join him. "Hey, Howard, you won't believe what happened to that black guy, Terry. The one with the scar."

"Spill it, the suspense is killing me," Howard said, sarcastically.

"Yesterday, he was telling me we shouldn't be hanging around together any more 'cause you're Jewish, and last night he was working on some piece of machinery and busted his hand real bad. Can't shoot any more. He'll be okay, but they're keeping him back at Da Nang."

"He tried that same garbage with me. Seems he has no idea we're all fighting the same enemy. He said if we were seen together again, we might catch some friendly fire. Shit, I have enough to worry about without having to keep looking over my shoulder, watching out for him."

"You did that to him?" Lastun seemed surprised.

"Look, I don't like that kind of hate from anybody. He's lucky I got him out of here."

After their indoctrination at Da Nang, Lastun, Howard and the other new troops were flown by helicopter to Pleiku, II Corps headquarters near the Cambodian border. Lastun was pleased to learn that he and Howard had been assigned to the same platoon, albeit different squads, as replacements for other troops who'd been wounded or whose twelve-month tour had ended. He thought Howard was pleased, too, because he tipped Lastun a wink.

Their new company had been pulled out of the field for a couple of days R&R, and Fishman and Wicker mustered into the company at Pleiku. They met in a conference room at HQ. The walls were too flimsy to filter out the noise of helicopter rotors and truck engines.

Captain Jim Dettinger, their company commander, led the meeting. "Our company's been ordered to establish a fire base near Phu Loc. G2 reports that there's an NVA unit operating in that area, and our job is to give them a headache. Any questions?"

Howard's and Lastun's platoon drew the "lucky" straw and got the job of securing the LZ—landing zone—so the rest of the company could be brought in safely. Four Hueys flew them to the designated spot and hovered a few feet above the ground while the platoon rappelled down and established a perimeter. The hilltop had few trees, but was covered in the tall, sharp-edged elephant grass that was the bane of the GI. One of the squads set up a picket line. Occasionally Lastun heard a burst of gunfire. He never knew if a real VC target had showed up, or if some anxious soldier was shooting at shadows.

The reality of being in a combat zone hit home. Lastun's heart thundered in his chest as he joined the other members of his five-man fire team, digging foxholes, and creating a network of interlocking fire lanes. The tall grass had not yet been cleared. When the wind blew, the grass rippled like waves on a huge lake. Despite his experience as a hunter and outdoorsman, the situation spooked Lastun. Every time he looked across the field, he envisioned the cone-shaped straw hat of a VC soldier bobbing toward him. But nothing happened.

The drill sergeant was right, Lastun thought. *This place does look a little like Fort Polk.*

The Hueys ferried the rest of the company in. With a secure LZ, each Huey performed a "dust-off," touching the ground only long enough for its eleven passengers to jump off.

Captain Dettinger assigned duties to each of his platoon leaders. Lieutenant Hendricks summoned his charges, which included Howard and Lastun.

"Sergeant Reilly, get some sling blades and start clearing this tall grass," Hendricks ordered. Reilly was Lastun's squad leader. "Go out about one hundred yards. Clear an arc extending from that tree," he pointed, "to that tree. We want the grass short enough so nobody can sneak in and surprise us. Got it? We've got a sunny day for a change. We'd better take advantage of it."

"Begging the lieutenant's pardon, sir," Reilly spoke in a gravelly voice, "but wouldn't it be easier to have one of those double-rotor Chinooks bring in a bulldozer and clear this hill? A dozer could do it in a couple hours."

Lastun liked the way his sergeant thought. He'd seen Chinook helicopters, huge choppers that carried artillery, trucks, and bulldozers. It would be no problem to do what Reilly suggested.

Hendricks frowned. "Now, Sergeant, you know the easy way is not the Army way. No, we'll be using armstrong equipment." He flexed his arm, making his bicep bulge. "Sling blades, axes, machetes, shovels. So, I suggest you hop to."

"Yes, sir." Reilly turned to his squad. "All right, men. You heard the Ell-Tee. Grab a sling blade and get to work. It's gonna be hot, so keep your canteens filled."

As Lastun moved away, he heard the lieutenant say, "Sergeant Fishman, have your squad fill sandbags and establish bunkers and machine gun nests along a line . . ."

A one-hundred-fifty man company could do a surprising amount of work when faced with approaching night and the threat of a VC mortar attack or stealth assault.

It would take a week to get all the details right, but by night-fall they had a clear field of fire, a barbed-wire perimeter, machine gun nests, and sandbag-lined trenches in which to sleep. Dettinger allowed the company to vote on a name. They chose Firebase Screwball.

That night, the group bivouacked in the area they'd cleared, since no buildings were yet constructed. Lastun pulled out a sheet of paper and pencil from his pack.

July, 1967

Dear Bizzy,

I don't think I'm supposed to say where I am, but I'm out in the field. We've had to do a lot of ditch-digging and sling-blade swinging, and we've had a few mortar shells thrown our way, but things aren't bad. (Lastun had resolved that as far as what he would tell Bizzy, things would never be bad.) *I've got your picture. Just about everybody has a picture of a pretty girl, but you're the prettiest. I look at your picture every night and think about you before I go to sleep.*

Love,

Lastun

13

A great deal of effort went into turning a hill into a fortified stronghold. The soldiers dug nine pits four feet deep, each over an area large enough to house fifteen soldiers.

"Just be happy it's monsoon season," Lieutenant Hendricks told them. "Mud is easier to dig than dry, hard-packed earth."

Then they built a wooden structure seven feet high from floor-to-ceiling, with a sloping entrance within the pit. The next step involved filling burlap bags with sand and stacking them around and atop the parts of the structure which protruded above ground. The result was a bunker—one for each of the company's squads.

They added bunkers for the officers, the company mess, and headquarters, plus a row of latrines—which Lastun called outhouses. The outhouses at home were set over holes dug in the ground. When the holes were almost full, Papa, and later Lastun, covered it over and dug a new hole. But at Firebase Screwball, the latrines were built far enough above the ground to set a fifty-five gallon drum cut in half under the hole to catch the waste.

Barbed wire already encircled the fire base, along with trenches and machine gun nests.

Sergeant Reilly's squad was assigned guard duty for a forty-five degree arc of the perimeter. Each five-man fire team drew an eight-hour shift. If they had duty at dusk, two of them crawled out beyond the barbed wire and set Claymore mines armed with trip wires. If the VC triggered them while trying a night incursion, they would alert the sentries. At dawn, two of those on guard duty went out to retrieve the mines. Problem was, the VC were very good at camouflage and often watched the mines being placed. So if they chose to attack at night, they just detached the trip wires or crept around them altogether. They also liked to steal the Claymores and use them against the Americans, or move them so the GIs would set them off while trying to collect them the next morning.

In addition to eight hours guard duty, the GIs had to perform routine maintenance such as burning the waste from the latrines or repairing bunkers damaged by nocturnal VC mortar attacks. On the day Lastun drew latrine duty, he joined a couple of fellow GIs in pulling the half-barrels of waste from under the seats and replacing them with empty ones. Then they mixed in diesel fuel and set the mixture afire.

"Hey, I know how to get Charlie to leave us alone," PFC Leon Dodge, another member of the latrine detail, said. Despite his caramel skin, freckles showed up on his cheeks like periods at the end of sentences. "We just put this stench upwind of their position. They'll run away for sure."

Lastun leaned on the shovel he'd been using to stir the mess. "All I know is, we ain't never goin' ta be able to hide from Victor Charlie. This stink carries for miles."

After the guard duty and grunt work, Lastun felt a level of exhaustion that made his fatigue at boot camp seem trivial. He thought he'd be so afraid of a night attack that he wouldn't sleep. But each night when he sacked out, he slept deep and dreamlessly.

After one span of work and guard duty, Lastun headed to his cot to get a few hours' sleep. As in every Army housing situation he'd encountered, the whites and non-whites voluntarily segregated into separate sections of the barracks. Before he could settle in, Leon Dodge spoke up.

"Hey, Wicker," Dodge said, "want something to ease you up?" He extended a hand-rolled cigarette.

In the last few months, Lastun had gained quite an education. If he hadn't been so dog-tired, he would have known Dodge's offer for what it was. But all the old-timers back in Satartia smoked hand-rolled tobacco, and Lastun thought nothing of it. He never smoked at home, but he wanted to be a regular guy. "Thanks," he said, and took a puff. In only a few minutes, he began to feel dizzy. That's when he knew Dodge had given him a doobie.

Marijuana—and other drugs—were a lot more common than Lastun expected. A surprising number of NCOs and junior officers just looked the other way as long as their units continued to function. Only the hard-asses got uptight about it.

Lastun didn't like it. It made him feel goofy. But he went along—just taking light puffs and inhaling little. Plus, it did relax him a bit.

And then there were the patrols. Each platoon took turns venturing out into the field to try to find VC dens and destroy them. Problem was, the VC had no uniforms and they didn't operate out of camps like the Americans. They looked and acted just like ordinary South Vietnamese civilians. That is, until they pulled an AK-47 from under a bag of rice and shot some GI dead, or tossed a grenade into a group of soldiers.

Once he'd completed several patrols, Lastun noticed how the locals seemed to defer to the GIs. They kept their heads down, eyes focused on the ground. Their behavior showed fear and trepidation—much like the coloreds back home deferred to whites.

He considered his own feelings. *Is this how a white man feels when dealing with colored?* Lastun wondered. *Is this what it's like being feared?* Lastun decided it made him uncomfortable having another person be so afraid of him, and that, he realized, was what made him different from whites back home. They reveled in their position of power over the coloreds.

Lieutenant Hendricks, Lastun's platoon leader, allowed the newbies time to get acclimated to their situation. While on patrol for the first couple of weeks, Lastun marched in the middle of the squad. Even with the coddling, he was jumpy. More experienced soldiers walked point or rear guard. The platoon sergeant accompanied Sergeant Fishman and his squad, guiding the new NCO in directing his charges until he grew comfortable with the patrol SOP; standard operating procedure.

But they couldn't stay virgins forever.

"Ready to walk point, Wicker?" Sergeant Reilly asked, as the platoon broke an overnight bivouac and prepared for another day's march. They were still in the middle of monsoon season and a steady rain had been falling for a day and a half. Visibility was lousy, and he discovered there were few feelings more miserable than being soaked to the bone. He'd also discovered why dry socks were so important. Back in Satartia, when he'd played in the creek for too long, his fingers got all wrinkly from the water. Wet feet did the same thing. But now, he wore army boots, and his feet and socks didn't get to dry out. Before long, the soft skin between the toes began to slough off, and a soldier's foot could become infected or worse. During rest breaks, they had to take off their boots and inspect each other's feet to make sure that jungle rot hadn't set in—and to change socks, if they had a dry pair.

"Anything you say, Sergeant." Actually Lastun was so jittery he feared he'd fire off a round by accident. But the sergeant said do it, so he did.

"Company HQ says we're heading into suspected NVA territory," the sergeant continued. "Unlike the VC, they'll be in camo uniforms. They'll also be more disciplined and have better armament, like machine guns and grenade launchers . . . so look sharp."

"Yes, Sergeant."

Two men actually led the platoon. One to walk point—watch for enemy movement—and one to clear a path through the dense underbrush. They avoided trails as much as possible since they were favorite places for booby traps. Lastun kept his M16 at the ready, while Leon Dodge walked beside him, using a machete to cut a two-foot wide lane through the sharp-edged elephant grass. The enemy usually didn't strike in daylight, preferring the dark of night for cover, so Lastun was surprised to see a darker, human-shaped shadow crouching in the shade of a banyan tree sixty yards ahead. The rain made him doubt himself at first, but he chose to trust his instincts. He raised his right fist—the military sign language for *stop*! Then swept his hand, palm down, toward the ground. *Get down!*

Lastun and Leon crouched together in the tall grass.

The NVA soldier must have realized he'd been spotted and fired an AK-47 burst in the Americans' direction.

The bullets whispered through the tall grass, sending Lastun's stomach into his throat. A bullet whickered off Dodge's machete and he dropped it like it had burned him. He unslung his M16 and fired. Lastun waddled two steps to the left to change his angle of fire and loosed a burst of his own.

The next few minutes seemed like hours, as soldiers on both sides fired blindly in the others' direction. The chatter of dozens of automatic rifles was deafening.

Lastun quickly realized the futility of their frenzy and held his fire, looking for a real target before taking a shot. Even so, the tall grass made it impossible to see if his shots had any effect.

The NVA soldiers withdrew after a few minutes and Lieutenant Hendricks called. "Cease fire!" The tang of burned cordite filled Lastun's nostrils. The squads regrouped to assess their damage. Not a single American casualty, aside from a few cuts from blades of grass and thorns.

"Good job, Wicker," Sergeant Reilly said. "You spotted that ambush right away."

"Just lucky, Sergeant," Lastun responded.

"Don't knock luck. Luck keeps us alive."

Lastun saw the wisdom of that. Even the veterans got freaky when a firefight started. Either you got shot or you didn't. Either you shot somebody or you didn't. *Luck.*

Lastun went with a group—including Lieutenant Hendricks and Sergeant Fishman—to check out the NVA soldiers' hiding spots for the ambush. Lastun almost decided the enemy had gotten away clean when he saw a bundle of black cloth lying under a bush near where the firefight had started. He looked closer and saw it was the body of a young woman. She held an AK-47 in one dead hand. *Kissy! My older sister!* Bile rose in his throat.

No, it can't be her. It just looks like her. Even with that understanding, he couldn't control his stomach. He leaned over and emptied his breakfast into the brush.

He swung around, checking where the woman lay in relation to the position he'd been in and the direction he'd been firing.

"You okay, Wicker?" Reilly asked.

"Reckon I shot that girl, Sergeant?"

Reilly looked back to make the same assessment Lastun had just made. "I don't think so. You were firing in that direction." He pointed.

Lastun exhaled. Maybe Sergeant Reilly thought he was disappointed, but he was actually more relieved than he should have been. After all, she'd been trying to shoot him and his platoon-mates. Seeing the woman's body also brought home another truth. *Women and men fight against the Americans in this war.*

That night, Lastun dreamed he'd killed his sister in the firefight.

The following week, Lieutenant Hendricks called Sergeant Reilly and Lastun to his tiny makeshift office. "Corporal Marks has been rotated out. His tour's over. I need a fire-team leader. Sergeant Reilly here," Hendricks nodded at the squad leader, "has recommended you. Effective immediately, you're promoted to corporal and you'll take over Marks' fire-team in Reilly's squad. Congratulations. Dismissed."

Near the end of September, mail call included a letter for Lastun. Usually, Bizzy put a drop of rose water or vanilla flavoring on the letter to add a scent from home, but Lastun could detect no aroma. He took a seat on the ground behind his squad's bunker and leaned back against the sandbag wall.

The envelope contained only one page. Bizzy's letters were always longer than that. She liked to show off her literary and penmanship skills.

September, 1967

Dear Lastun,

I love you. You know that. I need to ask you to do something for me. If Kissy writes, and she or your mama says something bad about me, please don't believe them. I would never hurt you.

Love,

Bizzy

14

Lastun's vision blurred. *What can this mean?* Something happened at home, only he didn't know what.

Howard Fishman, walking across the compound, saw Lastun's expression and stopped. "What happened to you, Wicker? You look upset."

Lastun handed him Bizzy's letter. "Reckon what does that mean?"

Howard scanned the page and chuckled. "I'd say your wife and your mom had a fight. Nothing to worry about. It happens all the time."

"You don't understand," Lastun said, shaking his head. "Bizzy and Mama got along like peas and cornbread. I ain't never seen them fight."

"How long have you and Bizzy been married?"

Lastun frowned, thinking. "*About a year.*"

"That's not long, you know," Howard said. He paused to watch another sergeant across the way chew out a private who'd been loitering. "Has your sister, what's her name . . . Kissy . . . ever fought with her mother-in-law?"

"Well, yeah, I guess so."

"You're making a mountain out of a molehill, and it's because you can't be there to smooth things over. Why don't you write your mom and ask her about it? I'll bet it's no big deal."

"Okay, thanks."

Fishman started to turn away, then stopped. "And don't let this bother you. People who lose focus are the ones who get dead, so, keep your head on straight."

Lastun nodded.

October, 1967

Dear Kissy,

Bizzy wrote and said she was worried you or Mama might say something bad to me about her. Did something happen? I can't believe ya'll would have a falling out. I love all of you too much to see bad blood between you.

Please let me know as soon as you can.

Love,

Lastun

More mortar bombardment. More patrols. The enemy — both VC and NVA — were crafty. While the Americans were obsessed with occupying territory and claiming victories, the enemy was busy inflicting casualties. They'd attack, then disappear before the officers could call in an air strike or artillery barrage.

Lastun's cool head in firefights drew the attention of Sergeant Reilly. It wasn't something Lastun wanted, but if he followed Sergeant Fishman's advice and stayed alive, he had to take the lead when things got dicey, to use one of Fishman's expressions.

"Runt, you and Dodge go out and pick up the Claymores this morning," Sgt. Reilly ordered.

"Yes, Sergeant," Wicker said. His boot camp nickname had followed him across the Pacific. It must have been recorded in his personnel file. He didn't mind. *It could be worse.*

The occupants of the firebase had kept the vegetation in the one hundred yard killing zone around the compound cut short, and the mines were placed at the outside edge of the KZ, where the heavy brush began.

He and Dodge eased out through a gap in the barbed wire, hoping the pale glow of early dawn didn't illuminate them too much for the VC, but did allow enough light for the GIs at the M60 to cover them.

A couple of bird calls sounded. "I think we're okay. The birds are singing," Leon Dodge said.

"I don't know," Lastun responded. "Them bird calls sounded puny to me. Might not be real birds."

"Oh, shit," Dodge said. He momentarily froze in his tracks.

Lastun twisted around and looked at the nearest machine gun nest. He pointed two fingers at his eyes, then turned his hand around to swing it in an arc, palm down, toward the edge of the KZ. Sign language for "keep a sharp eye out." That's what the machine gunner was already supposed to be doing, so Lastun's signal meant. "I've got a bad feeling about this."

He hoped the gunner picked that up. He knew he wouldn't get an acknowledgement; he could only hope his message had been understood.

He and Dodge reached the tree line and found the spots where the Claymores had been set.

They weren't there.

Dodge cursed. "Let's go back and tell them they got stole."

That was a possibility. They could have also just been moved. Either way it was bad news. But they had to look for them. If the Claymores had only been moved, Lastun and Dodge could still find and retrieve them without harm to the Americans. If they didn't get them, they would surely be used against the GIs either here on the firebase perimeter or somewhere else.

"We gotta look for 'em, Leon."

Leon looked like a whipped puppy. "I know it."

"We just go slow and easy. Don't step some place you ain't looked," Lastun said.

The two carried their rifles at the ready and walked in a crouch, studying the ground near their feet. Lastun had grown up hunting. He didn't even have to think. He allowed his instincts to assess each pile of debris, each mound of dirt. *Does it look natural? Would leaves fall in this pattern? Would rain or wind shape soil like this?*

He saw a cluster of leaves and twigs against the base of a nearby bush, and his gut clenched. A Claymore mine was about the rectangular size and shape of a hard-back book painted green. The debris at the base of the bush looked large enough to hide an object of that size. A straight line of soil extended out from the suspicious shape, right where Leon was about to step.

"Leon, stop!" Lastun shouted. But his buddy had already taken a shuffle step right across the hidden trip wire.

Lastun threw himself to the ground, back along the place he'd just walked, with his face turned away.

The Claymore exploded, vomiting dozens of ball-bearing sized pellets in an arc across the space in front of it. Leon's body was shredded by the fusillade.

A shrapnel pellet pinged off Lastun's helmet, but by throwing himself flat, he ensured that the shower of metal flew over his body.

Back on the firebase's picket line, the panicked M60 gunner loosed an extended burst which consumed his entire nine-yard long ammo belt. The shells chopped through the brush above Lastun, turning the vegetation into mulch. Other members of Lastun's squad joined in, emptying their M16 clips. Lastun wisely hugged the ground. It would take as much luck as skill to avoid a bullet.

Eventually, the firing died down as frenzied GIs responded to Sergeant Reilly's, "Cease fire! Cease fire!"

The world grew quiet. Dust and remnants of leaves floated in the air.

"Wicker, you okay?" Reilly shouted.

Lastun thought about staying silent, in case some of the enemy had stuck around. But he'd already learned that VC and NVA troops always bugged out when things got hot. He spit out a mouthful of dirt. "'m okay," he shouted.

"What about Dodge?"

"Claymore got 'im."

"Shit." Reilly didn't shout, but his voice carried so Lastun could hear him. Then he did shout. "Stay put. I'm sending a fire team out to get you."

That was an order Lastun had no problem obeying.

Reilly sent two fire teams, and a medic.

"Be careful," Lastun warned when they approached. "There's still one more Claymore out here, I think."

The soldiers formed a shield around Lastun and the medic.

"How did you not get hit?" the medic asked, as he checked Wicker over. "Not a scratch."

Lastun took off his helmet and inspected the nick carved by the mine's shrapnel. "I don't know," he said, "'specially since 'bout everbody in my platoon was shootin' at me."

"Don't get your panties in a wad," Jesus Gonzalez, a member of his squad said. "We were shooting *above* you. As long as you stayed on the ground—which you did—you were safe."

The second Claymore was never found, apparently taken by the enemy. Lastun figured they'd meet up with it sometime in the future while on patrol, or worse yet, Charlie would scoop out the explosive to make a Bouncing Betty.

Lastun steeled himself and looked at Leon's body. Dodge had been right on top of the mine, and he'd absorbed much of the shrapnel, which had probably saved Lastun's life. The front of his body looked as if it had been sprayed with red paint. Blood and guts spilled over the edge of the stretcher, and the medic struggled to push his entrails back up into his abdominal cavity. Lastun wanted to cry.

Once back inside the wire, Lastun received a round of consoling pats on the back.

"What happened?" Reilly asked, once the crowd moved on.

Lastun described the events. He tried to soft-pedal Dodge's negligence, but it was clear that his carelessness had cost him his life.

It took Lastun a long time to compose the letter. He struggled to keep his grammar sound and to avoid any indication that Leon had contributed to his own death.

October, 1967

Dear Mrs. Dodge.

Your son Leon was a good soldier and a good friend. His death hurt us all deeply, as I know it hurts you.

I don't expect you can find much good in this terrible thing, but I want you to know he was brave and respected. You should be proud of your son.
With my sympathy,

Lastun Wicker, Corporal
U.S. Army

Lastun didn't have Leon's address, so he gave Sergeant Reilly the letter with no envelope.

"May I read it?" Reilly asked.

Lastun nodded.

After he had done so. Reilly smiled. "This is good. Leon's mom will be grateful to receive it. I'll ask the LT to put it in with his letter."

"Thank you, Sergeant."

15

Lieutenant Hendricks' platoon earned a three-day respite for R&R. A quartet of Hueys ferried them from Firebase Screwball to Da Nang. If Lastun hadn't known better, he would've thought the war had ended; such was the party atmosphere aboard his chopper.

"Hoo, boy!" Sergeant Reilly shouted above the whack of the rotors. "Real beer, and women. You boys just remember to wear a raincoat. There's no telling what kinds of diseases those women have," he warned the soldiers.

I heard some of those hookers are VC and they deliberately got the clap so they could give it to us GIs," one of the platoon guys said. Lastun had heard the same rumor in boot camp, but he stayed quiet.

"VC women with VD weapons. How's that for strategy?" the soldier continued.

"Howard, you got a girlfriend back home?" Lastun asked.

"Nobody special," Howard replied. "There was a girl I was seeing, but a Jody got her after I left for boot camp." He used the term for a guy who stole a soldier's gal while he was away.

As far as he knew, Lastun was the only person in the platoon below sergeant rank who was married, although many others had girlfriends. The talk reminded him of his uncertain situation with Bizzy. He'd received no more letters since the mysterious one from his wife warning him not to believe any bad things his sister or mother said about her. He wished he could call somebody at home. But neither Lastun's nor Bizzy's parents had a phone. All he could do would be to leave a message at Kilgore's store. *Wouldn't that start the gossips up back home?* Same with the pastor of his church. Some of the worst gossips were churchgoers, including the pastor.

He watched the countryside flash by below. He was tempted to ask for extended leave, claiming some family emergency, so he could go and sort things out. But he knew it was out of the question. The captain, or colonel, or whoever approved such leave, would be like Sergeants Reilly and Fishman and see this as a "Dear John" situation. He'd get no sympathy.

Corporal Prescott scooted over to sit beside him. "For a guy headed for three days off, you look pretty glum, Wicker."

Lastun sighed. "Just wishin' I could keep on goin' 'til I got home."

"Copy that," Prescott said. "How much more time you got?"

"Eight months." Lastun leaned his head back against the 'copter frame and felt the throbbing vibration of the turbine engine overhead.

"Hmm, that's a while," Prescott said. "You'll just have to hunker down and ride it out."

That was a pretty good description of what he'd been doing so far. When he first arrived at the firebase, Lastun had been so scared he thought he'd piss his pants. The early patrols didn't make things any better. Then he began to see similarities between the behavior of the deer and other animals he'd hunted in Yazoo County, and the behavior of the humans in the forests. His epiphany came when he realized that the VC and NVA hiding in the bushes were just as scared as he was, and just as close to pissing their pants. He grew bolder, tempered with the caution of common sense. He still knew he could step on a mine, or eat a bullet, but he had come to realize that dwelling on that only made his fear worse. So he did his job, with as much care as he could.

123

Lastun said nothing more. He just closed his eyes.

The monsoon season was in its waning days and the base still dealt with sporadic rains that turned the bare earth between buildings into a quagmire. Only the plywood walkways allowed enough footing to get around.

Lastun found that many ordinary conveniences now attained the level of luxury. The firebase had offered only cold-water, gravity-fed showers, so Lastun's first action was to take a long shower under water as hot as he could stand it.

The second luxury involved breaking starch; putting on a set of clean, dry and pressed fatigues. He began to feel almost human.

Luxury number three required a visit to the mess hall where he found a wall-to-wall serving line offering many kinds of greasy, *warm* food. After four months of pre-packaged C rations and K rations, his choices seemed sinful. He loaded his tray with country fried steak and gravy, mashed potatoes and gravy, and apple cobbler.

He failed to account for how unaccustomed his stomach had become to such rich food. So his fourth luxury was the "pleasure" of being able to puke into an honest-to-gosh toilet bowl instead of the wooden cut-out seat of an outhouse-style latrine. He barely made it before his stomach emptied itself. He chose to wait a while before trying the mess hall again. Instead, he ambled to the temporary barracks for twelve uninterrupted hours of sleep.

Da Nang sat on South Vietnam's east coast, which opened to the South China Sea. The USO ran a perpetual beach party on a stretch of sand known as China Beach between the base and the bay.

Refreshed after his sleep, and after another more cautious trip to the mess hall, Lastun ventured over to find out what the

USO had to offer. He found several members of his platoon drinking beer. Lastun grabbed a can of Schlitz and went to stand beside Howard Fishman, who watched a pick-up baseball game in progress.

"Reckon do they have a broom handle and a Spaldeen 'round here anywhere?" Lastun asked the sergeant.

Fishman gave him a quizzical look. "Why do you ask?"

"Maybe we could get a game of stickball goin'."

The only broom handle they could find was still attached to a broom head. It was quickly beheaded.

Lastun held up the slender stick. "How in hell do you hit a ball with this little thing?" he asked.

Howard smiled and adopted Lastun's slangy drawl. "It ain't easy, partner, believe me."

Howard approached a Donut Dolly, a USO volunteer, and asked if they had a Spalding Hi-Bounce ball, which apparently was the real name for a Spaldeen. He was met with a sly smile. The lady rummaged around in an equipment locker and came back with a springy bronze-colored ball.

While the beach was large enough to handle the baseball game and a stickball game, there were enough soldiers from the Big Apple who deserted when the stickball game started, and the baseball game dissolved.

It felt wonderful to run in the sand, dive after fly balls, and generally forget that bullets and mortars were flying just a few miles away.

"Hey, batter, batter!"

"Swing batter, batter!"

"C'mon, Mr. Pitch, blow some smoke!"

It took a while for Lastun to notice that not one person had shouted, "Hey, look, he swings like a nigger washwoman!" or other such racist chatter.

The sun descended behind the tree-line on the western horizon and the game was eventually called on account of darkness.

"Reckon that Mei Li still has her bar outside of the base?" Lastun asked Howard.

Howard raised an eyebrow. "Why? Are you looking for some dope?"

"Unh-unh." Lastun shook his head. "She just seemed like a nice mama-san."

Howard smiled. "Ah, you want some female companionship. Not Mei Li herself, I hope. I'll bet she's older than your grandmother."

"Not that, either. Well, maybe just to talk to . . . nothin' else. You know I'm married."

"Do you remember how bad that beer she served tasted?"

Lastun said nothing.

Howard sighed. "Sorry, Lastun, but I'm bushed. I'm going to sack out for a while. See you later."

Lastun nodded. He still wanted to visit the bar. Maybe to recall some of the feelings he'd experienced when he first arrived in country. Mei Li had seemed nice and he wanted to talk to somebody who wasn't Army.

For some reason, Lastun thought the old woman would remember him. He hadn't thought about how many soldiers passed through her business, including those who visited the women in the back rooms. She gave him a gap-toothed smile and served up a mug of watery beer before moving on to the next customer. The beer was as bad as he remembered. The bar still smelled of sweat, tobacco and marijuana. The weathered wood was stained with it.

The men clustered around the tables gave off an angry, desperate vibe he'd been too green to catch on his first visit to the bar four months earlier.

126

This was a mistake.

As he rose to leave, he caught the eye of a big man sitting at another table with three of his buddies. *Goliath.*

The M60 gunner cut him off before he could reach the door. "Well, Runt, you just don't seem to learn, do you? Here you are breathing my air. Only you don't have the drill sergeant to save your ass this time."

His three buddies lined up behind him.

"No, no!" Mei Li ran up, shaking a bony finger.

For a moment, Lastun thought he was saved.

"You not fight in my bar. You fight, you go outside."

Goliath hadn't shaved in several days. He must have come right off the chopper to enjoy the bar's many temptations. He looked at his buddies. "You heard the mama-san. Let's go outside."

Two of the men grabbed Lastun by his biceps before he could move and gave him the bum's rush out the door.

The three white men took Lastun outside to a spot behind Mei Li's bar which was shielded from view. It also shielded them from most of the lighting. The men seemed to Lastun's eye to be shadows — demons.

Mei Li apparently used the area as a dumping ground for garbage, of piss pots, and no telling what else. The air stank.

Goliath seemed to notice Lastun's double chevrons for the first time. "A corporal, huh? Who the hell made you a corporal?"

Lastun had never been this afraid in the Vietnam bush. His voice betrayed him. He could not speak. An answer seemed unnecessary, anyway. His entire body trembled. Mei Li's noxious beer threatened to climb back up his gullet.

Stories that Papa and Mama Wicker told of beatings coloreds had taken at the hands of hateful white men back in

Satartia marched through his head. It seemed a waste to come all this way to die at the hands of white Americans.

"Strip off that shirt," Goliath commanded. "No need to worry about charges of striking a superior, though this nigger is no superior, I can tell you."

The giant's stooges pulled at Lastun's shirt and buttons popped. They yanked the garment off his shoulders, leaving him in pants and an olive drab T-shirt.

Goliath threw a punch. Lastun easily parried it. The big man hadn't gotten any faster since the last time they squared off.

Goliath frowned. "Hold him," he ordered his buddies.

"What's the matter, white man? You need help beatin' up on some colored guy? Why don't just me and you go at it? Make it even." Lastun was surprised at the venom in his voice. He knew this was going to be bad, but he couldn't resist a taunt. He was tired of playing the cowardly nigger. "You ain't learned much about fightin' since boot camp, have you?"

The two men grabbed Lastun's arms. He struggled, but there was little he could do to throw them off. Goliath was still Goliath, and Runt was still Runt.

Goliath launched a body blow into Lastun's gut, and he vomited the few ounces of Mei Li's beer that he'd drunk all over Goliath's shoes.

"Why you . . ." The giant aimed a right hook at Lastun's jaw. Lastun couldn't move his body, but he could move his head and he slipped the punch. He'd turned a potential haymaker into a misfire.

Lastun stomped the instep of one of the GIs holding his arm. The victim howled and released his grip. He then used his free hand to punch the guy holding his other arm.

In the meantime, Goliath threw a punch that didn't miss. Fireworks erupted behind Lastun's eyes, as the roundhouse landed under his left eye socket. He went down.

His mind kept yelling, *Get up! Get up!* But his muscles just wouldn't pay attention. Somebody's boot connected with his rib cage. His breath left him and wouldn't come back. A cloud settled onto his brain and the only thing he could do was curl up into a fetal position.

Goliath and his cronies seemed to be fighting among themselves. Occasionally, a foot bumped against Lastun's body, but it seemed as if someone was shifting his feet to keep his balance. A chorus of grunts and thuds accompanied the shuffle of footsteps.

Lastun fought against blacking out. He wanted to get up and fight, but he didn't have the energy.

After a while, Lastun felt a wet rag being gently dabbed against the spots on his face where Goliath had struck him. He opened his eyes to see a fuzzy shape outlined in the dim light. He groaned at the pain in his ribs and his head. He still couldn't draw a full breath.

"Well, Runt, I leave you alone for a while and you pick a fight with a mob. What am I going to do with you?" Howard Fishman had never called him Runt before, but Lastun recognized his gentle, teasing tone.

"What did you butt in for?" Lastun grumbled. "I had them right where they wanted me."

Howard laughed, and Lastun tried to join in, but after one short bark of laughter the pain stopped him.

"What happened?" Lastun asked.

"You first," Howard countered.

Lastun had to work to tell of his run-in with Goliath in boot camp, then of being ambushed by him and his two cohorts in

Mei Li's bar. "My first year at school, my principal got beat up by a bunch of white men because he got uppity. They burned a cross in his front yard. He wouldn't take it down, called it a 'badge of honor.' Not long after that, he disappeared." Lastun looked Howard in the eye. "I thought, 'Here I am in Nam, and some white rednecks gone kill me. It ain't fair.'"

Howard took a deep breath. "I decided I didn't want to hang in the barracks, after all, so I changed into civvies and came out to find you. I did. Find you, that is, being kicked around like a football. So I jumped in to help."

Lastun's eyes grew wide. "You beat up three white men, and one of them a giant?"

Howard chuckled and lifted a piece of firewood about the size of a baseball bat. "I had a weapon. They aren't dead, but I can say that you weren't the worst looking dude when the fight ended."

"I thank ye," Lastun said. He moved to get up, but the pain in his ribs and head drove him back to the ground.

"Anything broken?" Howard asked, a note of concern in his voice.

"My ribs are killin' me. Head, too."

"Let's get you to the infirmary and have them check you out. We can call the MPs from there."

Lastun made a second try and managed to sit up. He rolled over onto his hands and knees. With Howard supporting him, he struggled to his feet. "Maybe it's just me bein' southern and colored, but police ain't never been my friend. Let' just say I got mugged by some VC cowboys."

"Right outside the base?"

Lastun offered a misshapen grin made lopsided by his puffy cheek. "Them MPs will believe anything."

Howard moved into a shaft of light.

"Hey, you bleedin', too," Lastun exclaimed.

"Looks like I got mugged by the same cowboys," Howard responded.

Lastun put his hand on Howard's shoulder. "I'm beholden to you, man."

Howard shrugged. "That's what buddies do."

The infirmary operation was pretty informal. The doctor put Howard and Lastun together in a room that smelled of alcohol. A pretty nurse helped him. Her rank discouraged the two men from doing more than ogling her.

Then the doctor called the Military Police.

"You say you were mugged by a band of VC?" The soldier's voice revealed his skepticism. An armband with the letters "*MP*" encircled his bicep.

"Yup," Lastun said. The doctor had given him a shot of some kind of painkiller, and he was feeling a bit loopy.

"How many were there?"

Lastun looked at Howard and raised his eyebrows. "Three?"

Howard nodded. "Three."

"So three gooks beat up two American GIs." The MPs skepticism hadn't diminished.

Lastun shrugged. "They got the drop on us."

"What did they look like?"

"Asian," Lastun said, without hesitation.

"With slanted eyes," Howard added.

Lastun nodded. "And round hats with pointy tops." He lifted his arms as if trying to describe it with his hands, but the pain made him wince and drop them.

Still probing Lastun's torso with his fingertips, the doctor tried to hide his smile from the MP.

"And their clothes looked like pajamas," Howard said.

The MP sighed. "So they looked like every gook in South Vietnam."

"They must be in disguise," Howard deadpanned.

The MP frowned. "I don't suppose they, or you, had anything to do with the other three guys that came in all beat up earlier."

"Did one of them have vomit on his shoes?" Lastun asked.

The MP perked up. "Yeah."

"Wasn't us," Lastun said, with a head shake. "The cowboys must have hit them, too. Poor guys. Those VC muggers been working out of Mei Li's bar. That's why one of them vomited. Her beer will flat make you sick." He looked at Howard. "They must be on a spree."

"Yeah, I'm surprised you guys let them operate that close to the base," Howard said with a pointed look at the military cop.

The MP clapped his helmet on his head and rushed out as if on a mission.

The doctor, who'd been quiet, laughed. "I can't believe he bought that."

"Why did you put him on Mei Li?" Howard asked. "I thought you liked her."

"Not anymore," Lastun grumped. "She didn't try to stop those guys. She just told them to take me outside."

The doctor finished his examination. "Well, nothing's broken. Lots of bruises and contusions. Mild concussion. You should be okay after a couple of days." He shook his head. "I don't understand how you didn't at least get a cracked rib or two."

"That comes from eatin' poke salad for eighteen years," Lastun said with a straight face.

"What?" Howard asked.

"Poke salad. Beats Wonder Bread for makin' strong bones."

Howard just shook his head. "Doc, what was in that shot you gave him?"

Lastun spent the next two days in bed sleeping off the pain medicine and the effects of the beating, while Howard spent his time at the beach.

Once back at Firebase Screwball, the mail clerk gave Lastun a letter. It had probably travelled with them from Da Nang on one of the Hueys his platoon had travelled in.

November, 1967

Dear Lastun,

I know you asked about Bizzy in your last letter. I got to tell you that something bad happened to her just after you left last July. Real bad. Now she has run off. Your mama and me think you should just forget about her. Let her go and get on with your life.

I'm so sorry,

Kissy

16

Sergeant Fishman sat in the dusty cubbyhole of an office allocated to his platoon leader, making out the weekly duty roster for his squad. The stub of a cigar was clenched in his teeth, a habit he'd picked up in Nam. Replenishing his supply of stogies at Da Nang had improved his mood considerably. Private Eric Schultz, a member of Lastun Wicker's fire team, arrived slightly out of breath.

"Sorry to bother you, Sarge," Schultz said. "Corporal Wicker is in Sergeant Reilly's squad, but I know you and the corporal are buddies, sort of."

"What's the problem?" Howard asked.

"Well, Corporal Wicker is packing his duffel . . . like he's going somewhere."

"Did the LT give him leave?"

"You'd know that better than I would, Sarge."

"Okay, thanks, Schultz."

The private left, with Howard only seconds behind.

Lastun was in the enlisted men's quarters. Like all the bunkers, the building had a low overhead and felt cave-like. Dust from the sandbags on the roof occasionally sprinkled between the boards in the ceiling. His duffel bag sat on the end of his cot. His clothing was folded and stacked on the scratchy green blanket covering the cot, waiting to be packed. His eyes were red and puffy.

Howard adopted a casual air. "Going somewhere?"

"Home."

"Did General Westmoreland, or LBJ or somebody sign a ceasefire?"

Lastun cast his friend a weary look. "Nope."

"Well, then. I'm sure the LT and the captain won't let you go. You'll be AWOL. By the way, why are you going?" Howard kept talking, trying to get a handle on Lastun's motivation. He knew there was a problem of some kind between Lastun's mom and his wife.

Lastun tossed Kissy's letter at Howard. It fluttered to the floor.

Howard picked it up and read it, as Lastun resumed packing.

"Something happened to Bizzy? Something bad? Did she say what?" Howard asked.

"There's the letter," Lastun snapped. "You tell me. All I know is she ran away."

Howard was surprised. Lastun usually kept his cool, sometimes masking a much more unsettled mental state. "She ran away." Howard felt at a loss. All he could do was repeat the phrases in the letter.

Lastun stopped packing long enough to make eye contact. "I've gotta find her."

"You'll never make it to Da Nang, good buddy. The MPs will have you in the stockade as soon as you step off the chopper."

"But I can't stay here and do nothing!" Snot strangled his voice, and his words sounded as if he'd spoken under water.

"That's exactly what you have to do," Howard said. "I know it's hard, but you've got to stick it out. Finish your tour. Then you can go find Bizzy. If you stay here with me until our tour's finished, I'll help you look for her."

Lastun sat heavily on the edge of his cot.

"Look, maybe you can place a call home. Tell the captain you've got an emergency. Show him your sister's letter," Howard pleaded.

"Ain't nobody got no phone," Lastun's voice slid back into the old vernacular he'd been trying to get rid of.

Howard sighed. "Why don't you talk to the chaplain? Maybe he can help."

Lastun's conversation with the chaplain obviously didn't go well. After a few minutes he came out of the chapel and paused, looking around. He headed for the platoon leader's office.

Lieutenant Hendricks had taken over Sergeant Fishman's desk in the platoon office. He'd spread a topographical map over Howard's duty roster and studied lines of rivers, trails, and elevation contours.

When Lastun handed Kissy's letter to him and explained what he wanted, the LT looked like a harassed father whose child had asked for a toy he couldn't afford.

That's a big part of his job, Lastun realized through his distress. *To act as a father figure for a bunch of teenagers and twenty-year-olds who'd been thrown into a real-life horror story much scarier than anything told around a Halloween bonfire.*

While Lastun knew the lieutenant had his job to do, he still had to try to go home and find Bizzy.

Hendricks sighed. "Do you know how many 'Dear John' letters I see every week, Wicker?"

"But this ain't a 'Dear John' letter, sir." Lastun stood at attention before him. "You see that my sister said somethin' bad happened to my wife. She ran away. I got to go find her." Lastun hated the pleading tone in his voice, but he couldn't help it.

Hendricks wore an all-cloth camouflage hat with the sides pinned up. He pushed it toward the back of his head. "I know this is hard for you to hear, but the 'bad happening' is probably that she found another boyfriend and that she ran away with him. Your sister's just trying to break the news gently. Didn't she say to just forget about her?"

"But she's my wife! She promised to wait for me!"

"There's an old adage that says, 'Absence makes the heart grow fonder,' but from what I've seen, absence makes the heart forget." Hendricks sat back and adopted an authoritative posture. "You need to grow a back bone, soldier. I'm not going to give you leave. In fact," he indicated the map on his desk, "we've received orders to go on patrol tonight. You need to get your shit together and prepare your fire team."

Lastun opened his mouth to speak, but Hendricks cut him off. "Dismissed."

Lastun strode out of HQ and walked blindly across the compound.

Howard lingered nearby. He knew the answer Hendricks would give and he knew Lastun would be upset. He didn't even ask about the conversation. "Lastun, if you let yourself get distracted, you're going to get yourself killed . . . and maybe some of your squad, as well. Sergeant Reilly depends on you, and so do I. Are you up to it?"

Lastun's body still shook. After a few minutes, his breathing slowed and his wild-eyed look settled into a more focused expression. "I guess I'll have to be," he said.

Lastun went to his squad's bunker and instructed his fire team to clean their weapons and replenish their ammo, C-rats, and K-rats. The LT hadn't briefed the squad sergeants and the sergeants hadn't briefed the squads, but Lastun's instructions told them they were about to go for a walk in the woods.

Lastun brought his cleaning supplies and sat with his men and made his preparations as well.

Howard's warning about Lastun's responsibilities to his fire team had quelled his panic. He knew soldiers got killed in country. It was unavoidable. But the thought of causing the death of a fellow soldier because of his own distracted state was something he couldn't abide.

"Hey, Lastun," Eric Schultz said, "I heard you and Fishman got in a throwdown with a VC gang back at Da Nang." The fire teams were informal. Rank wasn't used in conversation unless somebody was in trouble. It was like when your mother called you by your whole name. "Lastun Roosevelt Wicker, come here right this minute!"

"Yeah," Lastun answered. "I got ambushed. Only the bushwhackers was American. Fishman saved my bacon. We just told the MP they was VC 'cause we didn't want to get tied up in a investigation."

"Why would GIs do something like that?" Schultz asked.

Lastun didn't say anything. He just continued to reassemble his clean weapon.

"Oh. It was because you're black. MPs wouldn't give you a fair shake," Schultz answered his own question. "Well, just so you know, not every white guy thinks like that."

Lastun finally met his gaze. "Like Howard Fishman."

Schultz nodded. "And us." He nodded toward the fire team, three of whom were white. "We've seen you in action. I'll fight alongside you any day."

The other white GIs made affirming noises.

Lastun just nodded, the lump in his throat too big to speak.

The patrol was delayed in departing the firebase. The VC loved the night and grew much more aggressive after dusk. The GIs liked to be in a suitable bivouac location with a secure perimeter by sunset.

"We didn't make it as far as we should have," Hendricks grumped when he called a halt and ordered the patrol to set up camp. "We'll have to double-time it tomorrow."

That was another no-no. A rushed patrol risked missing trip wires, booby traps, and land mines. This sortie was getting off to a bad start.

Lastun couldn't sleep, so he took an extra watch on the picket line. He couldn't figure out what Kissy meant when she wrote *something bad* had happened to Bizzy. She'd also written that she had *run off*. If she'd said she was *gone*, he would fear Bizzy was dead. But run off could only be interpreted one way.

But why did she run off? Had she run away with someone else, as the LT had implied? *Or had she run away from someone, or something?* Lastun sighed and refocused his attention on the mottled shadows of the starlit forest.

They made up little ground the next day. Heavy vegetation slowed their progress. SOP was to avoid trails, as that was where the enemy loved to set traps. Elephant grass and bamboo grew thick. It was hard to cut with a machete and the sharp edges of the grass blades cut back, leaving stinging lacerations on arms, necks, and faces.

Sergeant Reilly came back from a pow-wow with Lieutenant Hendricks. "LT says we're going to use the trail," Reilly said. "We're too far behind schedule." Then came more good news. "Wicker, you've got point."

Lastun had done just what his parents had taught him not to do. He'd excelled at something—woodsmanship. So it was natural for Reilly to put him on point, but dangerous. He knew that rushing and taking shortcuts increased the risks.

The sergeant knew what he was doing, though. By sundown, Lastun had spotted and helped the platoon avoid three booby traps. Two were pits, covered with forest debris, knee deep, so the VC could dig them quickly. *Punji* sticks—

sharpened stakes smeared with human dung—festooned the bottoms of the pits. When a GI stepped onto the flimsy cover, the soldier lost his balance as the top of the pit collapsed. The weight of the stumbling soldier drove the *punji* stakes through his shoe and then his foot. The dung almost guaranteed an infection.

The third trap was a springy tree limb, also with sharp, dung-covered stakes attached, and tied back to another tree. When a GI hit a trip wire, the loosed limb would snap across the trail at face or torso height. Lieutenant Hendricks was suitably grateful for Lastun's skill.

Hendricks summoned the squad leaders at dusk. He'd been on the radio talking to the company CO. Lastun hung close so he could eavesdrop. He didn't like what his gut told him.

"We need to keep going," Hendricks said.

"At night?" Sergeant Reilly's voice sounded incredulous.

The lieutenant looked at his watch. "We're already late. We were supposed to rendezvous with second platoon at seventeen-hundred. The CO's pissed."

Lastun grabbed his gear. He planned to find someplace to be invisible. "Wicker!" Sergeant Reilly shouted.

Too late.

"LT wants you on point again." Reilly sounded apologetic. "Sergeant Fishman's squad is due to lead, so you're going to work with him until we hit the rendezvous point."

"You know how dumb this is, don't you, Sarge?" Lastun asked.

"Yes, I do, and so does the LT. But the cap'n says go, so we go." Reilly took a deep breath. "We're already late. Doesn't matter to me if we're a little late or a lot, so be careful. Go slow until the LT says otherwise." He looked at the sky. "We'll have the moon for a while. Until it sets."

140

"Okay." Lastun walked over to where Howard Fishman had rallied his people. "I'm ready, Sarge," Lastun said to Howard.

"Let's go."

Dusk turned to night. As Reilly had predicted, the moon provided a weak light for a while. Lastun saw no trip wires or booby traps. He was tempted to relax a little. *Maybe the VC have pulled back, waiting until sunrise to worry about the Americans.* But he knew that would be a bad bet.

A leaf on a bush alongside the trail glistened in the moonlight. Too early for any dew to have accumulated. Lastun stopped, lifting his fist, the stop signal for the following platoon.

Howard came up beside him. "See something?" the sergeant asked.

"Yeah."

The two inched forward until they crouched in front of the offending leaf. Lastun studied the ground and the surrounding foliage. Too dark to see much. He'd have to risk it. He pulled his flashlight from his rucksack and flicked it on. He quickly scanned the surroundings again, making sure there were no other man-made signs. He then pointed the light at the leaf. It was covered in a red liquid.

Lieutenant Hendricks came up and joined the two. "Blood?" he asked.

Lastun extinguished the flashlight.

"Second platoon didn't use this trail, did they, sir?" Howard asked.

"No," Hendricks answered.

Lastun touched the red stuff with his fingertip. A little sticky. He touched his fingertip to his tongue. "Not blood," he said.

"What is it?" Hendricks asked.

"You know them nuts that the Vietnamese chew to get a buzz? Betel nuts, I think they call them," Lastun said.

"So somebody came down this trail," Howard observed, "and not long ago. The leaf is still wet."

"Yeah," Lastun said. His brain was in overdrive, trying to figure out what was going on.

Hendricks seemed to be waiting for Howard or Lastun to say something.

"Ambush?" Howard asked.

Lastun nodded. Then, realizing it was probably too dark, said, "Yup."

"If you can pinpoint where they are, I can call in some arty or an air strike," Hendricks said.

Followed by Hendricks and Fishman, Lastun walked along an upslope in the trail. When they neared the top, they crouched and began to duck walk, finally stopping at the crest on their bellies.

"There's a stretch of bottomland down there," Lastun whispered. "I can't see 'em, but I'll bet they're spread out on both sides of the trail."

"When we get back to base, remind me to requisition a Starlite night vision scope," Hendricks muttered to nobody in particular.

"I've got an idea," Lastun whispered. "Lieutenant, can you have the men spread out along this ridge, so they'll have a shooting angle into that low area?"

"Sergeant," Hendricks whispered.

Howard crept off to see that the LT's order was carried out.

Lastun rummaged around in his rucksack and pulled out a couple of packs of the items he'd bought back in Kilgore's store just before he'd left for Nam.

"Firecrackers?" Hendricks whispered.

Lastun unwrapped two packs of Black Cat firecrackers, twenty to a pack. Their fuses were woven together so they could all be lit at one time.

"When the platoon gets in position, I'll light these and throw them off over yonder . . ." The LT probably couldn't see him point his chin, but he'd understand, ". . . away from our location. Firecrackers don't sound much like M16s, but I'll bet the VC won't take time to figure that out. When the 'crackers go off, the VC will start shootin' toward the sound. That means they won't be shootin' at us. We can target their muzzle flashes and lay down on 'em. That way, we'll have the drop and the VC'll think there's more of us than there really is."

"Good thinking, Wicker," Hendricks whispered.

A few minutes later the platoon was ready. Lastun turned his back to the spot where he thought the VC hid, lit the two packs of firecrackers, and flung them as far as he could away from their position.

Popopopopopopop! To an unsuspecting ear, the fireworks really did sound like gunfire. All forty firecrackers sounded like a lot of gunfire.

Within seconds, the VC opened up, shooting toward the sound and flash of the fireworks. As planned, the GIs returned fire, aiming at the enemy muzzle flashes. The VC redirected their aim, but the Americans maintained fire superiority, until the VC mortar barrage began.

The enemy still hadn't decided where the American strength lay. Their initial rounds fell on the spot where the firecrackers had gone off.

Then some quick-thinking Viet Cong officer decided to launch a couple of flares. In addition to explosive rounds, a mortar can fire a flare which deploys a small parachute. This allows it to drift down slowly, illuminating the ground below it like a street lamp.

The mortar rounds fell nearer the GIs.

"Medic, I'm hit!"

Lastun recognized the voice.

Howard Fishman lay on an open section of the trail. It looked as if he'd been changing his position when an AK-47 round or a piece of mortar shrapnel caught him.

The VC weren't targeting Howard, yet. He was exposed, lit by a flare. They would wait for another American to come and get him, then they'd shoot the rescuer—and the next, and the next. They'd keep it up until the initially injured soldier died, or until the GIs gave up and waited for the firefight to end and hope the soldier survived.

So Howard Fishman lay exposed, which the VC wanted.

Lastun saw movement from the corner of his eye. Sergeant Mack "Doc" Carter, the medic, made his way toward Howard. In a couple of seconds, there would be two sitting ducks.

Might as well make it three. Lastun bolted from his cover and interposed himself between Howard and the enemy. He knelt and triggered a burst of suppressing fire toward the nearest VC position.

Doc grabbed Howard under his armpits and pulled him toward the covering brush on the side of the trail. Lastun's position blocked the VCs angle of fire.

A bullet clipped the rucksack on Lastun's back and another buzzed by his ear. With three targets, the VC fired in earnest. One stood up to get a better shot. Lastun dropped him.

A bullet clipped Lastun's boot heel.

As the flare began to burn out, Lastun spotted a forked tree. Instinct told him it would be a great firing position, so he put a round just above where the fork's "Y" joint formed. He saw a body fold back away from the tree.

Doc yelled, "Got 'im,'" just as the firing pin of Lastun's M16 clicked on an empty chamber. As he fell back, he ejected his clip and slammed a new one home.

Lieutenant Hendricks called retreat. Lastun and Doc formed a two-man cradle with their arms and carried Howard toward the rear.

The platoon reformed near where Lastun first spotted the betel nut juice.

"I've called in an artillery barrage," Hendricks announced.

The earth shook like a wet dog after a bath. The air split with the concussion of the high explosive shells.

Lastun lay back on the ground and thought about the fight. He hadn't had time to be scared. He bent his knee, so he could touch the gouged-out gap of his boot heel caused by the AK-47 bullet. He'd probably shot an enemy soldier before, but he'd never seen one fall from his shot and known for sure. He'd seen his shots take down two in this fight.

He thought he should feel something, but he didn't. *Too tired. Maybe later. It was a matter of survival. Them or me.*

After the battle, Lastun went to find Howard. He'd been taken to a triage area near a clearing. He and the other wounded would be helo-evacuated at dawn. His thigh sported a bandage.

"How *you* doin'?" Lastun tried to effect a Brooklyn accent, as he sat on the ground.

"I'm good," Howard said with a wan smile. "The doc gave me a shot of morphine."

Doc Carter came up and knelt beside them. "I've got good news and bad news, Sarge," he said to Howard. "Good news is you'll get a Purple Heart. Bad news is, a couple of weeks at the Da Nang meat factory, and you'll be back with us. This wound won't get you sent home." He looked at Lastun. "That's thanks to you, you crazy bastard. If you hadn't gone out there and

145

blocked their sight line, we'd both be in body bags. I still don't know how you missed getting killed."

Lastun held up his brown arm. "Victor Charlie couldn't see me very good. God gave me my own camouflage. First time bein' black was a advantage."

"Say what you want, but you're still one lucky bastard," Doc insisted. He snapped his fingers. "Oh, by the way, Lieutenant Hendricks is looking for you."

"Me?" Lastun touched his chest. "What did I do?"

Doc took a breath. "You're not in trouble. Sergeant Reilly wasn't as lucky as Sergeant Fishman here. He didn't get killed, but he got a million-dollar wound. He's hurt bad. He'll get sent home." Doc cocked his head to one side, "So, Sergeant Wicker, I'd say he's got a new assignment for you."

Doc was right.

"You know about Reilly?" Hendricks said to Wicker. "Captain's giving you a field promotion to sergeant and squad leader. I concur with his choice."

The matter-of-fact statement left Lastun marveling at the ironies of war. Sergeant Reilly hadn't even been evacked yet and he was already in the past.

"The VC ambush blew the timing of our mission. They've withdrawn now, but the rendezvous with second platoon has been called off," Hendricks continued. "As soon as the casualties are evacuated at dawn, we'll backtrack to the fire base."

Lastun noticed he didn't say *retreat*. "So my firecracker diversion didn't work," Lastun said. Disappointment tainted his voice.

"On the contrary. It saved our skins. Without that trick of yours, we'd have been massacred. You saved a lot of lives today."

December, 1967

Dear Bizzy

Kissy says something happened to you. Something bad, and you ran off. The Lieutenant thinks you probably went off with another man, but I don't believe it. I wish you would write and tell me what happened. You said you would wait for me.

When he finished writing the letter, Lastun took out his lighter and burned it. He had no idea where to send it.

17

"Ungh!" Waking from the dream always forced a grunt. Lastun leaned on his elbow and listened, wondering if he'd disturbed anyone. A couple of sleeping bodies shifted in their beds. Once the soldiers were safely in their own barracks, exhaustion made them deep sleepers.

The dream always repeated the same few seconds over-and-over, like a tone-arm on a hi-fi record player that kept getting bumped back to play the same few notes again-and-again. Only the dream was in images. *Lastun is kneeling in front of Howard and Doc. He fires his rifle, feels the shoulder-punch of the recoil, and sees the enemy soldier fall. Then he shifts his aim. Trigger-pull, recoil, and the second soldier falls. Repeat.*

The brass had called it the Battle of Phu Loc and declared it a resounding victory for the Allied forces of the U.S. Army and the Army of the Republic of Vietnam. Maybe a squad of ARVN infantry had been with the platoon, but Lastun hadn't seen any of them where the hot lead flew.

G2 also said that the U.S. platoon hadn't just been up against Viet Cong. The North Vietnamese Army had also been involved. In Lastun's experience, the VC didn't hang in against tough resistance. When things got wild, they usually bugged out. NVA didn't. Since the enemy had given as good as they got, Lastun believed Army intelligence was right. NVA infantry had been at Phu Loc.

Over the six weeks since the battle, things had stayed pretty quiet at Firebase Screwball. They'd run patrols and they'd had a few skirmishes, but nothing big. This led Lastun to believe the enemy had taken a beating, too, and they were hanging back and licking their wounds just like the company at FB Screwball. Unlike the brass, however, Lastun judged the encounter a draw.

Howard returned after a month. Except for a slight limp, he didn't look much the worse for wear.

Lastun met him at the helipad. "Hey, you okay? Looks like you got a hitch in your get-along."

"A what in my what?" Howard asked over the din of the rotor blades.

"You limpin'."

"Oh, that. The doctor says it'll go away in a couple of weeks. I see you made sergeant."

Lastun grinned. "Well, they needed somebody to run this place while you was gone." Lastun grew solemn. "Don't tell Lieutenant Hendricks I said that, okay?"

Howard laughed. "Don't worry, I won't."

"By the way, Captain Dettinger called a staff meeting for fourteen hundred hours."

Captain Dettinger had lost ten, maybe fifteen pounds in the time that Lastun had known him. That wasn't too unusual. Everybody lost weight in the field. He'd also gotten a lot more lax about shaving. He wore the same week-old beard that just about everybody else did. His XO, three platoon leaders, and nine squad sergeants sat in chairs in front of him.

"I don't know what you're hearing through the grapevine," Dettinger said, "but intelligence reports heavy NVA movement in all three corps areas. We assume additional arms and other war material are also being funneled in through the Ho Chi Minh trail." He paused, studying the group as he repositioned the Colt Model 1911 .45 in the holster on his hip. "The regimental CO thinks the NVA have something planned. The Vietnamese new year—Tet, they call it—is coming up at the end of January, in a couple of weeks, and both sides usually observe an unofficial cease-fire. The colonel thinks the NVA will pull something within a week or so after that."

Several men shifted in their chairs, as they processed this news.

The captain paced across the front of the room. "So, I want you to be alert, just in case Charlie can't wait. And I'm talking about before and during Tet." He stopped and stroked the stubble on his chin. "I keep remembering what George Washington did on Christmas morning at Trenton. Charlie might want to get a jump on things."

Patrols continued. While Lastun's squad was out on a foray, Eric Schultz stepped on a land mine.

He lost about twenty-five pounds in one second. Lastun cradled his head, while arterial blood spurted and bathed the ground where his missing leg would have been. "Hang on, Eric," Lastun pleaded. He took off his belt to try to apply a tourniquet on the bloody stump. "Doc's comin'. He'll get you fixed up. Chopper'll get you to Da Nang, and then you'll go home." He hadn't even called for the chopper. He knew that Schultz didn't have enough time, or enough blood to hold out. Two minutes before Doc arrived, he died.

The next night, Lastun had a new dream. He was back in Satartia, about to cross a stream, which wasn't a problem because he had a nice row of stepping-stones to use. Only when he made the jump to the first stone, it turned into a mine. He woke with the thunder of the explosion buffeting his ears and his heart pounding like an M60 on full auto.

He climbed out of bed and wrestled on some clothes. He then went out to walk the trenches and make sure the rest of his men were still alive. Sleep was over for the night.

The last week of January, Captain Dettinger announced that the company would move to Dak Tho, the site of an anticipated NVA attack after Tet. Apparently, the Army was undertaking a massive reshuffle of units and helicopters were unavailable. The company would have to travel in a convoy of deuce-and-a-halfs.

Sergeants Fishman and Wicker spent the morning making sure their charges were squared away. Everything packed, weapons and ammo ready to go, and everybody loaded on the trucks.

As they got underway, the vehicles kicked up their own dust storm. Lastun didn't know if the move was supposed to be on the QT, but he was sure every VC spy in the area knew they were bugging out. Maybe they didn't know where the GIs were going, but all they had to do was follow.

After two full days of travel, the company reached Dak Tho, where it joined up with the rest of the regiment. Lieutenant Hendricks summoned his staff.

"We're going to establish an outpost on a ridge right here." Hendricks pointed to a spot on his map. "The other platoons will deploy here and here, on each side of us. The other companies in the regiment will fan out to complete a circle around Dak Tho. We'll be the first line of defense in case of an NVA assault." He looked up. "They haven't been this aggressive in a long time. Personally, I think this is a bluff. If the enemy hits, it will be at Saigon or one of the larger bases."

Once the platoon reached its designated position, Lastun pulled his squad together. "LT thinks there's nothing to these rumors. Here's what I think." He looked around to make sure the lieutenant was out of earshot. "It won't hurt us to be ready for whatever Charlie tries to do. If I'm wrong and the LT is right, we just wasted our time. But if the LT is wrong, we'll be a lot less dead because we were ready." Lastun smiled. "Just don't tell him I said that."

Radios crackled to life on the morning of January 30th, the first day of Tet, and all the officers grew very alarmed.

Hendricks met with his sergeants again. "So much for the Tet cease-fire. The NVA hit a Marine post at Khe Sahn and they've also attacked Saigon, Da Nang, Hue, and a bunch of other places. So, we'd better get ready. There's no reason to think we're not on their list."

Lastun and Howard linked up their squads in a defensive line on the crown of a hill overlooking a chessboard of rice paddies. Hendricks established a command post behind this line. Doc organized a makeshift infirmary alongside Hendricks' position.

Nothing happened.

"They'll hit us at dusk," Howard predicted. "The VC and NVA prefer to fight at night."

Each squad established an M60 machine gun nest and loaded them with all the ammo the gunners could handle. In late afternoon, the squads set out Claymore mines at the limit of their range of M16 fire.

PFC Jimmy Lucas, Lastun's machine gunner, eyed the pile of M60 ammo sadly. "If the bad guys drop a mortar round on me, Sarge, it'll be worse than fireworks on New Year's Eve."

Lastun put his hand on Jimmy's shoulder. "We'll just have to hope Charlie's aim ain't that good."

"I feel so reassured," Lucas moaned.

Howard's prophecy came true. A couple of Claymores went off, alerting the GIs and, Lastun hoped, killing a few NVA troops.

"Okay, men," Lastun called, "don't waste ammo. Make sure you've got a target before you shoot."

As it grew darker, following Lastun's order became more difficult. Even so, Lastun could tell the enemy was advancing in force. This was no skirmish.

When the NVA got closer to the American lines, they opened up with mortars. The flying shrapnel, along with AK47 fire, forced the Americans to keep their heads down, allowing the enemy troops to close in.

The smell of cordite filled the air while enemy muzzle flashes flickered across the rice paddies like fireflies.

Lastun went to Lieutenant Hendricks. "How about some arty to slow them boys down some?" he asked.

"I've already called it in," Hendricks responded, "but Charlie is hitting everywhere. They're all tied up with other targets. We'll just have to slug it out."

Shortly after midnight, Lastun noticed that the Army platoon on his left was no longer returning fire, and the NVA had begun to advance into the platoon's former position. After shifting one of his fire teams over to counter the enemy's movement, he went to Lieutenant Hendricks' command post. "LT, I think we've lost our support on the left. In a few minutes, we'll be flanked, then they'll smoke our asses."

Howard joined them. "Same thing on the right. We're about to be surrounded."

Hendricks cursed and grabbed his radio handset. He put it down a few minutes later and said, "Damn, we're stranded. We were supposed to pull back, too, but the captain neglected to tell us. I reported a broken arrow." It was code for telling HQ that they were being overrun and needed help. "Nothing's coming. We're stuck." Bitterness soaked his voice.

"Reckon it's not too late for us to *di di mau*?" Lastun asked, using the term for "haul ass."

Lieutenant Hendricks shook his head. "We're pinned down." He scratched his chin. Before he could propose another action, his radio crackled again. He picked up the handset. After talking for a few seconds, he said, "There's a couple of F-105s out there with some napalm. The mission there tasked for got scrubbed and they're looking for some place to dump their payload. They can put it on our attackers, but we'll need to light a hand-held flare so they'll know where *not* to put it."

"But a flare will make it easier for the NVA to target us," Howard complained.

"Don't I know it," Hendricks said.

Howard thought for a minute. "LT, don't you have a Starlite scope?"

"Yep."

"How far out are the jets?"

"About ten minutes."

"I've got an idea. Lastun, you can help. Just do what I do." Howard grabbed a fifteen ounce C-ration can from his rucksack. Using a can opener, he removed both ends of the canister and dumped its contents. He now had a four-and-a-half-inch hollow tube.

Lastun repeated Howard's actions, using another C-ration can.

Howard rinsed out the inside of the tube with some water from his canteen.

"Doc, you got any medical tape?" Howard asked.

"Catch." Doc Carter tossed him a roll of two-inch cloth adhesive tape.

Howard fitted the hollow can over the lens of his flashlight and taped it in place. Then he gave the tape to Lastun, who did the same to his flashlight.

Howard pointed the flashlight at Hendricks, and quickly clicked it on and off, lighting the lieutenant's face for only a second. "Now we've got a line-of-sight beacon. Only the pilots

Lastun and I point at can see it. The NVA won't see a thing. Gimme your Starlite scope."

Hendricks handed it over.

"Ask the pilots to look for two flashing beacons. Once they spot them, have them barbecue the areas fifty yards on either side."

Hendricks clutched the radio handset, repeating Fishman's instructions.

The jets displayed no lights, making them invisible to anyone on the ground—anyone who didn't have a Starlite scope, anyway. Howard put the device to his eyes and scanned the horizon.

"They'll be coming in at about three hundred miles an hour. That'll give them only a few seconds to see your signal," Hendricks warned.

Howard said nothing.

Lastun heard the distant rush of jet engines, but he couldn't pinpoint the direction.

"There they are," Howard said. Excitement lifted his voice to a higher pitch. He pointed his flashlight beacon at a spot above the horizon and began clicking it on and off. "Lastun, point where I'm pointing, and rapidly blink your flashlight on and off."

Lastun followed.

"The pilots have acquired your signal," Hendricks said. He spoke in an enthused voice. "They're commencing their run."

Above them, the *whoosh* of engines grew louder. With the night scope to his eyes, Howard moved his flashlight beacon to track the movement of the fighters.

Lastun copied his movements.

It was too dark to see the jets or the bullet-shaped containers they dropped. Howard pulled the Starlite scope away from his eyes.

In the space of a heartbeat, a sun exploded around them. First, Lastun felt blistering heat, as hundreds of pounds of jellied gasoline ignited. Then his lungs lost their air, as the conflagration sucked up all the oxygen in their vicinity. Wind rushed by them, as the fire drew in air.

For a few seconds, the only sound Lastun could hear was the low thunder of burning fuel. As that sound subsided, it was followed by the shrill screams of immolated NVA soldiers. In the light of the flaming napalm, Lastun saw fiery bodies first moving, then falling. His lung function slowly returned, as the fire's need for air diminished. Lastun would now have a new nightmare to add to his collection.

18

The battle at Saigon went on for a week. The Army gained the upper hand and it was mostly a mop-up operation.

Hue was a different matter altogether.

American forces at Hue had to pry the NVA troops out with a crowbar. Each building was its own battleground. Troops cleared them one at a time, often reducing them to rubble in the process. The once beautiful city became a shambles. After a month, the enemy was driven out and the American and ARVN troops re-captured the city.

The NVA surrounded and besieged the Marine contingent in Khe Sanh. The Americans ran low on ammo and food, and I Corps had to resort to air drops for resupply. But, as in Hue, superior firepower forced the NVA to lift the siege and withdraw.

Lieutenant Hendricks was jubilant. He'd just returned from a regimental staff meeting at Pleiku. "We broke their backs!" He told the platoon sergeant and squad leaders. "They made a last ditch effort, like the Battle of the Bulge in dubya-dubya-two! Khe Sanh was their Bastogne!"

Lastun knew he was just repeating words the colonel had said, and the grapevine confirmed it. Twenty thousand NVA dead compared to less than five hundred Americans. In light of the enemy losses, the Americans had fared well, but Lastun knew the families of those five hundred would think differently. Lastun couldn't get over the idea of how close he and Howard and their fellow soldiers had come to being counted in that number. After a couple of months at Dak Tho, the company returned to Phu Loc. Once there, they stepped up their patrols. For the moment, at least, the enemy seemed to be regrouping. The patrols met very little resistance.

Howard Fishman's parents had been sending copies of the *New York Times* to him. Back in the States, the news was less optimistic. For the past three years, General Westmoreland and the brass had claimed the North Vietnamese Army was near collapse. If that was true, the press and Congress now asked, why had the NVA had been able to launch a surprise attack that had very nearly crushed the mighty U.S. Army? Westmoreland and LBJ challenged the use of the phrase, "very nearly crushed," but their rebuttal sounded weak and half-hearted.

"We've only got a couple of months left on our tour," Howard told Lastun at mess one day, "so I don't think it will affect us. But if the *Times* is right, and it usually is, this war won't last much longer. And it won't be because we've won. Things are so bad back home, President Johnson's not going to run for re-election."

Lastun shrugged. "All I know is my squad is tired of fightin'. When I first got here, I didn't even know what the word morale meant. Maybe I still don't. But I do know what it ain't, and it ain't here." He drew a deep breath and took a furtive look around. "The best thing me and you can do, Howard, is stay alive. I've still got one more mission to accomplish, but I can't do it if I die in Nam."

Howard said nothing. He only nodded.

Patrols continued to go on search-and-destroy missions, seeking VC hideouts. At least that's what happened on paper. News that the people in the States had lost heart filtered back to the troops. Suddenly, no one was gung ho. No one wanted to die for what was seen to be a lost cause.

The patrols went out far enough to be undetected by anyone at the firebase and camped for a few days. They fired off a number of M16 rounds and tossed a few grenades, so their ammo would be partially depleted. Upon their return, the platoon leaders filed fictional after-action reports about skirmishes that never took place.

Platoon leaders who were too vigorous in engaging the enemy were warned—subtly—by the enlisted troops in their command. If they didn't get the hint, a "friendly" grenade would land a little too close, or a "poorly aimed" M16 burst would take them out. The troops called this fragging.

After his initial excitement, Lieutenant Hendricks lost his shine. He was no dummy. He called his platoon together after setting up camp on one of their patrols.

"You never heard this from me, but the brass misread the situation after Tet. I see no need to risk my life or yours for a war we can't win." He studied the group, his eyes moving from face-to-face. "That being said, we can't rely on the enemy to cooperate. If we encounter a VC or NVA patrol, they *will* try to kill us, and we *will* have to defend ourselves. So from now on, we will not seek to engage, but we will defend. Are you on board?"

A sea of heads nodded.

"Good. Squad sergeants, post your sentries."

As Howard grew "short"—drawing nearer to the date he would rotate out and be sent home—his anxiety grew. While modern warfare rarely called for the use of bayonets in firefights, Howard found comfort in affixing his bayonet to his M16 barrel when shooting started—just in case.

During the first week of April, Dr. Martin Luther King, Jr. was assassinated while he stood on the balcony of a motel in Memphis, Tennessee.

When the news reached Nam, the black troops threatened to mutiny. Fist fights erupted between white and black soldiers. The company CO ordered that the two races be separated, sending each group to an opposite corner of the base for a cooling-off period.

Due to his skill and his unruffled demeanor, Lastun had become one of the more respected black soldiers in the company.

"What we gonna do, Sarge?" one of the privates asked Lastun.

Lastun closed his eyes for a moment and fought back tears. He remembered Mr. Hardy, his principal back at Yazoo County Colored School, and his defiance in the face of his white oppressors. He remembered how it had cost Mr. Hardy his life.

He remembered the Freedom Riders and their drive to register black voters in Mississippi. He remembered how his papa had run them off – not because he disagreed with what they were trying to do, but because he feared retribution from the white men who held power in the county.

He remembered men like Ellis Barber, and Goliath, and others, who continued to behave as if the black people were still slaves, subject to the white man's will.

And now Dr. King had joined the martyrs who'd given their lives to further the cause of racial equality.

Lastun opened his eyes and looked over the crowd of black faces watching him. "When I was drafted into the Army a year-and-a-half ago, the sergeant at the induction center said that I was the property of the United States Army." Lastun wiped a tear from his cheek. "He didn't know what them words meant to black men like me and you. Lastun lifted his chin and his voice. "Well, I am nobody's property."

His words generated an angry swell of curses from his listeners, mixed with words of agreement.

"But I am a U.S. Citizen and a American soldier,' Lastun continued. "If we riot because of this great man's senseless murder, we'll throw away everything Dr. King worked for. If we beat up them white men over yonder," he nodded toward the whites on the other side of the camp, "the way other white men have beat us so many times, the officers and the MPs will throw us in the stockade. Won't nothin' good come of that."

He took a deep breath. "Remember, not one of them was the one who killed Dr. King. Our hearts are broke, but we still have a job to do . . . 'cause like the LT said, the VC still tryin' to kill us.

"So we still gotta stick together, even with them white soldiers."

The crowd rumbled. Their words carried an undertone of disagreement and anger.

Lastun waited for the grumbling to die down. "But while we do it, we'll hold our heads high. They owe us respect."

The crowd murmured assent.

"We've saved their asses and they've saved ours. We'll expect respect from them. If we riot, they won't give us that respect."

Lastun picked up a bucket, turned it upside down and sat on it. He didn't know if what he'd said made sense, but he hoped it made his black friends stop and think long enough to allow their rage to evaporate.

When the two groups returned to their quarters, no more fighting occurred. Everyone felt the simmering anger, but the pot didn't boil over.

Later, Howard approached Lastun. "I heard from the grapevine you made quite a speech," he said.

Lastun gave him a sideways look. "I was so scared, I don't even know what I said."

"Whatever it was, it worked."

May. Just three weeks until Howard and Lastun rotated out. The LT had the platoon on patrol, marching in a wide circle which would bring them back to Firebase Screwball with a minimal risk of engagement.

The grunt on point failed to catch the absence of wildlife noises, a warning sign that some unknown persons were ahead, waiting. A sign Lastun would have recognized. A VC unit ambushed the platoon.

Howard quickly dispersed his squad along a skirmish line, connecting his left flank with Lastun's right. He grabbed and attached his bayonet. Their unofficial "rules of engagement" involved keeping their heads down and waiting for the VC to use up their ammo and withdraw.

Howard worked his way over to the LT's command post. "Think we can get some arty to flush these guys out?" he asked.

"On it," Hendricks said with a nod. "We aren't where we're supposed to be, but I can tell the CO we drifted out of position. It'll get me an ass chewing, but that'll be okay."

"Maybe when we engaged with them, they ran. We chased them and they made a stand here," Howard suggested.

That brought a grin. "I like your thinking," Hendricks said.

Howard wound his way back to Lastun. "Arty's coming. Just hang on for a while."

"Thanks for the news," Lastun said. "This bunch is stubborn. Thought they'd be gone by now."

Artillery shells thundered on a ridge a quarter-mile away.

"Don't that beat all," Lastun complained. "Somebody got the coordinates wrong."

The VC must have drawn the same conclusion and realized the American spotter would quickly correct the mistake. They burst from their cover, screaming and firing AK47s as they ran through the trees and brush.

Howard didn't have time to return to his squad. He grabbed a grenade from his belt, pulled the pin and heaved it. The device exploded in front of the enemy line. The concussion and shrapnel blast blew two of them off their feet just yards from his position. Howard got a good look at the contorted expressions on their dead faces.

The American line held fast, cutting down the enemy with automatic rifle bursts. The M60 gunner set up to protect the LT's position. The *chug-chug-chug* of his weapon sparked a feeling of assurance in Howard. The .30 caliber bullets chopped grass, branches and VC alike in a rain of mayhem.

Despite the Americans' entrenched position, they could only slow the VC advance. They must be at least company strength, Howard thought.

To his left, Lastun threw his last grenade and resumed his M16 fire. A trio of VC bore down on him, leaping over the bodies of dead comrades and screaming in high-pitched voices in a language Howard couldn't understand. He prepared to help his buddy when he caught a flash of black approaching from his right. A VC soldier wielding a machete made a beeline for Lastun.

With no time to aim, Howard fired his last burst from the hip and missed. His ammo was gone. Screaming his own battle cry, Howard lowered his rifle stock so the bayonet blade was angled upward and charged.

The VC appeared surprised by the danger from a new tack. Before he could shift to defend, Howard plunged his bayonet in an upward thrust under the enemy's rib cage. By his forward momentum, the VC impaled himself on the blade. His frantic machete strike swept harmlessly over Howard's head. His feet left the ground, and, for a second, he hung in the air atop the M16's barrel. Howard dumped his body onto the ground and turned to help Lastun.

His fellow sergeant took out one of the attackers. The other two lost their nerve and fled.

With the aid of the spotter, the artillery gunners finally found their proper target. The VC had enough and bugged out.

Lieutenant Hendricks had enough. He ordered a *di di mau* to the firebase. Although the platoon took substantial losses, the engagement was deemed a victory and Hendricks got a shiny medal to wear on his uniform.

Howard and Lastun got a few days shorter and counted their lucky stars.

June arrived. Howard and Lastun received papers ordering them to rotate home and granting them a thirty-day leave upon arrival in the United States. After that, they were to report for duty at Fort Carson, Colorado. A Huey took them to the air base at Da Nang, where they boarded a MAC flight to Travis AFB, near San Francisco.

Lastun stopped on the top step of the boarding ladder before entering the plane. He turned and surveyed the camp. The monsoon season had begun early and everything that wasn't wood or asphalt was mud again. At least the rain had paused momentarily, and he could get a sense of the desolation of the place. He shivered, remembering his arrival here twelve months ago, and the overwhelming despair he'd felt at the time. Through some combination of luck, fate or position of the stars, they'd managed to survive. He remembered the faces of the buddies who didn't: Leroy Dodge, Eric Schultz, and so many others.

Howard stopped at the step just below him and seemed to be saying his own silent goodbye.

Lastun realized that he'd gone up the steps ahead of Howard, and had thought nothing of it. Twelve months ago, he'd never have preceded a white man anywhere.

The two remained quiet while the jet's engines spooled up for takeoff. Acceleration pushed them back into their seats as the aircraft launched itself down the runway, and Lastun felt the subtle flip in his belly when the plane's wheels left the ground.

Lastun turned to say something to Howard, but his friend was already asleep.

That seemed like a good idea. He also was asleep almost before his eyes closed.

Howard's stirring roused Lastun from his sleep, too. Lastun glanced at his watch. "Six hours. I haven't slept that long at one time since . . . I can't remember."

Howard yawned and stretched. The dull thrum of the engines muted his voice. "Yes, it's amazing how peaceful things can be without mortar or AK fire."

Each man made a trip to the latrine. When they were settled back into their seats, the stewardesses began serving dinner.

"Ahh, baked chicken and roasted potatoes," Lastun said. "Beats C-rations."

Howard grunted. "Airplane food beats field rations, but not by much. You should taste the food at Katz's Deli on Houston Street in Manhattan. It's to die for."

Lastun shoveled a forkful of chicken into his mouth. "I'll take your word for it. I don't see myself ever gettin' to New York." The words came out mangled as he chewed.

"Don't say that." Howard took a sip of Coke. "You should come up to visit. I could show you the sights. I'll bet there's nothing in Satartia to compare."

"I know that's true, but first things first. I've got to find Bizzy." Lastun took a deep breath. "What are you gonna do when you get home?"

"Do you remember at Firebase Screwball when I promised to help you find your wife? Well, I meant it. I'm going with you."

Lastun put his fork down and stared into Howard's eyes. Something else he would have never done to a white man twelve months ago. "I know what you said, but that's above and beyond the call of duty. I'm not gonna hold you to that."

"You don't have . . ." He paused as the plane hit a pocket of rough air. Food trays clattered all around, but none fell to the floor. "You don't have to. I'll hold myself to it." He leaned back and struck a casual pose. "Besides, I ain't never been to Mississippi," he said, stretching his voice into a drawl. "I'd like a little time to adjust to stateside before I go home."

Lastun smiled. "Thanks, buddy."

They deplaned at Travis AFB, stopped at a nearby barracks long enough to change into their Class A uniforms. Each of their green dress jackets sported three sergeant stripes on the upper arms. Above the left set of chevrons, they wore the tan and green diamond and ivy insignia of the Fourth Infantry Division. Above their left breast pockets they wore a Combat Infantry Badge, signifying they had actually been shot at, and a sharpshooter badge. Each also wore a Good Conduct Medal, a Vietnam Theater Medal, and a Bronze Star. Lastun's Bronze

Star had been awarded for his actions at Phu Loc, while Howard's was for Dak Tho. In addition, Howard wore a Purple Heart.

They showed their leave papers to a guard at the base's exit gate and grabbed a bus for San Francisco International Airport.

When they dismounted the bus at the airport, Howard elbowed Lastun. "Maybe we should have worn our civvies."

"How come?"

Before Howard could answer, Lastun saw some of the crowd in the ticket area. Many wore long, unwashed hair, tie-dyed T-shirts, and grungy looking jeans. Most of the colored, including the women, had bushy, Afro-style haircuts, which made Lastun, in his close-cropped military hairstyle, feel almost bald. Several of the coloreds wore the long flowing tunics that some off-duty, black soldiers in Nam wore. They called them dashikis.

Lastun realized appearance was not what Howard referred to. The crowd looked at the two men in military garb the way a lion looks at lunch.

"Baby killers!" A woman near the front screamed at the top of her voice.

"Murderers!" Another shouted.

"Make love, not war!"

"Establishment pigs!"

The verbal abuse grew until Howard and Lastun were awash in the cacophony of the hate being directed at them.

Lastun looked at Howard and saw the pain in his eyes. Lastun felt it, too. They had just spent a year in a place where people tried to kill them every day. They'd faced death and dealt death in the service of their country. Instead of the gratitude they might have expected on their return, they were being treated as if they were the enemy.

Lastun wanted to grab his duffel and get out of there as quickly as possible, but he knew that wasn't the right thing to do. He leaned over and put his lips near Howard's ear so he could be heard above the insults. "Back home, I learned the worst thing to do was try to run from a vicious dog, it only stirs their instinct to chase and kill."

Howard nodded.

The two picked up their bags and marched with slow military precision through the crowd.

A white woman in a tie-dyed T-shirt and braless, spat. Her saliva struck Lastun on his cheek. He stopped, wiped the spittle from his face and gave the woman a cold-eyed, stone-faced glare.

Perhaps she saw in his expression what Lastun was capable of. What he'd done. The person he'd become. Her angry posture melted into one of fear, and she retreated into the crowd.

Lastun's and Howard's refusal to cower in the face of the mob dampened its anger. The group continued to seethe and grumble, but made no other efforts at confrontation.

They used their military vouchers to get tickets to New Orleans, boarded the plane and occupied their seats. "Well done, Sergeant," Howard said.

"Thank you, Sergeant," Lastun replied.

Airborne once again, Lastun's emotional fatigue from the confrontation at San Francisco took over and he drifted back into darkness.

Lastun snapped awake. The odor of burning flesh filled his nostrils. Flames surrounded the plane's cabin, and the screams of the dying . . .

It was a dream, the Battle of Dak Tho. He inhaled deeply and waited for his heartbeat to slow down.

Howard gave him a sympathetic look. "Nightmare?"

"I'll probly never get another good night's sleep," Lastun complained. "There's some sights and smells you just can't never forget."

"Tell me about it," Howard said. "I have them, too."

"How much longer 'til N'Awlins?" Lastun asked.

Howard glanced at his watch. "Two hours, I'd say." He shifted in his seat. "Have you thought about how you plan to find your wife?"

"I'll just start askin' 'round," Lastun said through clenched teeth.

"Do you think anybody'll talk to you?"

Although he smiled, Lastun's eyes were cold. "It's a small place. Everbody knows what happened, I guarantee. Kissy said Bizzy had gone away. Somebody'll know where." His smile widened, but there was no happiness in his expression. "There's more'n a few gossips in Satartia, and at least one of 'em is dyin' to tell me what she knows."

19

Their experience in San Francisco prepared them for another verbal assault, but Howard and Lastun found the New Orleans airport less frenetic and abusive. They still encountered a mob of pro-love, anti-war demonstrators, but it was less aggressive than its west coast counterpart. As before, the two soldiers conducted themselves with military aplomb.

They took a cab to the bus station and bought tickets to Yazoo City. Lastun led Howard to a spot near the rear of the bus.

Howard called him on it. "You know they can't make you sit back here," he said.

"Maybe not, but I'll bet there will be a big ruckus if I don't," Lastun countered. "I may have changed, but I guarantee the South hasn't. Besides, I've got other things on my mind. We can pick this fight some other time."

Howard nodded.

They sat in silence, watching scenery neither had ever seen as the bus pulled out of New Orleans on Highway 61.

After a while, Lastun said, "You was right."

"Of course, I was," Howard responded. "About what?"

"Us losin' the war. After what we seen in them airports, I can tell America is fed up with Vietnam. We maybe won Tet, but that ain't gonna matter none."

"Looks like we came home at just the right time, buddy."

"Roger that."

They had a short layover in Baton Rouge, but didn't change buses, followed by a similar pause at Natchez. Both were fascinated by glimpses of the broad, brown expanse of the

Mississippi River that occasionally appeared through the bus window. When they pulled in at the Vicksburg depot, they were considerably more rumpled. While sleeping on a bus wasn't wonderful, it beat the hell out of sleeping on the ground in Vietnam.

As they journeyed further into the interior of the country, and things grew more rural, they encountered fewer glowers that seemed related to their Army uniforms. The area that the TV reporters called "Middle America" showed a lot less animosity toward the soldiers. They did get a few bemused looks that Lastun attributed to the fact that a white man and black man traveled together.

They changed buses in Vicksburg and began the short trek up Highway 3 toward Yazoo City. As the miles passed, Lastun grew ever more watchful. Suddenly, he yanked the bell cord, and the driver pulled the bus to a stop in front of a weather-beaten roadside store. A single gasoline pump stood guard at the entrance. Alongside the store, a kerosene barrel lay on its side, supported by a wooden bracket. Assorted tin signs hawking *Winston* cigarettes, *Coca-Cola*, and *Martha White* flour, faded even more than when Lastun had last seen them, decorated the front and sides of the structure.

After dismounting the bus with their duffels, Lastun gestured toward the building. "Kilgore's Store," he announced.

They stepped inside.

"Lastun Wicker, is that you?" An old white man in denim overalls wobbled forward from the rear of the store, favoring his left side.

"It is, Mr. Kilgore. It's me."

"Well, you survived. Looks like you lost weight, though."

"Some. This is my friend, Howard Fishman," Lastun said, nodding toward his companion.

"Hmm, hmm." The temperature seemed to drop a bit.

"How do you do, Mr. Kilgore?" Howard said, extending his hand. "Lastun's told me good things about you."

Howard's accent was not excessive, but noticeable. The social temperature dropped a bit more. Howard recalled the three men, two of them New Yorkers, who'd been murdered during the Freedom Riders voters' registration efforts in 1964.

Kilgore executed a quick grip and release of Howard's hand. "You ain't from around here, are you?"

"No, sir," he said.

Kilgore turned back to Lastun. "Wasn't you the one that bought them Black Cat firecrackers offa me?"

"It was," Lastun confirmed. He suddenly realized that he hadn't once referred to Kilgore as "sir." "They came in handy over there, sir. Saved our skins."

"Izzat so?"

Lastun briefly recounted his use of the firecrackers in the Battle of Phu Loc. He touched the ribbons on his chest. "That got me this Bronze Star."

That tale warmed Kilgore considerably. "Well, I'm proud. I can tell everbody my firecrackers helped win a battle."

"Yeah, that'll make a good story for you, sir." Lastun rubbed his hands together. "We better get on to Mama and Papa's house."

"Here, I'll drive you over in my pickup."

Lastun looked surprised. "I don't want to trouble you none."

"No trouble. It won't take but a minute."

Kilgore locked the store and put a sign with a clock face on the door to indicate when he'd be back. The old man had a 1955 Ford F-100 pickup. Lastun didn't hesitate. He threw his duffel in the truck bed and climbed in after it. Howard followed. Kilgore didn't invite either to sit in the cab with him.

Once Kilgore had the old truck rattling down the dirt and gravel road, kicking up a rooster tail of dust, Lastun said, "He ain't never been that nice to me before."

Howard shrugged. "It's weird. People in the big cities treat us like the enemy. Out here in the country, a man in uniform gets respect he ain't ever had before."

The pickup stopped in front of an unpainted old house at the edge of the road, surrounded by a sea of green cotton plants. The two clambered out of the pickup bed and waved their thanks to Kilgore, who lifted his hand before driving off.

"This your parents' house?" Howard asked.

"Yep."

The structure looked small, but to Howard's eye was probably larger than most of the tenement apartments in The City. He wouldn't have said this aloud, but excluding the dust which seemed to be everywhere, the place looked neater and cleaner than he expected. The New York slums, where many blacks lived, were crawling with rats, cockroaches, and bedbugs. Garbage and debris lined the streets. Lastun's family might be poor, but Howard was convinced they lived better than they would have in New York City.

"C'mon." Lastun hoisted his duffel. "I want you to meet Mama and Papa."

Before they reached the steps leading to the porch, a time-worn black woman came through the front door. Age and children, Howard surmised, knowing what he did about the size of Lastun's family, had thickened her short body. She wore a white apron over a thin flower-print dress.

"Lastun?" the woman said. "Lawd, ain't you a sight to behold?"

"Hey, Mama," Lastun said.

173

The two wrapped up in a big hug. Mrs. Wicker made cooing and clucking noises as if she held a baby instead of a grown man. Lastun said nothing. He just held on tight. Howard stuck his hands in his pockets and studied his surroundings.

It seemed like minutes, but in reality only a few seconds passed before they broke apart. Mrs. Wicker wiped away a tear. Lastun's eyes were shiny.

"Mama, this is my friend, Howard Fishman," Lastun said. "He came back from Vietnam with me. We were in the same platoon."

Howard nodded. "How do you do, Mrs. Wicker?" He didn't offer his hand. He'd been taught that the woman decided if she wanted to shake hands or not, so he waited to see if Lastun's mother offered hers. "Lastun told me a lot about you." A little white lie. Once Kissy told him that his wife had run away, Lastun hardly mentioned his family. He'd also stopped writing them when they wouldn't respond to his demands for more information about Bizzy.

Surely, she'd seen Howard when she came out of the house, before she and Lastun hugged, but she looked at Howard as if she saw him for the first time. "Howard Fishman?" She pronounced his last name as if it were two words. "You Lastun's friend?"

"Yes, ma'am," Howard responded. "We've become quite close. He saved my life."

"And Howard saved mine," Lastun countered.

Mrs. Wicker seemed to hesitate. Howard could guess what she thought. During some of their downtime conversations at Firebase Screwball, Lastun had talked about how the races didn't mix back home. And now a white man stood on her porch. Her son called him friend. *What will she do with me?*

Welcome me in? Chase me away? Howard could only stand back and let things play out.

"I suppose you boys want somethin' to eat," she said.

Lastun glanced at his watch. "It is gettin' on toward suppertime, and we ain't had much today."

"Okay, y'all set on the porch and I'll throw somethin' together," Mrs. Wicker said.

"Where's Papa?" Lastun asked.

"He'll be along directly," she answered. "He's off at the gin. Now that the cotton's laid by, somma the men play dominoes over there." Mrs. Wicker offered her son a sly grin. "He thinks I don't know. He tole me he was gonna check cotton prices."

Lastun laughed. "Yeah, that sounds like Papa." He gestured toward the rocking chairs on the porch. "Take a load off, Howard. These are a lot better than them bus seats." He took off his uniform jacket. "Gimme your coat and I'll put it in the closet. It's too hot to be wearin' these things."

Mr. Wicker arrived in a ten-year-old Chevrolet pickup "Well, looky here!" he said as he surprised Lastun with a hug. "I'm so proud to see you."

Once out of his father's embrace, Lastun turned toward Howard. "This here's my friend Howard Fishman. He was with me in Vietnam."

"Pleased to meet ya, Mistuh Howard," he said, taking Howard's hand and pumping it. He showed none of the reticence his wife had shown. If he was surprised to find a white man on his porch, his behavior didn't reflect it. Howard suspected he was so happy to see his son, Lastun could have brought a polar bear with him and it would have been okay.

The trio settled into their chairs. Lastun began to relate a bit of his and Howard's experiences when Mrs. Wicker called everyone to supper.

Howard guessed at how difficult it was keeping the house dust free, since the air seemed to be laden with the stuff, but the interior of the small house looked clean and neat. Dozens of plastic frames occupied all the flat surfaces of the living room. They covered the mantel over the fireplace, several end tables, and a coffee table. The wood finishes on the furniture had been dusted so often the varnish had begun to wear off.

Howard looked at Lastun and cocked an eyebrow. "Brothers and sisters?"

"Lawd, yes," Mrs. Wicker broke in, "and nieces and nephews and what-not."

"Looks like a fine family," Howard observed, trying to curry a little favor. He'd been an only child. He wondered what it was like to be part of such a large family.

"Yeah, we been blessed," Mrs. Wicker said.

The kitchen table was laden with so much food that Howard feared it might collapse. Fried chicken, mashed potatoes, corn bread, black-eyed peas, corn on the cob . . . *how can four people eat all this food?* The aromas made his mouth water.

"Lastun, I think you'll soon regain all that weight you lost," Howard said. "Mrs. Wicker, this looks delicious."

Lastun's mother relaxed a bit. "Thank ye, kindly. But don't stand there and tell me how it looks. Set down and tell me how it tastes!"

Howard laughed. "Okay." He took the seat she'd indicated. The other three also sat, accompanied by the sounds of chair legs scraping across the bare floor.

"But first, let's have a blessin'," Mrs. Wicker said. "Abraham?"

The three Wickers bowed their heads. Howard followed their lead. While the others closed their eyes, he kept his open and watched.

"Thank ye, Lord, for bringin' Lastun and Mistuh Howard home safe from that awful place, and thank ye for providin' this good food Mama done cooked for us. Amen."

Halfway through the prayer, Howard realized that Mrs. Wicker had opened her eyes and studied him appraisingly.

Abraham Wicker picked up the platter of chicken, hesitated, and passed it to his guest. Howard concluded that Mr. Wicker, as head of the family, would have taken the first piece—thus the hesitation—before deciding the white man should serve himself first. Howard smiled and passed the dish back. "You first, Mr. Wicker," he said.

A surprised expression crossed Lastun's father's face. After a second, he nodded and forked a piece of chicken onto his plate, then returned it to Howard.

Protocol established, the dishes began their journeys around the table.

"Did Lastun tell you my father's name is Abraham?" Howard asked.

"You don't say," Mr. Wicker responded. "Well, he must be a fine man, then."

Howard joined the old man's laughter, quickly followed by Lastun and Mrs. Wicker.

The fried chicken had a crispy, battered crust over tender, warm meat. Howard didn't have to pretend when he complimented Lastun's mother. It truly was delicious.

Mrs. Wicker wouldn't let anyone help with the dishes, so the three men went back out to the porch. The house's interior trapped the heat, but the porch allowed a breeze, which cooled the air and dried the sweat.

Howard and Lastun removed their ties and stored them with their jackets in the bedroom.

Under prodding from Mr. Wicker, the two soldiers related a few war stories. Howard didn't need a cue from Lastun to minimize the bloody parts. When Mrs. Wicker joined them, the stories grew even tamer.

Sunset drove the light from the sky. No mention had been made of sleeping arrangements. Howard certainly had no intention of broaching that subject. He'd slept in swamps, with leeches for company. Wherever he wound up would be better.

Bullfrogs, crickets, and owls began their nighttime serenade. A year ago, Howard thought, I would have been frightened by all these strange sounds. But twelve months in the jungles of Nam had acclimated him. He returned his attention to the human voices.

"Come Sunday, I'm gone invite all yo brothers and sisters and their families by after church," Mrs. Wicker said. "We'll have us a reunion."

Lastun cleared his throat and leaned forward in his rocker. "I may not have time to visit, Mama. I got to find out what happened to Bizzy."

"I tole you, son," Mrs. Wicker said, "You got to forget about her and get on with your life." She spoke strongly, assertively, like a mother to a child.

"She is my life." Lastun's voice held a note of stubbornness.

"I raised you, Lastun Wicker! I changed your diapers! You think I don't know what's best for you?"

The porch grew silent.

Lastun broke the quiet. "I know you raised me, Mama. I know you love me. That's why I can't understand why you actin' this way. You know what the Good Book says. 'A man has to leave his Mama and Papa and cleave to his wife and they are to become one flesh.' You and Papa are my family, but Bizzy is part of me! Whatever has happened, it happened to me, too. I have to take care of my wife." He stood and paced along the porch.

Howard tried to be invisible. *Maybe I should go for a walk.* He feared movement would draw attention to himself.

A choked sob rose in Mrs. Wicker's throat. "Your wife was with child."

Lastun stopped pacing. Another long silence followed. He chuckled. "You got eight children, Mama. Do you think me and Bizzy just held hands that last night before I left home? Or the night before that?"

"But somethin' happened, Lastun. Else, why did she run away?" Mama's expression convinced Howard she knew more than she'd told.

"Tell me, Mama! Tell me what happened!"

"I don't know! Least not for sure. And I ain't gone repeat no gossip."

A porch board creaked as Lastun shifted his weight. "Well . . ." His voice was resolute. "I'm gone find out, Mama. Even if I have to turn Satartia upside down to do it." He stormed off the porch and into the darkness.

A third silence, broken this time by Mr. Wicker. Howard had forgotten he was there. "That boy just as stubborn as you, Shandra. If I was you, I wouldn't stand in his way."

"Excuse me, Mr. and Mrs. Wicker." Howard rose and quietly followed Lastun off into the night.

20

Darkness overtook Satartia. Stars shone through gaps in a partly cloudy sky, providing only a hint of illumination. Howard remembered seeing a scattering of outbuildings surrounding the Wickers' house when they'd arrived: a latrine-style outhouse, a chicken coop, an equipment shed, and a barn. *Lastun could have gone to any of those, or he could have walked into the cotton patch.*

Howard paused, listening for a sound, some clue as to where his friend might be.

"Lastun?" Howard whispered. A low whistle came from the direction of the cotton patch. Howard followed the sound. He stumbled a bit when he stepped from the smooth yard onto the cloddy, uneven dirt of the field, but quickly regained his balance.

"Back home in Brooklyn, we have these things called street lights. It lets you see at night," Howard said.

"Look at those stars," Lastun replied. "Can you see those in Brooklyn?"

Howard pictured his friend gazing up at the sparkly lights peeking through the spaces between the scattered clouds.

"They look just like the stars back in Nam," Lastun continued.

"Different ones, I think, but they look the same."

Both studied the stars in silence. At least, Howard thought, he's calmed down a little. But he was wrong.

"She is my Mama," Lastun spoke in a whisper, as if to himself. "She did raise me. She did change my diapers."

The clouds shifted in the breeze and a sliver of moon showed itself. An owl hooted in the distance.

"I've got a child, probly three or four months old." Lastun continued. He turned and the moonlight reflected in his eyes. "How'm I gonna raise my son if I don't know where he is?"

"It might be a daughter, you know."

"Yeah. My wife and daughter." Lastun reflected. "I got to find 'em. Reckon why she won't tell me where they went?"

Howard guessed the "she" referred to his mother. "She loves you—your mother—she loves you. Maybe she's just trying to save you some pain. Maybe she doesn't know where they are," Howard said.

Lastun didn't respond.

Howard decided this was an opportunity for a segue. "Is there a bar around here . . . someplace we can get a drink?"

"Well, they's a honky-tonk down in Vicksburg, and a blues place other side of Yazoo. Problem is, I can't go to any bar you can go to, and you can't go to any place I can. Welcome to the south." Lastun paused and shuffled his feet. "We could borrow Papa's truck and I could drop you off somewhere."

"No, that won't work," Howard said.

"C'mon," Lastun said after a moment's thought. He trudged over to the barn. Howard followed.

As they entered the wide passageway, Howard smelled the sour-sweet aroma of hay and the rank odor of manure. "I have to ask, what are you up to?"

"Hold on a minute." Lastun grabbed something that made a metallic noise. After a second, he struck a match and held it to the wick of a kerosene lamp. Dim amber light filled the space. He lowered the glass chimney over the flame, and walked into the last stall on the right and pulled back a canvas tarpaulin, revealing a stack of crockery jugs. "Hold this," he said, handing Howard the lamp.

"Isn't it dangerous to be using a lamp in a building with all this hay?" Howard asked. "It's just dead grass, after all."

Lastun gave him a sideways smile. "It ain't dangerous if you don't drop it. So don't drop it."

"Copy that."

Lastun picked up one of the jugs and blew the dust off it. "Papa's blackberry wine. If we can make do with this tonight, we'll track Jasper Curtis down tomorrow. He'll sell us some moonshine." Lastun uncorked the jug. He had no glass, so he hooked his finger through the handle and lifted his elbow, tilting the opening to his lips for a swig. He passed the jug to Howard, who copied Lastun's actions.

The wine was sweeter than the scotch Howard would have preferred, but it had the alcohol bite he wanted. "It sure has a kick to it," Howard said.

The two sat on hay bales and passed the jug between them, saying little. The fine dust from the hay made Howard sneeze and his eyes water. He knew from their time in Nam that Lastun was thinking through his problem, developing a plan of action.

Howard wanted to help, but he knew nothing of this country or these people. He could only rely on Lastun to set the pace.

A shuffle step drew their attention. Mr. Wicker appeared in the stall's doorway. "Y'all ain't done drunk up all my wine, have ye?"

"Not yet," Lastun said. "Come join us." He shifted so his father could sit beside him on his hay bale. "We'll go tomorrow and get some hooch from Jasper Curtis." He looked at Howard. "Jasper is white, but he's okay."

Howard suppressed a smile. He didn't think Lastun consciously thought about his need to comment that a person was okay despite being white.

"Most places, there's a white moonshiner and a colored one. A colored man can buy from the white bootlegger, no problem. But a colored bootlegger can't sell to a white man less'n the white bootlegger says it's okay."

"I don't suppose we could find any scotch, could we?" Howard asked.

"Well, Mississippi votes by county whether or not to sell liquor," Lastun explained. "Most counties, including Yazoo, is dry. That means it's illegal here." He gave a conspiratorial smile. "That don't mean you can't get it, though. Jasper might have some store-bought liquor, or he might know who does. We can ask him." He took a swig from the jug and passed it to his father. "'Course, people don't always follow the rules. A white man sometimes buys from the colored bootlegger. They just don't tell nobody."

Mr. Wicker took a swig from the jug and passed it to Howard, who took a sip.

Sweat on Lastun's face glowed in the yellow light of the lamp. The air was close in the barn and Howard realized he was sweating, too. He wondered if there was some place he could get his uniform laundered and pressed.

"Papa, do you know why Bizzy ran off? I don't see why Mama won't tell me," Lastun complained.

Papa leaned back and cupped his knee in his clasped hands. "She really don't know for sure, Son, so it won't pay for you to get mad at her. They's rumors, of course. They always is, but I ain't gonna repeat a rumor any more than your mama is."

Lastun snorted in disgust. "Reckon who does know, then?"

"For true? I ain't got the slightest idea."

Mr. Wicker pulled a pocket watch on a chain from his bib overalls. "It's gettin' late. I'd better get to sleep."

Lastun yawned. "Howard, you up to sleepin' in the barn tonight? It'll beat that Vietnam jungle, I guarantee."

Though it was dark, it didn't feel late. "Sure. This hay will be nice and soft," Howard said. He'd seen that the house had only one bedroom.

"Naw," Mr. Wicker objected, "y'all sleep on the bed. Mama wouldn't abide lettin' a guest sleep anywhere else."

"Nope." Lastun shook his head. "They's only one bed, and it belongs to you and Mama. Believe me, we've slept in worse places than this."

Mr. Wicker regarded the two for a second, apparently debating how much of a fight to put up. "All right, you'uns got the young bones. I'll see y'all in the morning. I'll tell Mama you said good night."

It seemed to Howard that Papa Wicker suddenly realized how close he and Lastun had become. "Good night, Mr. Wicker. Thanks for the wine, and tell Mrs. Wicker thanks again for dinner," Howard said.

Lastun found a couple of horse blankets to sleep on, but the two quickly decided the barn was too hot and moved to the house's front porch. The air was cooler there, and their sleep was long and peaceful.

21

The creak of a floorboard as someone moved inside the house woke Howard. Darkness still owned the sky. Lastun, silent as a ghost, was already up and had begun doing his chores as if he hadn't been gone this past eighteen months.

Mrs. Wicker, the one who'd been moving about inside, made breakfast for the three men. Having spent most of his adult life in a Gentile world, Howard didn't blink at being served pork sausage and bacon, along with scrambled eggs, biscuits and coffee.

Lastun nodded at the dollop of purple-black jam on his plate. "That's Mama's blackberry jam. After you taste it, tell me whether it's better than Papa's blackberry wine."

Howard knew a trap when he saw one. He also knew the solution: praise the woman. He took a bite of the biscuit and jam, smacked his lips and said, "Sorry, Mr. Wicker, your wine is good, but your wife's jam has you beat."

Papa Wicker leaned back in his chair and guffawed. He turned to Lastun. "Your friend ain't dumb."

All three faced Mrs. Wicker, who beamed. "I'm pleased you like it, Mistuh Howard."

"Call me Howard, please."

Her expression indicated that would never happen. It wouldn't be in her nature to call a white man by his first name.

"I s'pose y'all will want to borry my pickup to run around some today," Mr. Wicker said, wiping his mouth with a napkin.

"If it won't be no trouble," Lastun said.

"I'm pledged to help Mistuh Kincade haul hay. He pay a penny a bale. If'n you can drive me by his place, I'd be obliged."

"That's the least we can do," Lastun responded.

"You got some more clothes to wear?" Mrs. Wicker asked Howard. "I can wash and iron your army clothes, if you do."

"We've got some civvies—civilian clothes—in our duffels. We'll change after breakfast," Lastun said.

"Thank you, Mrs. Wicker, for offering to do that, and thank you for breakfast," Howard added.

"Oh, go on with you." Mrs. Wicker flapped her hand, as if shooing Howard's compliment away. But she was clearly pleased with his gratitude.

After dropping Mr. Wicker off at the Kincade place, Lastun drove along a dirt road beside an immense cotton field. The pickup sprayed a fantail of dust behind it.

"This land is so flat, the white farmers plant rows so long you can't see the end of 'em. Up until about ten years ago, we picked all this by hand. They paid us three cents a pound. Now they use mechanical cotton pickers. Cheaper for the farmers, but us colored hands lost money." Lastun seemed to be making small talk to fill the time while he drove.

Lastun came to a stop in front of another unpainted house. "This here's where my sister Kissy lives. Lastun's parents lived in a long, narrow building, what Lastun called a "shotgun house." His sister's house seemed to be made of two square structures covered by a single roof with a breezeway between. "They call this a dogtrot house, 'cause a dog can trot through that little walkway in the middle."

Howard didn't speak; he just took everything in.

Kissy looked like a younger version of her mother, only chubbier. She had a smudge of flour on her cheek. The two siblings went through a round of hugs and tears.

Lastun's sister installed the two men in the breezeway, where they were shaded from the sun and a soft wind dried the sweat off their skin. Kissy served sweet iced tea and joined them.

Lastun wasted no time. "Kissy, I aim to find out what happened to Bizzy, and where she ran off to."

"Have you talked to Bizzy's mama yet?" Kissy asked.

Howard noticed that Lastun's sister had dodged the question, but remained silent. This was Lastun's interrogation.

"No, I'm askin' you." Lastun's voice grew sharp.

Kissy flapped her hands, as if trying to shoo the question away, as she might a fly. "You know everbody's just tryin' to save you some hurt, don't you?"

"Well, it ain't workin'!" Lastun jumped up and began to pace across the porch. "It's like I been stuck with a knife and won't nobody pull it out. They ain't no pain worse than not knowin' what happened to the woman I loved."

Was Lastun aware that he'd referred to his love for Bizzy in the past tense, Howard wondered? Maybe it was just a mistake.

A drop of sweat slid down Kissy's cheek, or maybe it was a tear. The day was growing hot, and Howard didn't know if the moisture on her face came from the heat, or from stress, or from emotion.

"Did Mama tell you that Bizzy was in the family way?" she asked.

Lastun stopped walking. "You know that Bizzy and me are married, don't ya? Remember the shivaree?"

Kissy seemed to reach a decision. She smoothed the fabric of the apron covering her knees. "Somethin' happened right after you left. It wasn't her fault, Lastun. But she didn't know if the baby was your'n or not anymore!"

Lastun's complexion turned gray. Howard thought he might be about to faint; he shifted his weight, preparing to stand and catch him. But Lastun regained his balance, staggered to his chair, and sat. "Tell me," he commanded.

Lastun's sister took a drink of her tea, as if she were bolstering her courage with a slug of whiskey. "Bizzy walked to Kilgore's store, just like she does—did—all the time. Just like we all do. She bought a few things for supper and was walking back to her mama's. It was late in the day, almost sunset. Ellis Barber drove by."

Lastun's head rocked back, as if he'd taken a punch.

"You know Ellis Barber followed Bizzy around like he was a dog in heat ever since she started showin' curves." Kissy wiped a sweaty hand across her brow. "That's the horniest man I ever saw, and the drunkest, too. I reckon he never tried anything before, 'cause you was always around to stop him."

Howard wondered if she was aware of the guilt she was piling on Lastun's shoulders. She seemed to be saying what happened to Bizzy was Lastun's fault because the Army had drafted him and taken him away. Howard didn't think she'd deliberately harm her brother like that. Maybe she was punishing him for making her tell.

"Well, you was gone now," Kissy continued. "He pulled her into his pickup and hauled her off. Probly took her to Rainbow Swamp. Raped her. She was lucky none a Ellis' buddies was with him, or they'd a raped her, too."

Somewhere off in the distance, a dog barked. Lastun leaned over and put his face in his hands. His shoulders shook.

"She came in to my house about midnight, cryin'. Her clothes was tore to shreds and her face was a bloody pulp."

"How come she didn't go to her mama?" Lastun asked, without raising his face out of his hands.

Kissy looked at him as if he'd just proved he was the village idiot.

"She couldn't face her mama like that!" Kissy said, her tone incredulous. "She was afraid of what her mama would think; of what your mama would think! I got her cleaned up as best I could. Put salve on her cuts. Put her to bed. Sent word to Mrs. Polk that she'd come by and decided to spend the night with me." Kissy flapped her apron hem in an attempt to fan herself. "I knew Mrs. Polk would think that was odd, but I thought I could make her believe she was just lovesick...missin' you."

Lastun's shoulders began to shake again. Howard had never seen him cry before, and felt a lump grow in his own throat.

"The cuts and bruises was another problem. When I took her home the next day, I told her mama that she took a fall off the porch," Kissy continued. She looked across the road toward the tree line. Howard knew she was actually seeing nothing but the memory of the events she related.

Kissy glanced at Howard, seeking an ally, perhaps. "Mamas ain't as dumb as we think, sometimes. She knew somethin' had happened, but she knew Bizzy wasn't tellin, and she knew I was keepin' Bizzy's secret. So she held her peace."

Lastun lifted his head and sniffled. "Go on." He, too, stared off in the distance.

"When Bizzy missed her monthly, she knew. Oh, she didn't know who was the father. I knew what she wanted to believe, but she had doubts." Kissy glanced at Howard again.

Maybe she's uncomfortable talking about this in front of a strange white man, but Lastun's given her no choice.

"You can't hide somethin' like that for long," Kissy said. "Even before her belly started to grow. Sick ever mornin', food tasted funny, sore bosoms. Mama Wicker and Mama Polk both bided their time, waitin' for Bizzy to break the news." Kissy paused and waited for Lastun to meet her gaze. "She couldn't tell. She was afraid Papa Polk would take his shotgun after Barber."

Lastun nodded. "Yeah. He might of done that. Then he'd of been killed, too."

"And then Bizzy got afraid of what the baby might look like. If Barber was the father, it would of probly been high yeller. You know that a mixed child don't get treated right by neither whites nor blacks, even though there's a bunch around. Then she took off."

"But where'd she go?" A pleading tone filled Lastun's voice.

Kissy shook her head. She seemed relieved her ordeal of telling the story was almost over. "She didn't say. Up north somewhere is all I know."

Lastun glared at his sister, his jaw clenched. When he spoke, his voice was hard. "Who all knows this?"

"Nobody but Mama and Papa and Bizzy's mama and papa." Kissy sniffed. "I ain't sure how much they know, but ain't nobody knows where she went."

"She just up and disappeared. Didn't go to visit no cousins or aunts or nothing?"

"We was scared for her. We would've helped if we could. But she didn't give us a chance."

Lastun finished his glass of tea in one draught, put it on the porch floor, and walked toward Mr. Wicker's pickup without saying goodbye. Howard followed.

Once both were seated in the pickup, Lastun wiped his eyes.

"Do you believe everything she told you?" Howard asked.

"Everything but when she said nobody knows where she went. Twenty, thirty years ago, when a colored from around here went up north, that meant Detroit or Chicago." Lastun glanced at Howard. "Them's big places to search, so I hear. So we need to know more than that." He paused, tapping his fingers on the steering wheel. "Now that I think on it, I bet more people know about it than just our parents. Bizzy's best friend in school was Ruthie Warren. Maybe Bizzy talked to her." He pushed in the clutch and turned the key to start the vehicle. "Let's go find out."

22

Howard found the cross-hatched layout of the dirt and gravel roads that seemed to lead nowhere, confusing. *And the dust!* Every movement of foot, horse, tractor, and car or truck stirred clouds of the fine powder, which seemed even more stifling than the exhaust of thousands of cars, buses and taxis in mid-town Manhattan.

The pickup had only travelled a couple of miles when Lastun lifted his foot off the gas and the vehicle slowed. He studied a smudge rising above the horizon off to the right. "Smoke," he said. "Somethin's burnin'."

"How far away?" Howard asked. Gauging distances on this flat terrain was difficult. He pulled at the open neck of his shirt. The air had grown humid since sunrise.

"Not sure, but close. Five klicks, maybe." Lastun's hands closed more tightly on the steering wheel. "I think that's Mama and Papa's place."

Lastun floored the gas pedal, causing the light rear-end of the pickup to fishtail before gaining traction. He turned right at the next intersection of roads, and the Wicker place came into view.

"It's the barn," Lastun muttered.

Gray-black smoke boiled from the old, weathered-wood structure located behind the Wickers' house. As he bailed out of the now stopped pickup, Howard noticed that the slight wind blew the smoke—and sparks—away from the house. *Thank God for small favors.*

Heat radiated from the flaming building, turning the already hot day even hotter. Mrs. Wicker edged in toward the inferno, leaning forward as if she had to push against a wall of hell. She held a garden hose which spouted a puny stream of water.

"Mama, pull back!" Lastun grabbed the hose and tugged.

Mrs. Wicker felt the pull and turned. Lastun gestured for her to back away from the fire. She obeyed.

"Let it go, Mama," Lastun said, when she drew close. Perspiration soaked her skin and clothes, making her look as if she'd been caught in a rain shower. "That old barn is so dry, it'll burn like kindling," Lastun continued. "Ain't nothin' gonna put it out."

Mrs. Wicker looked back at the building just as the loft collapsed, scattering sparks. A wisp of smoke sprouted in the old woman's hair. A spark had landed, even against the wind.

Feeling a bit self-conscious, Howard extended his hand and patted the smoky spot, extinguishing the spark before it could sprout into flame.

Mrs. Wicker cast a suspicious glance his way, then seemed to realize what he'd done. Her expression shifted to one of gratitude. She instinctively patted her own hair.

"Was they any livestock in the barn?" Lastun asked.

"Naw, the mule and the cow is in the pasture. The chickens run as soon as the fire got hot. They was some hay and feed corn," she paused. "And Papa's blackberry wine."

"Uh-oh," Lastun said.

"Uh-oh is right. Yo Papa's gonna be in a bad mood tonight."

"How'd it start?" Howard asked. "Surely, it wasn't from us sitting in there last night. We made sure the lantern was out."

Mrs. Wicker made a shooing gesture with her hands. "Naw, it was a couple a white men."

"What!?" Lastun exclaimed.

"Two white men. Mr. Kilgore must of passed word to somebody. They said tell you this is a warnin'. Send the

Yankee back where he belong and don't make no trouble, else next time the house get burned." She looked at Howard. "Sorry, Mistuh Howard, it ain't yo fault."

"It sure feels like it," Howard said.

"It ain't. It's just these crazy white folks. Since that Freedom Rider thing a few years ago, they suspicious of every stranger. 'Specially Yankee strangers."

"Who was it done this?" Lastun asked.

"They had bandanas over their noses and mouths, cowboy like," Mrs. Wicker snorted. "Like that would keep me from knowin' who they was. It was Ellis Barber and Allen Glass, and they was both drunk as Cooter Brown, as usual."

Lastun crossed his arms and stared at the burning skeleton of the barn. The roof had now fallen in, and the smoky tongues of flame grew smaller as the fire ran out of fuel. At a distance, two pickups approached on the road. Thirty-five gallon barrels of water filled the truck beds. *Neighbors coming to help. Too late.*

"If anybody asks, black or white, tell them we've left. Papa can get somebody to take him to the Jackson bus depot tomorrow. That's where his pickup will be. Howard, let's get our duffels. We're gonna follow Ellis Barber's advice."

The two left Mrs. Wicker to explain to the neighbors. Once in the pickup and on the move again, Howard said, "How long will it take us to get to Jackson?"

"Not long. A hour. But we got other stuff to do first."

"Like what? It sounds like your parents may be in danger if I stay around."

"That's why I told Mama we was leavin'," Lastun replied. "If she tells everbody like I said, that'll buy us some time. We'll be gone by tomorrow, anyway."

Howard plucked at his lower lip, thinking, trying to figure out what Lastun had planned. "We still don't know where Bizzy went."

Lastun gave him a grim smile and nod.

According to Lastun, the former Ruthie Lamp was now married to Jonah Warren. "Ruthie and Bizzy was best friends in school," Lastun explained. "They was like sisters. I shoulda thought of her before. If anybody knows where Bizzy went, it ought to be Ruthie."

Another ten minutes of driving brought them to a square house built on a masonry foundation. The first house Howard had seen in the black community that was painted — white, in this case.

Jonah Warren was short and stocky; a couple of years older than Lastun. He wore bib overalls over long-handles with the sleeves pushed up to the elbow. He welcomed them in. "Ruthie's gone over to Belzoni," he said in answer to Lastun's question. "She's seein' to a sick aunt."

Lastun noticed Jonah's uncomfortable glance at Howard. "This is Howard Fishman. He's a Army buddy of mine from up north. He's okay."

Jonah nodded, but didn't relax.

"I wanted to talk to Ruthie about Bizzy, ask her if Bizzy said anything to her before she took off," Lastun continued.

"Set down, why don't you," Jonah said, keeping a cautious eye on Howard.

All three sat in wooden ladder-back chairs. For the first time, Howard realized, they'd visited a home without being served sweet iced tea.

"Bizzy come by to see Ruthie," Jonah acknowledged. "Told her she had to leave Satartia." He gazed at Lastun. "Guess you know why." Unlike the women they'd asked, Jonah showed no reluctance to talk about the crisis.

"I know," Lastun affirmed. "Did she say where she was goin'? Detroit, maybe? Or Chicago?"

"Nope, neither of them places." Jonah rocked back in his chair. "Said she was goin' to some place called Hollum. Never heard of it, myself."

"I ain't, neither," Lastun said with a frown. He looked sick.

An itch started in the back of Howard's brain. He'd spent a year listening to Lastun's drawl, plus another couple of days listening to everyone in Satartia mispronounce words. He felt sure Jonah had mispronounced the name of a place he knew.

"Did Bizzy say why she was goin' there?" Lastun asked.

"She had a relative that had lived there some years ago, she said. She hoped she was still there. Aimed to try and find her."

"Hmm," Lastun mused.

"Did she mention any other places nearby?" Howard asked.

Jonah stroked his chin. "She say it was a big city. She seemed sad that she wouldn't be in the country. But some place called Center Park was close by. She aimed to go walkin' there when she could."

Lastun stood. He looked hopeful. "Well, that's something to work with. Thanks, Jonah. You've been a big help."

The two said their goodbyes to Jonah and clambered back into the pickup. The sun had climbed to its apex. Although it was mid-day, neither mentioned lunch.

Howard turned to Lastun. "Bizzy said Hollum, but I think she meant Harlem. And it's not Center Park, it's Central Park. Harlem is in New York, not far from where I grew up in Brooklyn."

"That's great!" Lastun exclaimed.

Howard grew solemn. "That's still a big place. Harlem is just a neighborhood in upper Manhattan, but there's easily a half-million people there."

Lastun sighed. His exuberance faded, but didn't disappear. "It's still a place to start."

"How many people live in Satartia?" Howard asked.

"I don't know," Lastun replied, frowning. His fingers rubbed the steering wheel, anxious to get a move on. "Two hundred, give or take."

"That many people live in two, maybe three buildings in Harlem."

Lastun regarded his friend, wide-eyed.

"I just want you to know how big this job is."

"Don't try to talk me out of this! I got to try."

Howard faced front and stared out the windshield. "Let's get to it, then."

"They's one more thing I got to do," Lastun said.

Howard's head snapped toward his friend, wary of what Lastun had planned next.

"Ellis Barber raped my wife and burned my parents' barn. I've got a score to settle with him," Lastun said in answer to the unasked question.

"Where would he be?"

Lastun looked up to gauge the sun's height. "Mama said he was drunk when he lit the barn on fire this mornin', and it's just now 'bout noon. He probly got drunk on hooch, but that means he ain't workin' today. I bet he's hangin' out at Stu Chappell's pool hall, just this side of Yazoo City." He reached for the pickup keys, still dangling in the ignition.

"Will anybody else be there?"

Lastun paused. "I imagine there'd be a few. Most people would be workin' this time of day, but they'd be two or three bums like Barber."

"All white?"

"Oh, yeah," Lastun said.

"I reckon so," Lastun admitted. He thought for a minute. "Remember at Da Nang, when Goliath and his buddies beat me up, and you took 'em on and whupped 'em?"

"Yes."

"Well, what are you worried about?" Lastun cranked the pickup.

23

During the fifteen-minute ride to Yazoo City, Howard's apprehension over the upcoming confrontation grew. He had no way of knowing what or who they'd face. But Lastun was determined to see this through. During the previous year, each had held the other's life in his hands. And they had survived. Howard hoped their bond would be strong enough to overcome this crisis, too.

Stu's Pool Hall was in a low-slung, cinder-block building whose windows were covered with tar paper to keep out prying eyes. The two paused just inside the doorway to allow their eyes to adjust to the dark interior. The low ceiling and dim lighting enhanced the furtive atmosphere.

A muted burble of voices faded to silence. Everyone had stopped talking when the stranger and the black man walked in the door. Like lambs to the slaughter.

A bar extended from the entry door along the narrow end of the building. Lastun had said that Yazoo was a dry county. No alcoholic beverages could legally be sold here. But the odor of whiskey and beer told Howard that a variety of alcoholic beverages were stocked below eye level behind that bar.

Only one of the two pool tables in the center of the room was in use. Four grungy white men stopped their game to stare at the pair of intruders. A wooden rack filled with pool cues hung on the long wall beside the empty table. A couple of circular tables with chairs occupied the back. A multi-colored Wurlitzer juke box played a country-western tune being sung by a nasal, twangy-voiced singer.

Dead cigarette butts filled many of the ashtrays around the space, and the air was foggy with left-over smoke.

Now that he could see well enough to avoid tripping over something and falling on his face, Howard strode purposefully to the cue rack and grabbed two sticks, handing one to Lastun, who'd followed along behind.

"Hey, whatta you think you're doin'?" one of the four, a fat man, at the other table demanded. His words slurred as he spoke.

"Thought we'd play a game of pool," Howard answered casually.

"Not here, you ain't," the same guy said.

"Oh, is this a private club?" Howard asked. As he spoke, he glanced at Lastun, seeking some guidance from him.

"You might say that," the man said. "No niggers or Yankees allowed."

"Well, then, Mistuh Barber, we might as well get down to it," Lastun finally spoke, prompting a sigh of relief from Howard. "You and me got a bone to pick."

While Barber was in no shape to fight, the other three were slender and muscular—and less drunk. They began to fan out, surrounding Howard and Lastun, and blocking their path to the door. Not the kind of odds Howard favored.

"Look fellas," Howard said to Barber's companions, "this is between Wicker and Barber. Why don't we just stand down and let them settle things?"

"Hardly a fair fight," one of Barber's cronies said. He was middle-aged with a scruffy brown beard. Howard labeled him Beard. "Ellis is drunk, and Wicker here is younger and stronger."

"'Bout as fair as it was when Barber raped my wife, or when he burned my parents' barn this mornin' . . . when only Mama was there," Lastun responded.

Trying to make his action look unintentional, Howard picked up a pool ball and began lightly tossing it up and catching it. Howard knew Lastun would need about two seconds to take Barber out. The other three or four would be more difficult. In a pack situation like this, at least one—maybe two—wouldn't want to fight. They'd hang back, hoping the rough stuff would be over quickly and they wouldn't have to participate. Howard could usually identify those by the looks in their eyes. They would be furtive. Instead of sizing up their opponent, they'd be looking for a safe corner to hide in.

None of Barber's cohorts had that look. All three seemed to be evaluating their two opponents, choosing which one to attack first. Two of them—Howard labeled them Slim and Red—seemed to have chosen Lastun, the runt, as their first target. Beard, the one Howard deemed the most aggressive, held Howard's eye. This is the man that spoke. "You boys are outnumbered four to two."

"Five to two," the bartender added. His words helped Howard better assess their situation. The bartender pulled a cut down baseball bat wrapped in cloth adhesive tape from behind the bar. It was about the size and shape of a cop's nightstick.

"They's one thing y'all haven't taken into account," Lastun responded. "You see, you white men made one mistake when y'all drafted me into the Army. Y'all learned me how to kill."

The pool hall grew silent.

"Aw, hell," Barber snarled, "let's do this." He charged Lastun, swinging his cue stick like a baseball bat.

Part of the training Howard and Lastun had received in their AIT involved fighting with pugil sticks. Adaptive training, they called it. Learning how to fight with what was handy; improvise. Lastun dropped to one knee, allowing Barber's clumsy swing to pass harmlessly over his head. He thrust the heavy end of his cue stick into a spot just below Barber's sternum, paralyzing his diaphragm and rendering him temporarily unable to breathe. Barber doubled over, his mouth formed a big "O," looking very much like a beached fish gasping for oxygen.

Howard saw this out of the corner of his eye. He'd already targeted Beard, the guy who'd been watching him, and let fly with the pool ball he'd been holding. Howard's nemesis was no dummy. He'd already figured out Howard's plan and sidestepped. The move wasn't a complete loss. The ball flew past his target and struck Slim in the gut.

The fighters' movements resembled a dance, where each person moved in a prescribed series of steps; thrusting here, parrying there, spinning, ducking, swinging.

Red made for Lastun, who'd taken the moment to whack Barber in the temple with the heavy end of his weapon. Barber was now out for the duration –concussed, and possibly dying, if he didn't start breathing soon.

Red swung his stick, striking Lastun on his left cheekbone, knocking him down. Lastun responded by hitting his attacker in his shin.

Beard charged Howard, swinging his pool cue. Howard parried.

The bartender came around the end of the bar, seemingly undecided about who to go after. He chose Howard.

Slim, who'd taken the pool ball in the gut, was now up and headed for Lastun. But he misjudged his trajectory and moved within Howard's reach. Howard jabbed him in the ear.

The bartender swung for Howard's head. Again, he blocked the blow. But Beard struck home with a thrust to Howard's stomach. He bent over, and the attacker whipped his cue around to hit Howard above his left eyebrow.

Still on his knees, Lastun slashed his cue in a vertical arc and clubbed Red on the crown of his head, taking him out.

Blood trickled from Slim's ear, where Howard had jabbed him with his cue, but he picked up the ball Howard had thrown and launched it back. It missed, caromed off the wall, and rolled on the floor in the midst of the melee.

The bartender swung his club again. Occupied with fending off Beard, Howard took a glancing blow to the tip of his nose. Tears blurred his vision. He swung blindly, clipping Beard on the chin.

Slim stood over the still kneeling Lastun. He'd dropped his weapon, so he punched him in the jaw. Lastun swung his cue stick up into his attacker's groin.

Lastun grabbed the ball rolling across the floor and launched it toward the bartender. It hit him in the back of the head, flooring him.

Beard seemed startled when the bartender went down, giving Howard time to crack him with a right cross. A knockout punch.

The sudden quiet unsettled Howard. He hesitated, waiting for an attack from another quarter, but none came. He scanned the room, checking the layout. Everyone was down except for Lastun, who knelt, as if praying.

Howard's walk was more of a stagger as he made his way over. "Hey, buddy, you okay?" He sounded as if he had a cold.

Lastun coughed and spit a gob of blood before speaking. "I did better than last time. I didn't pass out. Least I don't think I did." He touched the left side of his face. "I think my eye is swole shut."

"It is," Howard confirmed. "The entire side of your face is swollen."

Lastun cranked his head around, so he could focus his right eye on Howard. "I wouldn't brag if I was you. You got a broke nose and a knot the size of a walnut over your eyebrow."

Both grew silent as each poked and prodded, identifying bruises and cuts. Howard looked at Lastun and started laughing. Lastun joined in. Howard identified the emotion; relief at having survived a life-threatening experience. He'd felt it before.

"We better light out 'fore these yahoos wake up," Lastun said.

"Good idea," Howard agreed. He surveyed the group one last time. Ellis Barber looked unusually pale and still in the dim light. He knelt beside him and looked closer, feeling his neck for a pulse. "Lastun, I think he's dead."

Lastun struggled to his feet, brushing the bloody pool ball aside with his toe, and tottered over beside Howard. "I think you right," he said. "We really do need to get gone. I didn't aim to get you tied up in a killin', Howard."

Howard stood. "Too late to think about that now."

As they approached the pickup, Lastun said, "I can't see too good. You drive. I'll give you directions."

"Where are we going?" Howard asked.

"Jackson bus depot."

24

"Let's sit in the last row," Howard said, as they boarded the bus. "Don't give me that look. There's more room back there and we'll be further away from the crying kids."

"Whatever you say," Lastun replied.

Just like on the bus from New Orleans, the whites tended to sit in front, and the black passengers occupied most of the seats toward the back. Howard's eye was used to a more random pattern on the buses and subways of New York, but he realized that to Lastun this was business as usual.

They chose to carry their duffels onto the bus, and had to maneuver them as they walked down the aisle so as not to hit any passengers, which would certainly have caused an incident. The last row gave them plenty of room to stretch out, and their duffels made good foot rests. They were both exhausted and hurting from the fight only a few hours earlier.

"I don't know about you, but I think I can sleep all the way to Atlanta," Howard said kicking off his shoes.

"'Bout right, I'll be hungry for breakfast by the time we get there," Lastun said.

"Me too. Shit, we forgot to eat dinner."

"We make a stop in Birmingham around midnight, maybe the coffee shop'll be open. Come to think of it I'm not sure I want to be seen with you in Ala-freekin-bama in the middle of the night." Lastun said. His swollen face made his smile lopsided.

"Amen to that. We can split up when we get off the bus. The way we look now, it would be an invitation to anybody looking to start somethin'."

Howard saw that none of the other passengers seemed to take more than casual notice of them, but he did see the driver's curious stare in the rearview mirror before the bus pulled out.

Howard closed his eyes, but sleep was still distant. He couldn't fathom how different life in the south was from any part of America he knew. Hell, he felt more at home among the South Vietnamese than he did with the whites in Mississippi — and safer too. Even the undeserved deference he received from black people made him uneasy. Without Lastun at his side he probably would have been regarded as one of those "Yankee agitators". With the exception of the time he spent in the barn with Lastun and his Papa drinking blackberry brandy, Howard never felt any more ease with the black folks of Satartia than he did with the whites he encountered there. He was an outsider, and he felt a profound sense of isolation, which would have been unbearable without Lastun. Even in Vietnam, he was with his comrades. He thought about how Lastun must have felt out in the white world, and then again, how he'd react to the sensory overload of New York.

If the whites of Yazoo County knew he was Jewish, he probably would have wound up in a shallow grave like Goodman, Schwerner and Chaney. Instead, he was an accomplice to the murder of a white man, Ellis Barber. Perhaps in another place further north, the crime might be manslaughter, maybe even self-defense. Now, he pictured himself a fugitive from the Yazoo County Sheriff, who at that moment might be issuing an APB for two murderers — one white, one black. But for the moment he felt safe and heading in the direction of more familiar places. And finally he could sleep.

Lastun had a lot on his mind, too. He couldn't figure how to begin to find Bizzy and her baby in a city of eight million people. Then it hit him. *The baby is mine.* He was a father, even though he'd never even seen a picture of his child. He refused to accept any other possibility. Now he had to find his wife and his child—his family. The uncertainty of how he would proceed, even with Howard's help, left him uneasy and anxious. He tried to take comfort in knowing that—in Mississippi, just as in Nam—Howard had proven his friendship, but he didn't know if that would be enough to overcome the obstacles they could be facing in the concrete jungle. Whatever visions he could conjure of New York, he knew they were almost certainly wrong.

Lastun didn't wake Howard when the bus pulled into Birmingham. He also chose not to leave the bus. Even as a battle-hardened veteran, he was in no mood to show his black skin to the denizens of the Birmingham, Alabama Greyhound terminal at midnight. Thirty minutes later, the bus was moving again. With Birmingham behind them, Lastun finally fell asleep.

About twenty miles out of Atlanta, Howard awoke. Seeing the sun shining through the front window of the bus, he knew where they were even before looking at his watch. It took him several tries to wake Lastun. They managed to clear their heads just as the air-brakes jolted the bus to a stop. They were the last to exit, and, dragging their duffels, followed their noses to the terminal coffee shop.

Howard opened the door, and saw a young black woman approach carrying a baby. He held the door and gestured for her to pass first. Lastun froze. The woman eyed Howard cautiously and passed without smiling. When he saw the expression on Lastun's face, he realized his mistake. He looked around and was relieved to see that other people were more concerned with getting their breakfast than what Howard had done.

"What the hell were you thinkin'? We're still in the south. White men don't hold doors for black folks here. Didn't you learn nothin' in Satartia?" Lastun hissed.

At first embarrassed by his *faux pas*, Howard suddenly became angry. "Look, my mom raised me to be a gentleman and hold the door for ladies. It's who I am. It's what I do."

He was also angry at what happened to his friend's wife, angry about the beating they took, and angry that the archaic notions of racial supremacy still persisted more than a century after the Civil War. *This is America, what the hell kind of people are these?*

"Order a coffee for me, I have to make a call," Howard said.

Howard wanted to contact Jeff Malloy, a friend from his college days at NYU.

Jeff had managed to avoid the draft by landing a desk job with the FBI while attending Columbia Law School. Today was Saturday, and Howard hoped to catch him at home.

"Hey Jeff, this is Howard." After a pause, "Howard Fishman."

"Yeah, Howard, sorry man . . . it's been a long time. You back stateside?"

"Stateside and in Atlanta. I know it's kind of short notice, but I really need to talk to you. A friend of mine has a problem and I need some advice." The urgency in Howard's voice was evident.

Jeff had enough experience on the job to recognize a plea for help. It was always for a friend, and always urgent. He wanted to know more, but Howard would only talk in person; it was a familiar scenario.

"Sure, buddy, give me your twenty."

Howard gave him the name and location of the diner.

"Got it," Jeff said, "give me about an hour. I live outside of town."

"Thanks, man," Howard said before hanging up. He put another dime in the phone and dialed.

"One dollar and twenty-five cents more please," a female voice prompted.

Howard deposited the coins and waited for his call to be connected. He felt guilty about not making this call as soon as he got stateside, but needed some time to adjust and to decompress before returning home from the surreal world he'd lived in for the past two years. Not that he could ever have considered the time he spent in Mississippi as any reality he could relate to. He could already see things had changed, and he wasn't even back on his home turf.

"Hi, Mom . . . it's Howard."

"Howard, are you okay? Where are you? Are you coming home? Wait, I'll call your father to the phone. Abe, it's Howard, come down."

Howard was surprised a woman her age could manage to say all that in one breath.

"Yes, Mom, I'm okay. I'm . . . in Atlanta now, taking the bus. I should be home in a few days." He had to shout over the sound of a bus pulling out of the terminal.

"Son, are you okay?" His father asked the same questions again.

"Yes, Dad, I'll be home in a few days," He no longer had to shout. "I wanted to ask you if it's okay to bring one of my army friends home for a while?"

"Of course, as long as you're coming home you can bring the whole army. Your mother will probably start cooking today. I know there'll be enough food." His father's voice trembled. Howard realized his father's great sense of relief upon learning his son was at home and safe. *Home, maybe. But safe? Not yet.*

While waiting for Jeff, they finished breakfast and ordered more coffee. On the third cup Howard knew it was time to get Lastun's thinking adjusted.

Before he could start Lastun spoke. "Look over there."

"Where?"

Lastun pointed. "There, at the wall, over the water fountain."

A porcelain drinking fountain was mounted on the wall.

"Yeah, a water fountain, so what?" Howard asked.

"See the rectangle of old paint above it?" Lastun pointed again.

"Yeah, what are you trying to say?"

"There used to be a sign there. It said *"WHITES ONLY"*. It looks like they probably took it down while we were away. See the wall to the right, about ten feet down with the plywood panel over it? That was where the *"COLOREDS ONLY"* water fountain used to be."

Howard nodded.

"That is what life was like for us black folk here in the good old U. S. of A. when we left for Nam."

"Well, my brother, I'm glad as hell things are starting to change."

They raised their coffee mugs.

"Listen," Howard said, "I called a friend here in Atlanta. He works for the FBI. He may be able to help us find Bizzy and the baby, but don't let on about what we might have to do. If he knows, he'll try to stop us. Get it?"

"Yeah, I get it, but do you really think he won't know?"

Howard thought for a moment. "No, but he's a friend and I know he'll do what he can to help."

They ordered some peach pie so they could hold the table until Jeff arrived. They didn't speak while they ate their pie. Both men eyed the diner and the other patrons with curiosity born out of a long absence from such surroundings. Forks and knives clinked against plates, as customers ate their breakfasts. A haze of cigarette smoke filled the room. Waitresses called orders to the fry-cook, while others patrolled the tables looking for coffee cups and glasses of Coke that needed filling.

By the time they finished their pie, Jeff Malloy showed up wearing a dark suit, and a narrow black tie over a white shirt, looking squeaky clean and polished.

Howard jumped up. "Jeff, over here."

They greeted each other like long-lost brothers. "Man, it's good to see you made it back okay, but you really do look like shit," Jeff said.

Howard thanked Jeff for meeting them on such short notice. Howard and Lastun were still badly bruised, and hadn't shaved or showered in two days.

"Yeah, I suppose we do look like two pounds of crap in a one pound bag. Jeff, this is Lastun, the guy who—in more ways than one—is responsible for me being here."

Jeff and Lastun shook hands. Lastun noticed that this white man took no apparent notice of his skin color.

"Well, let me thank you for that. If Howard hadn't dragged me through some of my undergraduate classes, I wouldn't be here today, either." Jeff's body was slim and muscular. His hair was light brown.

"Man, you wear a suit on Saturday?" Lastun asked.

"Please excuse my country-bumpkin friend here," Howard offered.

"It's okay. Yes, I dress like this any day of the week I'm working. We got an APB for a salt and pepper team coming up to Atlanta to cause trouble." Jeff said without expression.

Lastun's eyes widened. Howard suddenly felt queasy. Had he heard about the bar fight and Ellis Barber's death? *No, that's not possible. Jeff is just messing with us.* He saw Lastun's expression and laughed out loud to put him at ease.

"Shit, you just pullin' my leg." Lastun said before Howard's laugh infected him as well. Shaking his head, Jeff waited for their laughing fit to end.

Howard explained their last few days in Mississippi, the beating they took, and more than he'd planned to tell about Bizzy and the baby Lastun regarded as his own. He never mentioned the death of Ellis Barber.

"So let's see if I've got this right," Jeff said, looking at Lastun. "You two are lucky enough to return home from a year of in-country fighting, and now you want to go up to the middle of Harlem to find and rescue a runaway Negro girl and a baby . . . from guys that make the VC look like Girl Scouts? Is that what you're telling me? Your chances of survival would have been better back in Nam."

"I can tell you never been to Vietnam, Mr. Malloy," Lastun said, with acid in his voice, "else you wouldn't say they looked like Girl Scouts."

"Maybe not," Jeff said, "but I know what usually happens to young women who run away to New York. Unless they get very lucky, the outcome is never good. At this point Lastun, you have absolutely no idea what kind of shit storm you're dragging my friend here into."

"He's not dragging me, Jeff. We've been to hell and back together. I want to do this."

"So can you help us find them?" Lastun asked, completely disregarding Jeff's last remark.

Howard felt surprised. He thought Jeff's remark would have hit Lastun like a punch in the gut.

Jeff rolled his eyes. "Look, you guys need to clean up and get some rest, then we can talk about it. I live alone, so I'm taking you to my place for a couple of days. After some down time we can see what we can figure out, unofficially." Jeff said.

While driving them, Jeff considered the situation he'd been presented. He was from New York, and was no racist, but he didn't like Lastun for a couple reasons. First, he was getting his friend Howard involved in something that could turn out to be a suicide mission. Second, he didn't like southern blacks generally — not because of their skin color, but because he believed they were weak for not fighting back against white oppression.

Jeff admired strength and abhorred weakness. He thought they were taking the easy way out instead of standing up for their rights. He didn't have the same opinion of northern blacks. To Jeff, the absence of separate drinking fountains and rest rooms meant everything in the north was just fine. For an educated FBI agent, who, unofficially, supported the civil rights movement, he was remarkably myopic.

But it wasn't just blacks. When he was younger he didn't like Jews either, for the same reason. He couldn't understand why they didn't fight back against the Nazis. Many of Jeff's friends in college were Jews. Over time, he thought he'd learned to understand how things were over there, but that was Germany.

To Jeff, Howard was different. He was strong and stood up for what he believed. He served his country and was now backing a friend who needed him. For that reason, he wanted to help them, but could do little because of his position. Jeff knew his best option was to try to talk them out of doing something incredibly stupid.

Howard and Lastun spent the next two days at Jeff's place in a suburb of Atlanta. It was the first time Lastun had been in the home of a white person. That took some getting used to, but for now a shower and clean clothes were more important.

During the day, while Jeff worked, they rested, watched daytime television and let their wounds heal. At night, the three of them would drink beer and talk about the old days, as well as the days to come. The country was changing at an alarming rate, and two men who had been overseas for a year had a lot to catch up on.

Jeff had a contact in New York working undercover narcotics cases in Harlem. From the old picture of Bizzy that Lastun carried, they were able to find a match to some mug shots in the NYPD organized crime files. The photos from the telefax he received were black and white, and grainy. Bizzy's brown skin made it hard to see her features clearly, but the shape of her head and the angle of her jawline left no doubt in Lastun's mind, and he said so. Bessy Polk—aka Bizzy—had been arrested several times on prostitution charges, and bailed out by a Lester Freeman, aka Mr. Gold. Bessie Polk's address showed her living in a building on 127th Street in Harlem, owned by Mr. Gold. That information was a matter of public record, and Jeff knew that Howard would have been able to find it eventually.

Jeff saw their expressions and was immediately sorry he'd given them a head start. "Look, you can't do this. NYPD has a Tactical Response Unit that won't go in there, even with guns and the force of law. Besides, there are more than a dozen ongoing investigations. There are undercover officers investigating not only prostitution, but drugs, weapons, money laundering, racketeering . . . it's all a way of life up there. Attorneys General from the city, state and the Southern District of the Justice Department are involved. You could be endangering some of our people. Without a scorecard, you won't know who you're dealing with. And if you wound up in the middle of an operation going down, they won't know you're not with the bad guys."

Lastun sighed. Howard gave Jeff a dead stare. His resolve unshaken.

Jeff saw their looks. He got up and paced the room, trying to find the words to make them realize how hopeless their mission was.

"Bottom line is, the best I can do is to bump this file upstairs and see if the Special Agent in charge wants to do anything."

On their last night with Jeff, he took a more serious turn and directed his words to Lastun.

"I know you have got a lot going on in your head right now, but you have to listen to me. You're from the south. You just spent a year in a green jungle. Now you're going to the gray jungle. Not just any city, but New York City, and you can't even begin to imagine what it'll be like. Where you're planning to go, Harlem, there are no rules of engagement. It doesn't matter what color skin you have. If anyone thinks your nose is where is doesn't belong, they'll kill you, plain and simple. The only advantage you have is some natural camouflage. That just means it'll take them a little longer to spot you. Once you open your mouth, it's game over. How white bread here thinks he can fit in is beyond me. I'm not even suggesting you call the police because I know how it is up there at the 126th precinct. Asking them to find one drug whore in Harlem is like trying to find one particular piece of hay in a haystack. And the pimps don't do their work in Harlem. They mostly run the whores in the Deuce."

"The what?" Howard asked.

"Yeah, that's what they call it now. Forty-Second Street between Sixth and Eighth Avenue and all around Times Square. Some of them even run up Central Park West to Eighty-Sixth."

Howard and his friends usually hung out in the Village, but he knew the area and was surprised at Jeff's description of how bad it was now.

Lastun had no idea what they were talking about. He just stared at Jeff. *Whore.* The word shocked him. He wanted to call Jeff out for calling his wife that name. Then he realized that based on the police records, Jeff was technically correct.

"Please don't call my wife that word," Lastun said.

"Sorry, man, I know this is tough." Turning to Howard, Jeff said, "Stay away from Sherman Park on Seventieth; that's where the addicts hang out and the drug deals go down. They call it Needle Park now. Those animals will kill you for your shoes."

"Things have gotten that bad while I was away?" Howard said.

"Yes, they have," Jeff said, turning back to Lastun. "Honestly, I still think you want to try to play hero, but once you get up there and take a look around, I hope you're smart enough to turn and run as fast as you can back to whatever little town you came from." Jeff immediately realized that this young black man would not be deterred, and loyal Howard would stand by him in New York just as he did in Vietnam.

Before boarding the bus, Lastun gave Jeff an envelope addressed to *Mr. and Mrs. Abraham Wicker, RR1 Box 342, Satartia, Mississippi.*

"Jeff, please mail this for me," Lastun said.

"Sure thing, I'll take care of it this morning." Jeff said.

July, 1968

Dear Mama and Papa,

Howard and I are going to find my wife. I won't say where. As you can guess, I don't expect I'll ever be able to come back.

I love you. I always have and I always will. I just wish you had been honest with me and told me what you knew about Bizzy without making us go out and find her on our own.

Your son,

Lastun Wicker

25

When they left Mississippi, Howard wanted time to heal and adjust to his surroundings. As the bus wended its way north from Atlanta, he folded thoughts of their mission with those of home, his parents, old friends, and somewhere in there, what he was going to do with the rest of his life, after he helped rescue Bizzy and the baby.

Jeff's warnings resounded in his head, making him question the wisdom of his and Lastun's plan. He'd spent most of his life in and around Brooklyn. Of course he'd been to The City many times, but never ventured to Harlem. Nobody went there unless they belonged there. He'd heard warnings from his parents and others over the years, and Jeff's tales only reinforced them.

Lastun tried to get his head around some of what Jeff had said, but it was no use. His small town upbringing, and the two years in the Army left him ill-equipped for life outside of Mississippi. Still only twenty years old he was totally unprepared for the task he had set for himself and his friend. The only thoughts that made sense to him were of the Bizzy he once knew, and his baby.

The bus made an overnight layover in Winston-Salem, North Carolina.

"Let's ask the ticket clerk. I bet there'll be another bus going north before morning," Lastun said.

Howard shrugged. "Maybe we should take some time to think about what Jeff said. There might be another way to do this."

Lastun's expression hardened. "If you want to back out, you can. You don't owe me nothin'."

"This isn't about owing anybody anything." Howard sat heavily on a bench. The bus depot was not overly busy, but a scattered few travelers moved about the station. "We're partners, joined at the hip, but can't we at least talk about this?" He scratched his chin. "How long has Bizzy been in New York?"

"I don't know." Lastun ran his hand over his hair. "Six, seven month's maybe?"

"And I'm sure those have been hard months for her. Jeff said so. I know this is hell for you. But if we rush in without having a plan, all we'll do is get killed . . . and maybe Bizzy and the baby, too." Howard regarded Lastun closely. "Where is she?

Lastun looked confused. "You know where, Harlem."

"And where's that?"

"New York. What you tryin' to say?"

Howard leaned forward and put his elbows on his knees. "A Hundred and Twenty-Seventh Street, to be precise. How exactly do you plan break into a building on a hundred and twenty-seventh street in Harlem, and how do you plan to get Bizzy and the baby out of that building?"

"I don't know."

It was exactly what Howard wanted Lastun to realize. "That's right, you don't, and neither do I. Not yet, anyway. But I know some people who may be able to help. Right now, we need to pause and let our brains catch up with our hearts."

"Okay. Besides, it don't look like we have much choice since there won't be another bus till morning, anyway."

Forsythe County, North Carolina was a dry county, but the lounge near the bus depot allowed patrons to bring their own liquor if they paid ten dollars a head for set ups, glasses and ice. They had each bought a bottle of Jack Daniels in Atlanta.

When Howard and Lastun sat at a table in the bar and ordered set ups, the white bartender said, "Niggers can't set out front here. If y'all want to set together, you'll have to go out back."

"I'll sit out back. You can sit here," Lastun said.

"How long are we going to put up with this shit? No, I'll sit with you," Howard said loud enough to be heard by everyone in the bar.

The bar had a dingy back room with old paint-chipped furniture. The black bartender eyed Howard with the same suspicion blacks did in Satartia, before bringing the glasses and ice to their table.

"I thought things might be better here." Howard sipped his whiskey.

Ice clunked in Lastun's glass as he took a drink. "Do you remember about eight years ago when a bunch of colored students set at a lunch counter at a Woolworth's store and wouldn't move?"

Howard frowned. "Yes."

Lastun pointed. "Well that was in Greensboro, about thirty mile that way."

"How do you know that?"

"I saw the sign out on the highway, that's how I know. I remember it 'cause when I was in the sixth grade, my teacher brought in some newspaper, and we talked about it in class."

"She didn't get into trouble?"

"She would have, if she got caught."

Howard shook his head. "I still think we should have stayed out front, and stood our ground like they did."

"I hear you, brother," Lastun said with a nod. But we've got other fish to fry, and just like in the jungle, we need to keep a low profile. Besides, I don't think any contact with the local police would be a good idea right now."

"You do have a point there," Howard said, before emptying his glass and refilling it.

They reminisced about some of their more memorable experiences in Vietnam. A black Marine in uniform overheard their conversation and walked over to their table. "Excuse me, Sirs, but I couldn't help overhearing you."

Lastun was surprised by the smoothness of his speech. He definitely wasn't from the Deep South. "The two of you were in Vietnam?" The single stripe on his sleeve informed them that he was just out of boot camp.

Lastun touched his chest. "I'm Sergeant Lastun Wicker and that's Sergeant Howard Fishman. Care to join us?"

"I'm PFC Cordell Lewis," the black man said as he sat.

"Where you from, Cordell?" Lastun asked.

"Gary, Indiana."

He was on his way back to Parris Island, returning from home for his orders to ship out. He wanted to hear what it was like over there. Lastun paid for another set up and they poured him a stiff one.

"Why did you decide to join the Marines?" Lastun asked.

Cordell grinned. "I wanted to leave home because I was tired of my parents telling me what to do."

"How did that work out for you?" Howard asked.

Cordell's smile grew wider. "I think you know the answer."

The young private laughed along with his new friends at the irony of his decision. Lastun noticed he showed no uneasiness about sitting at a table with a white man.

Feeling the effects of the liquor, Lastun – now more relaxed felt compelled to impart some war wisdom to the private.

221

"Your gunny sergeant probably told you this, but don't move anything you find on the trail. Charlie likes to set booby traps," Lastun warned, in a slightly slurred speech.

"You need to rely on your instincts, but remember survival in the jungle is a team effort. You have to be a team member to survive. Every member of the team depends on every other member, and you need to have their backs, if you want them to have yours," Howard counseled, holding his liquor a little better than Lastun.

"I know that well. Gunny told us that almost every day."

If somebody sends you to get a left-handed monkey wrench, or a fifty foot roll of flight line, they just tryin to put one over on you. Those things ain't real," Lastun said.

The next morning, Howard hoped the Marine didn't take all of their "remember the time" stories too literally. He would find the reality much more terrifying. Memories of pain are dulled by time and alcohol, and the mind has a way of filling in blanks with things less likely to cause nightmares. Last night, as they told their stories to PFC Lewis, the details became less horrific and more heroic.

Perhaps out of empathy, or out of a sense of gratitude for surviving their year in hell, both Lastun and Howard—each in his own way—said a quiet prayer for the young Marine.

After an early breakfast in a nearby diner, and a little hair of the dog to blunt the effects of their hangovers, they boarded the 8:30 bus for Washington, DC. They spent most of the morning sleeping. By 10:00 AM, they had crossed the border into Virginia, their direction now northeast. The distinction was not only geographic, it was metaphysical. Even though the state had been part of the former Confederacy, both men had the unmistakable feeling of change. The weather grew cooler, the trees were different, and they could feel the social effects of the changing latitude.

In Richmond, their stop was extended to allow time for lunch at the terminal coffee shop. That also gave them a chance to go to the restroom and wash the sleep from their eyes. Howard noticed his bruises were a little less colorful, but his nose was still crooked and would probably remain so. That was the other reason he wanted to delay his arrival in New York. He wanted more time for his wounds to heal before his mother saw him. Howard saw Lastun examining his wounds and noticed the puffiness around his eye had diminished.

Howard was oblivious to a change which screamed at Lastun. That was the relative ease with which whites and blacks shared the space. Blacks did not seem to consciously alter their path through the terminal to avoid whites. Friendliness had never been an attribute of bus terminals, but people just seemed to go about their business without the tension that existed between the races further south.

They had a different driver when the bus left Richmond. Their next stop was Arlington, VA, at the Pentagon. In addition to women traveling with children, almost half of the passengers were men in uniform. Each of the branches were represented. Most of them outranked Lastun and Howard, who had been in civvies since Mississippi.

It was dusk when they left the Pentagon and drove along the George Washington Parkway, passing the entrance to Arlington Cemetery. The driver wheeled the bus onto the Memorial Bridge entering the district at the Lincoln Memorial and circled around it to Constitution Avenue, riding past the site where Dr. Martin Luther King gave his "I Have a Dream" speech only five years before. Receding daylight was quickly replaced by flood lamps, illuminating government buildings and national monuments. The slow-moving traffic allowed time for them to see the Washington Monument on their right and the back of the White House on their left, as the massive Capitol Building began to fill their view through the windshield. Too soon, the bus left the Capitol Mall and began to weave through dreary side streets to the bus terminal.

On the bus to D.C., Howard's general apprehensions about going home and their mission hadn't diminished. He nudged Lastun in the ribs. "We got waylaid by our Marine friend and didn't have a chance to talk about our plans once we get to New York. Let's lay over another night and finish our talk."

Lastun's expression grew glum. "I want to go on. What's wrong with goin' on?"

Howard didn't respond.

"You got me over a barrel. You know that don't you?" Lastun said. "I'll stay and we'll talk, but not by my choice."

Howard considered Lastun's words and understood his feelings. He also knew that at this point, Lastun had no basis to understand the difficulty of the situation they were about to get into. That would come later. For now, Howard needed to keep things on track his own way.

"I know you're beginning to doubt my commitment to helping you, but nothing's changed. I'm in this with you, but rushing in is a sure way to guarantee failure. You've got to trust me on this."

The flickering neon of the Capitol Motel was a block away. The ticket agent in Richmond told them about the motel, and Howard had called to reserve a room. The greasy spoon on the corner would serve them both dinner and breakfast the next morning.

The feelings of pride and awe most people experience when seeing Washington for the first time was denied to Howard and Lastun. A year of jungle combat, another skirmish in the American South and the prospect of the battle that lay before them erased those emotions.

26

When they checked in, the clerk had shown no reaction to renting a room to two men, one white and one black. Lastun wondered if they'd finally traveled north of some imaginary line where socialization between races didn't matter.

The room had two shabby double beds, a wobbly chair, a writing desk and a small black-and-white TV, with a rabbit ear antenna on top. The bed linens were clean but looked worn. Howard saw a cigarette burns on the bedspreads.

"Ahhh," Lastun sighed, as he took his shoes off and lay back on one of the beds, positioning the pillow so he could sit semi-reclined.

Howard went into the bathroom and returned with two small glasses and poured two fingers of whiskey in each. "Neat," he said, before pulling the chair out and positioning it so he could rest his arms on the chair back while facing Lastun. He downed half of his drink and took a deep breath. "Okay, let's talk."

Lastun nodded.

"I'm worried that when we get to New York," Howard said, "you plan to rush off to Harlem and barge in through Gold's front door and take on everyone in the house. That just won't work."

Lastun sat up on the bed, downing an equal measure of the whiskey.

"And I'm worried that you've lost your stomach for this fight. I'm thinkin' that you're just delayin', stoppin' at every town, putting off our getting to New York and getting this thing done," Lastun's tone was challenging.

Howard sighed. Before he could speak, Lastun continued.

"When I first got to Nam, I was lost. We both were. We each had to rely on somebody to tell us where to go and what to do.

"Now I got that same problem. Like you telling me last night that I don't know where anything is in New York. And you're right. I don't even know where Harlem is. I need you to be my guide. If you don't want to help me take on Mistah Gold and his bunch, that's fine. Just show me where his place is and I'll take it from there."

The old chair creaked when Howard stood. He didn't look at Lastun as he paced over the threadbare carpet. "I will help you, Lastun . . . I'm in this with you to the end, that isn't the point. But I know we have to do this with clear heads. I don't want anger to drive you into doing something that will turn this into a suicide mission."

Lastun emptied his whiskey glass. "So tell me what you want me to do."

"The thing is, I don't know much about Harlem, either. It was the place we always stayed away from. But I do know some people who can help us," Howard said.

"So what are we waiting for?"

"Tomorrow morning, before we leave Washington," Howard explained, "I'll make some phone calls. By the time we get to New York, we'll have a couple more guys to help us . . . I hope."

"Okay, buddy, I'll leave it to you."

During breakfast Howard decided to modify their travel arrangements. Tired of riding the bus, he calculated that—for only a few dollars more—they could take the train from Union Station to Penn Station in New York. He didn't have to work very hard to sell the idea to Lastun.

They took a taxi to Union Station. Howard didn't need the schedule. He knew trains ran frequently between the two cities. The ticket agent told them there was an express leaving in forty-five minutes. Howard knew the trip would take less than four hours.

Lastun watched the two duffels, while Howard made some phone calls.

The first one was to Isadore Feinstein, a college friend, who now worked the crime desk for one of New York's major tabloids.

"Izzy, this is Howard Fishman."

"Hey, man, I heard you were back in the states. Didn't know when you would be in The City."

"Actually, I'll be in Penn Station at three ten, on the train from D.C. One of my army buddies is with me. Can you meet us?"

"Not a problem, I hope you guys can spend the night. We can go out to one of the coffee houses in the village like we used to."

"Sounds like a plan." It wasn't exactly what Howard had in mind, but he agreed for now.

The second call was to Phil Romano, a NYPD cop, and the son of one of Howard's father's old army buddies. Phil's dad had been a precinct captain in Queens. Howard and Phil were friends since childhood. He left a message for Phil to call him at Izzy's house that evening.

Next, Howard called his parents and told them he would be home the following day, not mentioning that he would be staying overnight with Izzy. He had two reasons for this. One was to allow time for some strategic planning. The second, was a feeling of apprehension. It had been growing inside him since they left Mississippi. He knew that bringing a *shvartza* home would be a shock to his parents. It would be awkward and he would deal with it. *But not yet.*

27

Once they left Washington, Howard began to feel the exhilaration that comes with the last leg of a journey home.

Lastun felt uneasy. Even though he'd been to Vietnam, he never felt so far from home as he did now. Basically, it was the mirror image of the way Howard felt in Mississippi.

With these radically differing perceptions, the two watched the scenery change from rolling hills and farmland to rivers, seaports, and industrial areas. Even the sky seemed different. The combination of latitude and industrial pollution turned it to a pale blue grey color instead of the deep blue they'd gotten used to in Vietnam, and Mississippi, for that matter.

Traveling through New Jersey and getting closer to New York, Howard began to feel the familiar energy that comes from a city of over eight million people living, working and playing in one of the most important places on the planet. New York is the place where money happens, and makes everything else possible. Traveling into The City always gave him a feeling of vibrancy and enthusiasm. He remembered describing this feeling to his parents. They said they felt it, too. It endured through depression, war, cultural shifts and more, reflecting both the best and worst of everything in America simultaneously.

These were feelings he could never describe to Lastun, or anybody else who hadn't been to New York, and certainly not to someone whose whole world revolved around a cotton farm in the American South.

Lastun was lost in his own thoughts of rescuing Bizzy and his child, and bringing them home – and where that might be.

Even with Momma and Papa still there, Satartia could never feel like home again. Not after everything that happened while he was away, and after he returned. Regardless of his feelings, the death of Ellis Barber made it a moot point. Once he rescued Bizzy and his child, they would have to decide as a family where home would be.

No conversation passed between them, as New York towering buildings came into view. Lastun began to feel awed by the immenseness of the skyline that filled his field of vision. The sensation was strong enough for him to wonder, for a fleeting moment, what it would be like to live in a place so dense with buildings. Still miles away, the scale of the buildings was beyond his imagination.

The skyline vanished as the train descended under the Hudson River, fifteen minutes from Penn Station.

Izzy looked like a giant elf with a full beard and glasses. His five-foot-ten-inch frame carried his two-hundred-eighty pounds well. He was leaning against a pillar, with his arms folded. When Howard and Lastun emerged from the stairway leading up from the platform, he ran to greet them. He greeted Howard with a giant man hug that lasted long enough to reveal the depth of their friendship. Howard introduced Lastun, and Izzy threw his arms around him and patted him on the back.

Lastun should have been shocked. Instead he was amused, almost giddy. The lively and to him surreal atmosphere of Penn Station. Along with the greeting he received from Izzy, suddenly broke the tension he'd carried within him since they left Mississippi. The only time he'd even shaken a white man's hand was with Howard and Jeff. Now, this big elf stormed out of the crowd and greeted him like a long-lost brother. He wondered if this was what life was like for blacks in the north, or if it was just a New York thing—or just an Izzy thing. It didn't matter. The experience was exhilarating and his outlook suddenly became brighter than it had been in a long time. Jeff was a nice enough guy, and offered them hospitality, but he never got that warm fuzzy feeling he felt immediately upon meeting Izzy.

On the way out of the station, Howard insisted they stop at Orange Julius. "Ya' know I've been jonesing for one of these since we hit the states. Lastun, you gotta try one."

"What is it?

"It's something like an orange slushy, only a thousand times better."

Howard bought three large size drinks, not giving Izzy a chance to refuse. They watched as Lastun took a sip. His eyebrows went up. "Good," he said, and took another gulp.

Howard and Izzy watched as Lastun put his hands over his face and doubled over.

"Brain freeze," Izzy said.

"Sure looks like it," Howard replied, as they both broke out in laughter.

"What the hell was that?" Lastun said, regaining his composure.

"Yeah, you're not supposed to drink those things so fast. We'll explain it on the way. Let's get going," Izzy said.

They took a cab to Izzy's apartment in a newer building in the East Village.

Before getting into the cab, Lastun stopped to gawk at the scene before him. One after the other, buildings as tall as mountains lined each side of the street as far as the eye could see. *And the din!* Car horns, people shouting, and the Doppler effect of the sirens from unseen police cars and ambulances on other streets. Looking down the street, he could see more people at one time than there were in all of Yazoo County.

To Howard, the décor in Izzy's apartment was college-dorm chic. Posters from rock concerts on the walls, two book shelves made from bricks and boards, an old leather couch, and an old footlocker like they had in the army served as the coffee table. Because he had been to Jeff's townhouse, this was not Lastun's first impression of how white people lived. Certainly not impressive by most standards, to Howard it was a lot more comfortable than their stay in Lastun's home in Mississippi.

"Just big enough to lay your head, and a few good friends," was the way Izzy described the place.

In the privacy of the apartment, Howard told Izzy why he brought Lastun to New York, and what they had to do.

"I hope you don't mind. I invited Phil Romano to join us tonight. I thought he could help us. I know you've worked with him," Howard said.

"Shit, you don't need a cop, you need a freakin' army. Do you guys have any idea what you're getting into?" Izzy asked, his ruddy complexion turning red.

This sounded familiar. Howard and Lastun nodded.

"Bullshit!" Izzy bellowed. "You guys have been away for two years and think you're going to lead a charge into Harlem like it is some bamboo village in the jungle?"

"Not exactly," Howard answered. "You're going to help us."

Lastun looked sideways at Howard.

"I know this won't be easy, but it's doable. I had a lot of time to think on the way up here. It wasn't till Jersey that figured it out."

"Thanks, but there are several young ladies counting on me to keep them company on cold nights, and several bartenders that depend on me for a living."

Lastun laughed at the idea of an overweight hairy elf being a ladies man.

"Sorry man, I just . . ."

Howard walked over to Izzy and framed his face in both hands. "This *boychik* was a real chick magnet when we were in school."

Izzy pushed his hands away. "Jeez, man, I thought you were going to kiss me."

The doorbell rang. "That must be Phil," Howard said.

Phil Romano gave the impression of being one of the most affable guys you would ever meet. And he was, unless you were one of the bad guys, then Phil might be the last person you would ever want to meet. Howard and Phil were about the same age. The difference was that — while Howard was in college and in the army — Phil had spent the last six years in the battlefields of some of the worst neighborhoods in the city. By this point, he'd seen it all and wore more than one bullet scar to show for it.

Howard and Izzy knew this. Lastun didn't.

After all of the introductions, Izzy brought out some beers.

"Lastun? What kind of name is that," Phil asked.

Izzy perked up. "Yeah, brother, tell us the story."

Lastun looked at Howard, who nodded encouragement.

"Well," Lastun said, wearing an embarrassed expression, "Mama had eight kids, me bein' the youngest. According to Papa, when she got through birthin' me, she said 'that's the last one, so we gone name him Lastun."

Izzy laughed so hard he spilled beer on his shirt. Phil and Howard joined in.

"Now that's a good story," Phil said, "that's a good name."

After a few more beers, and getting tired of the small talk, Phil leaned in. "So, Howard, why don't you tell Izzy and me what kind of important business you need our help with."

"We already gave Izzy some background," Howard said. "Lastun, I think you should tell Phil the whole story."

Lastun leaned back in his chair and took a deep breath. "Just a few days after I left to go to Vietnam, a white man named Ellis Barber raped my wife and she got pregnant. Only she wasn't sure if the baby was mine or Barber's. Least that's the way my sister told it when me and Howard got back last week."

"That really sucks, man," Izzy said.

Phil was angry. "You know how many times I've heard stories like that from relatives looking to find daughters, sisters or sometimes even wives that ran away to this city?"

Howard already knew the story, but hearing Lastun tell it now, in New York, made him angry again, and further hardened his resolve to reunite Lastun with his family.

"I reckon she got scared and run off." Lastun paused and looked pensive. "I wondered why she might want to do that. I think she knew I wouldn't hold what happened against her, and I wouldn't. All I can figure is that she was afraid if it was Barber's baby, its colorin' would be all wrong. High yeller they call it. She knew that a baby like that, growin' up in Satartia, would be tormented somthin' awful at school." Lastun shrugged. "So she took off to Harlem. Kissy, that's my sister, said she knew somebody that was supposed to have went there."

Howard summarized their visit with Jeff Malloy in Atlanta. He explained what information Jeff was able to obtain from an undercover source, and how they identified Bizzy and Mr. Gold from FBI and NYPD crime files.

Phil recoiled at the sound of Mr. Gold's name. "Shit, you guys don't mess around. You picked the most bad-ass pimp in the city. God help you on this one. We've been workin' to put that SOB away for years, but he always manages to slip through our fingers."

"God ain't been too helpful lately, I think I'd rather have the police on my side now." Lastun said, looking directly at Phil.

The room was silent, while they collected their thoughts.

"She's been arrested for prostitution a few times," Lastun continued, "I guess that was after she birthed her . . . our baby."

"Not necessarily," Izzy said, "some men like to—ow!" Phil elbowed him sharply in the ribs.

Lastun's eyes teared up. "I don't even know if the baby lived or not." He took a deep breath and squared his shoulders. "Anyway, we got an address where she's supposed to be, and we goin' to get her and the baby out."

"Boy, you guys got *chutzpah*," Phil said.

Lastun look puzzled.

"That means brass balls, sort of," Howard explained.

"Shit. I'm a writer," Issy said, "and I can't come up with stuff like that."

Phil leaned back in his chair. "Man, that sure is one screwed up place you come from, no disrespect intended,"

"None taken." Lastun said, maintaining eye contact.

"I don't suppose we'll ever know if your wife found her friend," Phil said, "but men like Gold hang out at bus and train stations. They spot the new arrivals, men and women, and they move in. They con them with an offer of a place to sleep and a meal. Most of them are scared and lonely, and they accept. Then they rope them into prostitution by getting them hooked on drugs. It's a whole new kind of slavery. I'm sorry man, but I'll bet my next paycheck that's what happened to Bizzy."

Lastun's expression turned ashen at Romano's mention of slavery. "Man, this sure is one screwed up place you got here. No disrespect intended."

Phil chuckled. "None taken." He turned. "Howard, you know I'd do anything to help you. And Lastun, you got balls, comin' up here from the south like Grant ready to take Richmond, or somethin', but this is more complicated than you can imagine. Gimme a coupla days to think about this and I'll get back to you, okay?" Phil said.

"Sure, but only a couple of days," Lastun said. "We really have to make this thing happen."

"You two crashing here?" Phil asked.

"Just for tonight. Then we'll be heading over to my folks place in Brooklyn," Howard said.

Phil and Izzy exchanged glances and looked at Howard, who understood exactly what they meant and shrugged. The exchange meant nothing to Lastun.

"Okay then, I'll be in touch. In the meantime don't be a schmuck, got it? Phil said pointing his finger at Howard, then looking at Lastun. "That means you, too."

"Right. I got it," Howard said.

Lastun looked puzzled, but took his cue from Howard. "Yeah, right, I got it, too."

Lastun felt strange. This trip was about rescuing his wife and baby, and somehow Howard, Izzy and Phil made him feel left out, even though they were willing to help.

If Lastun had known the word, he would have said he felt marginalized. The fact is, they were a group of old friends, and knew how things worked here. And Lastun was the stranger. The thing is, he was so used to having to do everything for himself, this was the first time he'd ever been offered help and he didn't know how to react. The fact that his new friends were white added to his emotional confusion.

Out of earshot, Howard walked Phil to the door.

"Hey, your buddy there, is he going to be alright? He looks a little edgy."

"Don't worry about him. It's just his first time in the big city. Besides, I wouldn't be here if he hadn't saved my ass over there."

"I hear you, but, remember what I said." Phil said and closed the door behind him.

When Howard returned, Izzy said, "Hey guys, it's early and I don't want to spend the night here on my *tuchus*. A new bar opened up near the Cellar Door. How about it?"

The bar was much nicer than any Lastun had ever been in. Lots of shiny surfaces and a strobe light that made everyone's movements look jerky. But the thing that surprised Lastun the most was that the crowd included blacks and whites — dancing, talking, and drinking — and nobody seemed to notice or care about skin color. There were even a few mixed race couples. *Back in Yazoo County, this would cause a riot.*

"You okay?" Howard asked. He had to shout to be heard over the din of conversations and music.

Lastun looked around the room. "I just ain't never seen anything like this. I wish Papa could see it. But even if he saw it, he wouldn't believe it."

Izzy leaned toward Lastun. "Believe it, brother!" He raised his glass. "You're not in Dixie anymore."

The trio didn't get in until almost dawn. True to Howard's expectations, Izzy invited some girls from the bar to join them for a pub crawl.

Even Lastun got caught up in the atmosphere and energy of The City, especially after several glasses of bourbon had taken a very hard edge off. For a few hours he was able to forget exactly why he was in New York. And for the first time in his life, in his own country, he was able to relax in a room full of black and white people, and have a good time.

"Whew," Izzy sighed. "I needed that break. I've been putting in a lot of overtime at the paper." He put his arm around Lastun. "I'm telling you brother, if this mission of yours works out, I'm getting the scoop on this story."

Breakfast never happened, but the three did venture out for lunch at around one o'clock.

Howard would wait to hear from Phil before going ahead with the rescue, but he knew they would need to do a recon before they could form a workable plan. That was common sense.

They planned to meet again at Izzy's place to work out the details. With that thought on the back burner, and mixed feelings of excitement and anxiety, Howard set off for Brooklyn, with Lastun in tow.

28

They descended into the subway station a few blocks from Izzy's house. Below ground thousands of people hurried to and from trains in a vast maze of tunnels. The first thing Lastun noticed was the smell. It was a combination of ozone from the electrically driven trains, urine, and aromas from unknown sources gave him a momentary queasy feeling. Overhead signs with names of streets, train numbers and arrows pointing in different directions meant nothing to Lastun, as he followed Howard who seemed to instinctively know which passage to take. Near stairways, vendors sold newspapers and candy. Spray-painted graffiti, words Lastun only learned in the Army, covered much of the space on billboards that lined the walls with advertisements for everything from cars to sporting events. Lastun was uneasy in this confined environment and felt Howard's hand on his shoulder.

"It's okay man," Howard said, "just go with it."

Lastun tried to grin, but his expression was more of a grimace. "It's just a lot to get used to, you know? Trains running through caves, the noise, the smells, and so many people, strangers so close."

"You made it okay in Nam. You'll be okay here. Just hang tough," Howard said.

Lastun nodded.

At one point in the maze, Howard went to a booth and bought some metal coins with holes in them. "Subway tokens," he said, giving one to Lastun and depositing the other in the turnstile and where he passed through. In trepidation, Lastun watched how Howard and several other passengers got through before imitating their motions and passing through the machine, using his hand rather than his body to push the bar.

Howard watched and tried not to laugh.

The train jolted out of the station and screamed through the tunnel making several stops before passing under the East River to Brooklyn. Lastun felt his ears pop as they descended. The lights on the train blinked off and on several times as the train changed tracks in the underground labyrinth.

Lastun watched the other passengers, who seemed oblivious to the noise, flashing lights, and strange smells. Some even slept sitting up through the chaos. Lastun showed no outward sign of how close he was to a panic attack.

On the other side of the river, still underground, the train made several more stops before emerging into daylight on tracks that were elevated high above busy streets filled with cars and trucks. They were eye level with many of the apartment building windows that lined the street only a few yards away. They were moving too fast for Lastun to see inside.

After one of the stops, Lastun leaned over to Howard. "Was it scary for you when we were in Mississippi?" he asked.

Howard's brow creased. "We'd just gotten back from Nam, which was a whole lot wilder than Mississippi, so no, it wasn't scary for me." He smiled at Lastun. "Besides, I had you with me. But I can see how you would find all of the noise and crowds a little intimidating." He put his hand on Lastun's shoulder again. "But don't forget, now, you have me with you."

Lastun blinked, swallowed hard, and relaxed a bit.

When they got close to their stop, Howard stood up and walked toward the door. Lastun followed. They exited the train with the crush of other passengers, and descended a long stairway to the sidewalk.

They stood on one of the busiest shopping streets in the Bensonhurst section of Brooklyn. Small shops lined both sides of every block. Groceries, butchers, produce stands, clothing stores and some that seemed to sell a little bit of everything. Every one of them had more stuff than Lastun had ever seen in Mr. Kilgore's store. Howard caught the aroma of his favorite kosher deli from a block away. He was home.

29

Howard's parents lived in a brownstone house in the middle of a block lined with nearly identical buildings with no spaces between them. Once a tree-lined street, now only a few old oak and elm trees remained. Patches of hardened earth where other trees once stood now served as places for dogs to do their business.

It had been only a year since Howard had his thirty day leave before shipping out to Vietnam. But in this moment, it felt as if he'd been gone for a decade. He had grown up on this street and, in his memories, it was always the same from the time he was little until the time he went into the army. The street now looked older, narrower, lacking the vibrancy he remembered. It was as if the street had shared his experiences, and they both aged a lot in the two years he'd been away. He would soon realize that his wasn't only the neighborhood that changed. Howard stopped in front of one of the houses and looked up.

Suddenly, he was filled with the emotions he'd repressed during the hundreds of terrifying nights in the jungle, surrounded by M16 fire and mortar explosions when he was sure he'd never see home again. It was a feeling that every combat veteran experienced when returning home.

Strangely, Lastun, who spent almost his entire tour of duty worrying about Bizzy never experienced it, or at least never showed it, but instinctively understood Howard's emotional release and tried to comfort him.

After a while, Howard sniffled. "Thanks, man, I don't know what happened. I guess I tried too hard to forget what it was like, ya' know?"

Lastun did know. He knew in the only way a friend who'd been with him through most of those terrifying nights could. Once again, he held back his own feelings.

Lastun was struck by the closeness of the houses. There was no yard or garden space. Back home his closest neighbors were a quarter-mile away. Here, the neighbors were right on top of one another. The exterior of the building looked worn and weathered, the cement stairs leading to the front door were worn down by decades of footsteps, creating a path to the front door.

He wondered if he was up to the task he'd set for himself, though he would never express these doubts to Howard. This city was so different from anything he'd experienced or expected that his mission to rescue Bizzy might be more than he could handle, even with Howard's help. He'd overcome so many obstacles he never thought he could—like Goliath and Ellis Barber. The thought gave him hope and he squared his shoulders, resolving to do what must be done.

"That window up there, that's my bedroom," Howard said, pointing. The curtains moved at one of the other windows. He motioned to Lastun to follow him up the stone stairs to the front door, which opened as Howard reached for the handle.

A stocky, bald man past middle age who was wearing an undershirt opened the door and threw his arms around Howard. "Rachel, it's Howard. He's home!" the man shouted back inside the house.

"Lastun, this is my father Abe. Dad, Lastun is the reason I'm here now."

They shook hands. Lastun was still not used to doing this with a white man. Howard's mother came running from the kitchen at the back of the house and nearly knocked Howard over as she threw her arms around him, crying tears of joy.

Howard introduced Lastun to his mother, who without offering a handshake, said, "So nice to meet one of Howard's friends."

"Look at you, Howard, and your friend. You're both so skinny! Somebody would think the army didn't feed you. Come sit down. Abe, see if the boys want a drink . . . maybe some wine. I'll have dinner on the table in a few minutes." She returned to the kitchen.

Howard's mother's reaction to the return of her son reminded Lastun of their return to his family's home just a little more than a week ago. It made him sad and he fought to hide his emotions.

It was almost five, and Abe poured a glass of wine for Rachel, and something stronger for the boys and himself.

Abe and Rachel left for the kitchen. "I think dinner is almost ready," she called behind her, as she walked to the back of the house.

Now bolstered by the whiskey, Lastun took everything in; the furnishings, the space, the number of lamps and light fixtures. "You grew up here, in this house?" he asked.

"Yes."

Lastun noticed the carpeting and all of the polished wood furniture. There were things on almost every surface. Tchotchkes, Howard called them.

"You didn't tell me you was a rich kid," Lastun said with affect.

"I'm not. This is what we call middle class. If there's time, I'll show you where the rich people live."

"Do any black people live around here?"

"No," Howard said, "this area is mostly Jewish people. A few blocks over is another neighborhood called Bay Ridge. Over there, people are mostly Italian and Irish."

"Where do the black people live in this city?" Lastun asked, noticing Howard's evasion.

Howard mentally cringed. He knew where the black people lived. And he knew there were some middle class blacks who lived on the fringes of the white neighborhoods—but only a few. Most lived in slum neighborhoods. Every borough had them, and they were horrible.

"You'll see that too," Howard promised.

They heard voices from the kitchen. Abe and Rachel seemed upset, their voices raised but muffled. The only word Howard heard clearly was *shvartza*, and he knew what it was about. Lastun would figure it out later.

Abe came out and ushered them into the dining room. The table was set for four, but the quantity of food made Lastun wonder if more people would be showing up.

They dined on brisket, *kasha varnishkas*, vegetables and casserole—food Lastun had never seen before, but enjoyed eating.

Rachel told Howard everything that had happened in the family, the congregation, and the neighborhood since he'd been gone.

Lastun was polite and well-spoken, and eventually Howard's mother outwardly accepted his presence in their home.

Abe wanted to know everything, from what it was like on the front lines in Vietnam to how their trip to New York went. After a while, he and Rachel excused themselves to prepare coffee and dessert.

"I don't think your momma likes me," Lastun said.

"It's not like that," Howard stammered, "it just takes her a while to get used to strangers."

Lastun understood his meaning but remembered his manners, just the way his mama had taught him.

When Abe and Rachel returned from the kitchen, Lastun said, "Mrs. Fishman, I want to thank you for a wonderful dinner. I haven't eaten so well since the last time I ate at my mama's table."

Rachel's expression softened. "Thank you, Lastun. And by the way, what kind of name is that, anyway?"

Abe cringed while Howard tried not to laugh as Lastun told his story once again.

Rachel asked how many of his siblings were boys, and Abe wanted to know if they had been in the service, too.

Lastun told the Fishmans about his family, parents, brothers and sisters, and that he was the first one in his family to graduate high school, and the first to go into the military. He explained how the whole family worked the farm, and how all of the children had to help with the field work, picking cotton, and growing their own food.

Howard's parents listened attentively and asked questions. They told Lastun that they never knew how hard life was for people down there. They understood because their parents had also grown up in appalling poverty in the *shtetls* — ghetto villages — in Poland and Russia. Every day was a struggle for survival. And just when things seemed to be okay, there would be *Pogroms*; bands of thugs, sometimes soldiers, who would ride through the *shtetls,* shooting people and destroying whatever they could. A chill ran through Lastun, as he remembered the men wearing white hoods carrying torches and sometimes ropes, terrorizing black folks who gathered in family celebrations or at church. Sometimes, they'd drag someone away and they'd never be seen again.

"Seems like both our peoples have suffered hard times. I learned in school about how Nazi Germany and Hitler killed so many of y'all in World War Two. Up 'til 'bout a hundred years ago, my people was slaves, right there where Mama and Papa live now." Lastun's expression grew wistful. "My great-grandparents on both Papa's and Mama's sides was slaves within about fifty miles of Satartia." He lifted his chin. "It just ain't fair that some people would treat other people like that. And it still goes on. When I was in elementary school, the Klan burnt a cross on my principal's yard. When he got sassy, they took him off and nobody ever saw him again." Lastun stopped and looked embarrassed. "Sorry, I didn't mean to carry on so."

At the end of the evening, Lastun and Abe and Rachel Fishman had arrived at a place they'd never expected to be. It was a place of greater understanding. None of them realized they had only scratched the surface.

At the end of the evening, Howard showed Lastun up to the guest room, with its own private bathroom and shower. That night, in the most comfortable bed he'd ever lain in, Lastun slept like a baby, and dreamed of Bizzy and of his family in Mississippi.

30

Howard Fishman knew that, even for sophisticated Americans, visiting New York for the first time could be a daunting experience. When he was in high school, one of his father's Army buddies from Kansas visited with his family. They were so wide eyed about everything; the number of people hurrying about, so many tall buildings, signs everywhere, and more taxis and buses than they ever imagined.

The social and political turmoil of America in the late 1960s was magnified in New York. Howard had to adjust to a climate which was very different from the one he left. He tried to put himself in Lastun's shoes. *How would a young black man, who grew up in segregated rural Mississippi, take all of this in?* In the best of times, New York could be intimidating. But now the mood of the country created a new dimension of chaos. Howard was truly concerned about the ability of his friend to comprehend the very different attitudes and sensibilities of the biggest city in the country. The task ahead of them only intensified his concern.

On Monday morning, Howard's father left for work at 7:30 AM.

Rachel made his usual breakfast of orange juice, one slice of toast, one soft-boiled egg, and coffee. Bacon, of course, was unknown in the Fishman household.

Afterwards, she made a more substantial breakfast for Howard and Lastun; pancakes, scrambled eggs, a pile of toast and a large pot of coffee. Rachel believed breakfast was the most important meal of the day. Actually, in the Fishman household, every meal was important, which was why Rachel

Fishman spent a good part of each day shopping for food and preparing meals. Sometimes, Abe referred to this obsession as a depression-era mentality. People of their generation, who grew up during that period of extreme privation, were prone to obsessing over food. He could never grasp the fact that the Wicker family, along with many other families—especially black—continue to live in a perpetual state of privation.

Howard didn't bother to explain this to Lastun. During the time he spent with the Wickers in Mississippi, Howard saw that black people in Yazoo County—and by extension, in much of the rural south—still lived in depression-era poverty. And as Lastun would learn on this day, some parts of Brooklyn were no better, maybe worse.

During breakfast, Howard received a call from Phil.

Phil said he was still checking things out and would have word for them on Wednesday. "In the meantime, don't screw around. Ya' know what I'm talking about, right?"

"Yeah sure, I won't do anything. I got it." Howard said. But, he didn't see anything wrong with taking his country friend on a sightseeing tour of the "Big Apple."

After thanking Rachel for breakfast, they left the house. Once outside, Howard told Lastun about the call from Phil.

Lastun clenched his fist and banged the stone railing next to the stairs repeatedly.

"Lastun, listen to me."

Lastun turned to face Howard, fire in his eyes.

"Remember in Nam, when we planned a mission? We sent out scouts, studied maps and organized. Sometimes we even planned an escape route, if we got ambushed along the way. If this thing is going to work, that's the way it has to be now . . . in this jungle." Howard was emphatic.

Lastun's muscles began to relax. His head knew Howard was right. His heart ached.

"Look," Howard continued, "just because we're not, I repeat, not going to take any action before we hear from Phil, we can still plan. I have some ideas, but I need you to be cool until then. Can you do that?"

"I suppose I'll have to," Lastun grumbled.

Howard walked down to the street.

"Where are we going?" Lastun asked.

"Down the rabbit hole. Fasten your seat belt."

"Huh?" Lastun grunted, and followed.

He took Lastun on the scenic route, walking several blocks through the modest, but neat streets in the neighborhood, to the busier shopping street. Howard had been away for two years and he could now see the changes in the neighborhood he'd grown up in.

He'd tried to keep up with current events. His parents would include some front sections of the New York newspapers in their monthly care packages. He still had no way of knowing the toll that the war, recession, and social upheavals were taking on American neighborhoods, but apparently not yet in Yazoo County.

They walked for several blocks to a train station and climbed the stairs to the elevated platform.

"This isn't the station we were at yesterday," Lastun said. He had a keen eye and was beginning to see the patterns of the city, the same way he could recognize a squirrel hiding in the shadows on the branch of a tree, or Charlie in a shaded thicket of bamboo.

"Good call," Howard said, "you're noticing things. Like I said, we need these two days for you to get used to the lay of the land."

Lastun knew Howard was right. Besides there was no point in arguing. After eight months of wondering, another couple of days didn't really matter, especially if the wait would increase their odds for success.

The elevated tracks plunged underground, and they got out of the train and stood on the platform.

"What are we waiting for?"

"Another train."

"What was wrong with the train we were on?" Lastun asked.

Howard gave Lastun a strange look. "Nothing, but it wasn't going where we wanted. We need to take one of the trains on the other side of the platform to get us where we're going."

Lastun shook his head in confusion.

"Follow me." He walked Lastun over to a map of the subway posted on a board about three feet square, suspended between two pillars on the platform. The map was behind worn and scratched Plexiglas, with large parts covered by spray paint, but the part Howard wanted to show him was still visible.

"This is a map of the city subway system. All of these straight lines are the different train routes. The colors are the different trains. We were on one of the red trains. We started here," Howard said, pointing to a spot. "Now we're getting on the blue lines, which will take us to this point in Brooklyn."

Lastun read the printing on the map near Howard's finger. "Brownsville?"

"Yes, that is another section of Brooklyn. Remember I told you I lived in Bay Ridge? Well, this is another part."

They took the train that ran on the blue line. Lastun noticed that after each stop some of the white people got off and more black people got on. Some men wore black berets on top of shorter Afro hair; others wore headbands in the same kind of prints as their dashikis. Some of the black women wore strong perfume which mixed with the usual subway smells. At times, he thought he was going to be sick.

After a while, Lastun became aware of other passengers noticing them. He and Howard were dressed differently, and Lastun's close cut hair was decidedly out of place.

"Let's go," Howard said when the train stopped, and hurried out of the car down the platform and up the stairs to the street.

Lastun stayed close. When they were outside, he looked around.

"This sure don't look like where we came from."

"No shit," Howard said.

Here, the streets were just as busy, but different. Almost all of the people on the street were black. Not all the people had the same distinctive appearance Lastun noticed on the train, but most of the younger ones did.

Even the stores that were open had iron bars or grating in front of the plate glass windows. Shabby men sat in the doorways between some of the stores, many holding paper bags with protruding bottle necks.

Howard walked down the street, keeping close to the curb. Lastun stayed next to him.

"Keep your head up, act relaxed and just walk. Look around, but don't eyeball anybody, got it?"

"Yeah, be cool. I got it." Lastun said. The last time he felt this wary of his surroundings he was glad to be carrying his M16A1, serial number 72176287. He missed that old friend.

They stopped at a corner before crossing. There was a poster on the side of a boarded-up newsstand. It announced an event at the Central Park Mall the following week. Somebody named Angela Davis would be appearing with Huey Newton and Ossie Davis. They crossed the street and saw several black men with black jackets, and black berets. The set of their lower jaws made them look angry and menacing. It was a primitive gesture, and it raised an innate sense of danger in Lastun.

When two of the men stepped out in front of them Howard saw the Black Panther insignia on their jackets. The men were clean shaven and had expressions Lastun had never seen on black faces—pride. Pride in their blackness. Pride no white man could dismiss.

That said, they were young and their experiences were limited to the city streets they inhabited.

The Panthers had no idea the men they were facing were hardened combat veterans. They had killed with bullets, as well as knives and bayonets in close combat.

For a long moment, they just stared at Lastun and Howard.

"What's a brother doing on this street with a honkie?" one of them asked, thrusting his face inches from Lastun's.

"He ain't no honkie. He's my army buddy." Lastun didn't know the word honkie.

The two men laughed at Lastun's ignorance, and their demeanor became more menacing. When they spoke, they raised their voices loud enough for everyone around to hear. A crowd began to form.

"Am I seeing a brother and a honkie just back from killing yellow people in Vietnam walking down our street like they have a right?"

"I do believe that's exactly what we're seeing," the other man replied loudly.

"Look, man, we don't want no trouble," Lastun said.

Howard remained silent with his hands in his pockets.

"Well, if you are not looking for trouble, then please tell me exactly what in God's name you two are doing here in the first place?" the first man shouted.

"I think we must have gotten off the train at the wrong station," Lastun said softly, glancing at Howard for support.

He remembered how he felt when the white men spoke to him at the cotton mill when he was a boy. He couldn't understand why a black man he didn't know would be so hostile.

"You sure as hell did get off at the wrong stop," a voice in the crowd shouted.

Woop-Woop. The short bursts of the siren from a police cruiser, red bubble light flashing, arrived to investigate the gathering crowd.

A white police officer got out of the car. His black partner called in a 10-50 — disorderly group — and gave their location.

As the police officer approached, one of the black men said in a loud voice, "Mr. Johnson, I think I smell pig shit, do you?"

In an equally loud voice, the other man replied, "Why yes, Mr. Leonard, I do believe I smell pig shit, and the smell is getting stronger."

The onlookers murmured. Howard and Lastun remained silent.

The crowd parted as the officer approached.

"Well, if it isn't Mr. Leonard and Mr. Johnson."

"Good day, Officer Halloran. Are you here to harass black people having an orderly gathering? Do you plan to deprive us of our constitutional right to assemble?" He held his chin high and appeared to look down on the officer even though they were about the same height.

Another police cruiser pulled up behind the first, lights flashing.

Officer Halloran heard the door slam and held up his right hand, It was the same signal Lastun and Howard used in the green jungle when one of them sensed danger, and they wanted the rest of the squad to hold back.

Officer Halloran ignored the black militants and looked at Lastun and Howard, eyeing them up and down. Clearly, they didn't belong here. He took his hat off and ran his hand up his forehead, pushing his hair back before putting his hat back on.

Howard read this as a gesture to show he wasn't intimidated.

"What in the name of sweet Jesus are you two numb-nuts doing in this neighborhood?" He didn't wait for them to reply. "Never mind, I don't give a rat's ass. You two are going to go down that stairway," he said, pointing to the nearest subway entrance, "and get on the next train that pulls in. I don't give a shit where it's going, as long as your dumb asses are on it. Do you understand?"

Howard and Lastun nodded.

Messrs. Leonard and Johnson looked on in amusement.

"Now move, before I take you in for inciting a public disturbance!"

Howard and Lastun took off for the stairs.

Officer Halloran said, "Mr. Leonard, Mr. Johnson, you may continue exercising your constitutional right to assemble." He turned and walked back to the police cruiser. The officers in both police cars watched the crowd that stubbornly refuse to disburse. When he was sure they would not pursue them, he drove off and the second car followed.

While the Panthers and the police were having their pissing contest, Howard and Lastun bounded down the stairs, jumped the turnstile, ran down the platform and boarded a train just as the doors were closing.

They sat in silence, sweat pouring down their faces. Other passengers looking too much like the street people they'd just encountered watched them while they tried to catch their breath and get their heart rates down. As the train made stops, they saw other Black Panthers boarding the train and riding one or two stops before leaving.

Howard and Lastun stayed on the train, as it passed into Queens and continued to Jamaica Station. The number of black passengers decrease and the number of white passengers increase to what Howard thought were normal proportions.

"Let's get some coffee," Howard said.

They descended to street level and entered a luncheonette.

They sat in a booth and a young black waitress approached them. Taking only cursory notice of Howard, she looked at Lastun and asked, "What can I get you? The coffee is fresh and so is the apple pie."

Lastun looked at Howard, who nodded.

"Two cups of coffee and two slices of apple pie, please," Lastun said.

The waitress walked away.

"You wanna' tell me what in the hell we were doing back there?"

"Scary, wasn't it?" Howard said calmly.

"You damn well know it was. What were you thinking?" Lastun raised his voice.

"Well, my friend, that was the watered down version of what Harlem is like, only in Harlem we wouldn't get a greeting by the welcoming committee. They'd just have beaten us into the pavement and then, maybe, wondered who we were."

"You serious?"

"Serious as a heart attack, man. That's why everybody thinks the idea of a rescue mission in Harlem is pure insanity."

"Then what the hell am I supposed to do, just abandon my wife and baby? You know I can't do that." Desperation was in his voice.

"I know, I know. We are going to do something. And we need to plan. But whatever we do, we have to be smart about it. You see why the police can't help, you saw how much respect those Panthers had for the cops."

"Panthers?" Lastun asked.

"Shit, you don't know about them? The Black Panthers are a militant group of civil rights activists," Howard tried to explain. "You know Dr. King believed in nonviolence right?"

Lastun nodded.

"Well, they don't. Those men with the black berets think you're a race traitor for hanging with a honkie. That's street talk for a white guy . . . me."

"Why did they call me brother?" Lastun asked.

"Because they believe all people of color—black, yellow, brown or red like Comanche—are brothers and sisters who must stand up against their white oppressors, and they believe all whites are oppressors," he said in a hushed tone.

The idea of reverse racism—blacks being prejudiced against whites—seemed unfathomable to a black man who grew up in the south calling all whites sir or ma'am.

"Can the Panthers help us in Harlem?" Lastun was groping for hope.

"No, the guys in Harlem are black and the Panthers consider them brothers, too."

"So they see all whites as bad, even if some are good . . . and all blacks as good, even if they're bad," Lastun thought out loud.

"Pretty much."

Lastun shrugged. "What kind of place is this? What's going on here, it's all so . . . different. Even the waitress, she acted like you didn't exist."

"This is my city. I grew up here. How the hell do you think I feel coming back from serving my country and finding black people here hate me for being white?" Howard asked.

The coffee and pie arrived. Their blood sugar had tanked somewhere on the train from Brooklyn. They'd just finished

258

eating when the waitress returned with the coffee pot to ask Lastun if he wanted a refill.

"Two, please," he said.

The waitress sighed, filled both cups and put the check on the table.

Before she could move, Howard slapped a ten dollar bill on top of the check and held his hand on it.

The waitress glared at him.

He smiled at her and moved his hand, "Change, please."

Lastun watched her walk away. He saw her skirt swoosh as her hips swayed. Her long slender black legs reminded him of Bizzy.

She returned, put the change on the table, glared at Howard and walked away.

"Mind telling me what that was all about?" Lastun asked.

"When I put the money on the table, she realized that I had the power to decide whether she makes anything on this transaction," Howard said.

"And that's supposed to make her like white people more?"

"No, but it shows her who has the power."

"Isn't that her point?" Lastun asked.

"Yes, my friend, exactly. But as long as we're expanding your vocabulary today, what I did is a passive form of *white backlash*. You see, I'm angry at this whole situation, too. Look, I don't have to explain my feelings to you. Our friendship is the reason we're both still alive and sitting here eating apple pie and drinking coffee," Howard said.

"I know that, man. It's just that this whole thing is like a dog chasing his own tail. Where does it end?"

"I don't know, but I hope we live long enough to see things turn right for everybody," Howard said.

"Amen to that."

"Speaking of living, exactly what were you going to do back there if the cops hadn't shown up?"

Howard gestured for Lastun to look under the table.

Lastun glanced down and saw Howard holding a knife handle. He moved his finger and in a flash a five inch blade appeared.

"What the —?"

"It's called a switchblade. I won it in a poker game. They're illegal, but like the man said, I'd rather be judged by twelve than carried by six," Howard said smugly.

"So now that you're back from Nam and in the big city, you're, what, a killer now?"

"Not a killer, a survivor. Like you. We did it in Nam and we did it in Yazoo County."

"And what did you think I would be doing while you were flashing that blade around?"

"Same thing I did for you behind Mei Li's bar," Howard said.

"Well, why didn't you pull that while we were in that fight at Stu's in Yazoo city?"

"I didn't have it with me," Howard explained. "I didn't think we'd have trouble, so I left in my duffel. I knew we were going to Brownsville today, so I came prepared.

"While we're on the subject," Howard countered, "surely, Barber and his boys had weapons, but they didn't pull them. I wonder why?"

Lastun scratched his chin. "Their guns would've been in their trucks in the parking lot. Like you, they didn't expect trouble. But they would have had stickers like that," Lastun nodded toward the switchblade. "They just didn't have time to get to em'. Everything happened pretty fast."

"That it did."

"Can we get out of here? I'm getting tired of watching that waitress eyeball us," Lastun said.

"Sure, let's go into The City."

They took the train from Jamaica to Penn Station.

31

"How about gettin' one of those orange things again?" Lastun asked.

They bought two giant sized Orange Julius cups.

"Man, these things are good," Lastun said. "Working the farm in the summer these would have been great. Where we goin' now?"

"Back to The Village. You didn't get to see anything when we went to Izzy's the other night, I think you'll find it interesting. We can walk," Howard said.

"How many klicks is it?" Lastun asked.

Howard laughed. "This is New York City. We don't have klicks here."

"Well, then how many miles is it?" Lastun persisted.

"We don't use miles, either." Howard said as they reached street level. "Look, we are on Thirty-Third Street now, and we're going to Third Street. That's thirty blocks. Going north or south, there are about twenty blocks to a mile. We also have to go two blocks crosstown. Those blocks are much longer, so that's roughly another quarter mile, so it's probably a little under two miles to where we're going, and we don't have to double time it so you can look around."

As they walked, Lastun tried to see everything. It was like trying to juggle images with his eyes.

The streets were filled with yellow taxi cabs and black limousines that seemed as long as a school bus. "Why are all of the taxi cabs yellow?" Lastun asked.

Howard didn't answer; he just watched with amusement as his wide-eyed country friend tried to absorb the scene: thousands of people hurrying along the sidewalks. Stores, without steel bars over the windows, lined every block, and the streets were filled with cars. Buses and delivery trucks spewed black diesel smoke. "I'll bet there's more people in New York City than in the whole state of Mississippi!" Lastun observed.

Howard smiled. "Could be."

"And look at all these eatin' places," Lastun said, gesturing toward the restaurants and food carts on every block. He sniffed the air. "I smell hot dogs and pizza and . . ." He put names on all of the aromas he could identify.

"Look at the signs," Howard pointed. "Gyros, bagels, Chinese food . . . you name it."

"How come there ain't more fat people here?"

"Because so many people walk."

"Yeah, and faster than the cabs. They oughta ride the trains. That's even faster still."

"It's called the subway," Howard corrected.

Lastun grew morose. "Reckon where Bizzy is now?"

"The place Gold is keeping her is on Hundred and Twenty-Seventh Street in Harlem. We'll get a look at it later. Just be patient. Everything we're doing today is preparation for what we're going to do."

Lastun tried to get his bearings, but in the concrete canyons of the city, he couldn't tell where the sun was, even though it was early afternoon.

Howard took Lastun by the shoulders and turned him around. "Look up."

Three crosstown blocks away, one building towered over all the others.

"What the . . ." Lastun said. Looking up made him dizzy.

"That's the Empire State Building, over one hundred stories high. About eleven hundred feet to the top of the antenna. If we have time, we can take the elevator up to the observation deck, that's near the tip where the building starts to get narrower. All of the windows in that building are offices, and thousands of people work there every day. Look at all of the other buildings. They're full of working people too."

"Other than when we flew over to Nam, I've never been that high off the ground. Not sure I want to do that now," Lastun said.

"Let's go." They walked toward Seventh Avenue and turned south.

"Sure do have a lot of fine looking women in this city," Lastun said.

"Yes, we do. I didn't realize how much I missed that," Howard said, as his mind wandered. Before he went into the Army, he had a girlfriend named Karen. She dumped him for a med-student before he even shipped out. Jody was the name they gave to any guy that took your girl while you were in the service, and the "Dear John" letter is how you found out about it. Even if the relationship wasn't that serious, as was the case with Karen, receiving that letter when you are nine-thousand miles away always hurts, and makes the loneliness even more intense. Howard tried not to remember that feeling now.

After a few blocks, Lastun had learned to observe the *Walk, Don't Walk* signs at intersections, and Howard explained about jaywalking, which was against the law—not to mention unwise.

At one intersection, Howard had to pull Lastun back to the curb when he heard the wail of a police siren speeding toward them on a cross-town street.

An hour later, they arrived at Washington Square Park, the dominant feature being a quarter size replica of the famous Arc de Triumph in Paris.

Hundreds of people crowded into the park and the central fountain area. They were mostly hippies, men, women, white and black, many about the same age as Lastun and Howard. Many chanted slogans demanding equal rights for all, and "Hell no we won't go," was heard over the din in several areas of the park.

"Shit! What's that about?" Lastun asked.

"Those are the spoiled kids who are afraid to leave their comfortable homes and serve their country like we did," Howard said.

"Hey asshole, what'd you jus' say?" a long haired hippie shouted in Howard's face.

"You freakin heard me. Now get outa my face, while you have a chance."

Lastun stepped between them and the hippie chose to back off, screaming, "Baby killers!" and spitting at them as he did. Lastun lunged at him and he ran. "Chicken shit."

Usually in pairs, police wandered through the crowd. Patrolmen on horseback, also in pairs, were stationed near each entrance to the park. Lastun was surprised to see horses in the city.

Many of the girls were barely dressed, showing off as much skin as they could without being arrested. The standard uniform for non-conformists consisted of brightly-printed fabrics, called tie-dye, with lots of beads around their necks. Some wore pendants that looked to Lastun like a chicken foot in a circle. Howard explained that was the symbol for the peace movement. Almost all of the black people wore what Lastun now knew was the Afro hair-style; few wore their hair cropped short as Lastun did, and none of them straightened their hair the way some black women did in Yazoo County.

Some played guitars and sang folk songs. Others lit fires in trash cans. Women took off their bras and burned them, and some men burned their draft cards. One hippie burned the American Flag. As a black man, having just returned from combat less than a month before, he understood the protests for equality, but protesting the war and disrespecting the flag he'd seen so many die for, stirred an outrage he had to fight to contain. Many of their buddies were still fighting for their lives in the jungle right now and the juxtaposition of those two thoughts was almost too much for either of them to fathom.

The escalation of protests and the growing hippie movement since Howard had left New York, surprised him. He knew from his own recent experience in Nam, and in Mississippi, that these hippies truly had no idea what went on in the real world. He also knew that if he hadn't been drafted, he might have been one of them. The thought revolted him.

Some Black Panthers, proudly displaying their uniforms, walked through the crowd, making their presence felt without making a sound.

To Howard and Lastun, this looked like ground zero for the protest movement. Both were not yet aware of far larger gatherings in many other American cities from New York to San Francisco, which was in fact the epicenter of the hippie movement.

While Lastun read protest signs and watched some of the scantily clad black girls, he was wrenched back to the reality of why they were in New York.

"Howard, weren't we supposed to hear from Phil today?"

"He said not till tomorrow, but I spoke with him this morning and he'll be meeting us at Izzy's tomorrow. Besides, I think we both need a little more time to get acclimated. It looks like a lot has changed here, while I was away."

32

Tired and a bit overwhelmed, the two men took the train back to Brooklyn. On the way, Lastun asked about the way the black people lived in Brownsville.

Howard described the decaying tenement buildings, rusty plumbing, rats, roaches, and over-crowded living conditions. Civil rights groups sued the city for lack of code enforcement, but little progress was ever made. Workmen couldn't go into high crime areas to work because their tools and building materials were stolen. It was a vicious circle.

"Your home may be small, but even without a television or dishwasher it's a whole lot better than what poor people have here, stacked up in those shit boxes. Momma Wicker is a good homemaker and your family has good food, good water and clean air," Howard said.

Lastun couldn't begin to imagine the conditions Howard described. "Reckon Bizzy has to live like that?" he asked.

"Probably." Howard's expression was sad.

They arrived home in time to meet Abe walking up the street.

"How was your day, Pop?" Howard asked, as he kissed his father on the cheek.

Lastun was surprised to see two men express such affection—especially kissing on the cheek. When he saw his Papa, each would give a nod, and maybe a smile.

"Good, very good. Mrs. Lebow was in with her son. He just returned from the war in one piece, thank goodness. Mrs. Benson said her son would be leaving in a few weeks. I wish they would end this *farkakt* war already."

"You and a lot of other people," Lastun added. The word Abe used was unfamiliar, but he got the meaning.

Howard's mother had prepared another feast for them. Abe and Rachel enjoyed relating all of the stories and gossip about family members. They went through the list of all of Howard's uncles, aunts, and cousins; their weddings, divorces, and funerals. Through it all, Rachel Fishman kept a close eye on Lastun, something Howard noticed and Lastun appeared not to.

After dinner, they retired to the living room to celebrate their son's safe return. Mr. Fishman poured glasses of schnapps for all of them. They toasted *l'chaim* — to life. Abe explained the meaning to Lastun.

Most soldiers who were lucky enough to return from Vietnam usually didn't care to discuss their experiences in battle. Men who'd served over there would never ask and people who hadn't been there could never understand.

After the second glass of schnapps, Howard mellowed and decided to share one story with his parents. "Our platoon was on night patrol in the jungle. We were advancing on a known enemy position when a mortar shell landed near me and I was thrown into a trench. Lastun was about twenty yards to my right and saw what happened. I had a shrapnel wound in the hip which turned out to be minor, but I was in shock from the blast. The enemy was advancing and the sergeant yelled for us to retreat, but I couldn't move. Lastun turned back, jumped in the trench and carried me to our rear position. If it wasn't for Lastun, I wouldn't be here now."

The room was silent. Howard's father's eyes were wet. He remembered the horrors of his own experiences in combat.

Sobbing, Howard's mother walked to Lastun and threw her arms around him. "Thank you for bringing our son home," she whispered.

"It wasn't anything. We were in combat. Any one of us would have done that. I just happened to get there first."

"But you did," Howard's father said, taking Lastun's hand.

"Yeah, but he didn't tell you about the time he saved my life," Lastun replied.

"In combat, everyone is a hero, and most of the stories never get told," Abe said.

"Amen to that," Lastun added.

They sat and talked for a long time.

Lastun realized that, in many ways, Jewish families were a lot like his own family. The fathers were the bread winners, but always deferred to their wives in matters of the home and child rearing. Both mothers worked hard to prepare meals for their families. There was love and respect and pride. He began to feel at ease.

Howard excused himself to make a phone call.

By the time he returned, Rachel had officially welcomed Lastun as part of the family, and invited him to all future family functions—including Howard's wedding. "I should live so long," she said.

"I hope you don't mind, but we have to go out for a while. We still have a lot to catch up on, and I know you two will be getting to bed soon," Howard said.

"It's so late, I don't understand it. But what can I do? Just be careful," Rachel said.

Howard kissed his mother and father good night and left with Lastun.

"Where are we going now?" Lastun asked.

"We're going to meet Izzy. We have to do something before we speak to Phil tomorrow. I'll explain when we get there."

They took the train into the city. After changing trains twice, they walked up to street level one block from Izzy's apartment.

"Ya' know, this subway thing is a pretty convenient way to travel, once you get it figured out," Lastun said.

Izzy welcomed them. "Hey, you guys want a beer?"

"No thanks, we're going out."

"Okay, I know this club that previews new music acts on Tuesdays . . ."

"No, not that kind of going out. This is business. You have a car?"

"Yeah, still have that white '63 Falcon."

"Perfect," Howard said.

Howard explained their need to do some reconnaissance in Harlem before they heard from Phil. Howard had the address Jeff gave him and wanted to check out the buildings and surrounding area.

"You guys are crazy. We could get killed," Izzy argued.

"Not if we go around four in the morning. It will still be dark and most of the action, you know what I'm talking about, will be over for the night," Howard said.

Izzy thought for a while. "Okay, but only if my friend JJ comes along."

"Who's JJ?" Howard asked.

"JJ's a good guy. Definitely a little weird, but reliable. Trust me," Izzy said.

Howard knew not to ask any more questions. Izzy worked the crime desk, so JJ probably had some connection to things he didn't want them to know about. The fact that Izzy wanted him in on the mission meant he would be useful in some way.

Izzy made a call.

A little after one AM, JJ arrived wearing sunglasses. Black and wiry, he and Izzy greeted each other warmly.

"Glad you could make it," Izzy said.

"Anything I can do to help a brother, man," JJ replied.

"Thanks. Did Izzy tell you what this is about?" Lastun asked.

"Just enough to convince me that you and white bread here—no offense, man—must have gotten too much of that Agent Orange stuff in your head. You got any idea what you're getting into?"

"By now, everybody's told us what a cluster this could become. Do you want in or what?" Howard said, wasting no time.

JJ sat back and said, "Like I said, I gotta help my brother here, so why don't you give me a heads-up on what's goin' down."

Howard nodded, and Lastun began.

He told them what he knew had happened in Mississippi, the letters from Bizzy, and the tip that she was in Harlem. It was the first time Howard heard Lastun tell the whole story. It was hard for him. His voice was strained as he finished.

Then Howard explained that they 'd gotten an address from "a friend in Atlanta" with contacts in New York. He deliberately left out the part about Phil, a cop, also being involved.

JJ agreed to help.

It was already after two o'clock, and he suggested they leave about three.

"How many klicks . . . miles . . . blocks is it to Harlem?" Lastun sputtered.

"We're on Third Street and we are going to Hundred Twenty-Seventh Street, off Seventh Avenue," Howard said, adding the last part for JJ and Izzy's benefit.

"Shieet," JJ said.

"Double that," Izzy added.

"That's only six miles," Lastun said.

They looked at him. "Nobody around here uses miles. We just know how far a hundred twenty-four blocks is," Howard said. "But I think it's the location they're concerned about, not the distance."

"Oh."

"Are you guys in or what?" Howard asked.

"A brother's got to help a brother," JJ said. "But one thing, we take my car. Ain't nobody in Harlem be seen driving a shit box like you got, Izzy."

They went in JJ's black, '63 Lincoln Continental. It was clean but the shine had long since weathered away, and Howard could see the suspension was bottomed out.

"This won't stand out?" Howard asked.

"Not where we be goin'."

In New York, the cross streets are one way and 127th was westbound. They found Mr. Gold's house, number 423, in the middle of the block. It was a run down four-story brownstone sandwiched between another one of the same height and a five-story building that probably wouldn't have stayed upright on its own. A black man who would have dwarfed Goliath stood outside the front door, smoking a cigarette.

JJ had good timing. The streets were nearly empty. Mr. Gold had the girls back in the crib, and lights were visible through windows that weren't boarded up.

JJ cruised around the block once, and then again. After his second pass, he pulled into a parking space and got out leaving the motor running.

"You guys stay here. Izzy, move over to the driver's seat — just in case."

Nobody wanted to ask, "In case of what?"

A police cruiser slowly rode by, eying the Lincoln and its occupants, but it didn't stop. A few minutes later, a lone pedestrian walked past them approaching from the front. He looked at them and kept walking.

That bothered Howard. It was like the way Lastun recognized when things didn't look right in the jungle. Howard's senses were attuned to the city. He knew there was something wrong when a black man sees two white guys in a car with a brother at 4:00 AM, in this neighborhood, and just walks by like it's nothing. Howard didn't say anything, but he saw that Izzy picked up on it, too.

"Wait," Lastun said. "I'm comin' with you."

JJ shook his head. "It'll be too dangerous."

"Why tell me what you see on your recon when I can see for myself?" Lastun's voice was obstinate.

JJ paused, caught a glance from Howard, and shrugged. "It's your show."

"Wait up," Howard said, when Lastun opened the door. "I'm coming too."

"Ya wanna call your mother and see if she wants to tag along?" JJ snapped.

"Lastun's right. We need to see the layout, so we don't get blindsided when we go in for real," Howard insisted.

"Like I said, it's your show, but if you're going you'd better move fast. We can't stay here much longer."

"Izzy, you stay in the car and keep the motor running," JJ said.

"You got it.'

The three men got out of the car and hurried into the shadows. They could see the guard in front of the house light a cigarette. JJ counted off the number of buildings from the corner to where the guard stood.

"There's no way we can get near the house from the front. We have to take one of the alleys around to the back," JJ said.

On the cross street, they found an alley that ran the length of the block behind the buildings. The only light was from the street lamps and diminished as they made their way past piles of garbage, old furniture, appliances and dead rats. The smell reminded Lastun of the back of Mei Li's bar, making him even queasier.

"That's number four twenty-three," JJ whispered, looking up at the back of a five-story building. "See the fire escape? We can climb the fire escape to the roof and jump down to the roof of four twenty-five. Then we use the trap door on the roof to get in the building on the top floor. That's the easy part."

"Why don't we just use the fire escape on four twenty-five?" Lastun asked.

"Because we could be seen from the windows. Four twenty-three looks vacant, so we won't be spotted climbing up," JJ said.

Lastun looked up and around. "What about the buildings on the other side of the alley. Won't someone spot us from there?"

"It is a possibility, but it'll be late and dark. Besides, in this neighborhood, people mind their own damn business."

They retraced their steps to the car. Izzy slid over and JJ took the wheel. Not wanting to attract attention, he slowly wheeled the big car around the corner and headed for 5th Avenue, which ran down the east side of Central Park.

JJ continued sharing his plan. "Like I said, getting in isn't the problem. We don't know what we'll be facing inside. We don't know how many mokes we'll have to deal with, how much hardware they're packin' or where in that hell hole Bizzy or the baby are. A building that size can have fifteen or more rooms. Then, if you get really lucky, and find them before they kill us, we still have to get them out past the front door and past the guard.

They rode in silence 'til they got back to Izzy's place.

"Thanks, man," Howard said, "now we have to figure out the rest. When we do, you still want in?"

"Too late to back out now."

33

Rachel heard the boys come in just before dawn and didn't wake them for breakfast at the usual time. When she did hear them getting up, she busily prepared the same full breakfast they had the day before.

After eating, they sat with Rachel drinking coffee and listening to her tell stories of family lore and what life was like when she was a child. She knew Howard had heard them a thousand times but enjoyed her new audience and was happy to answer all of Lastun's questions.

About two o'clock, Howard received a call from Phil. He said they would meet at Izzy's house at seven.

Before their meeting, Howard wanted to show Lastun a little more of the city by daylight. Again they took the train to Penn Station but now walked north, up 7th Avenue to where it intersected Broadway at Times Square.

Even millions of flashing lights and miles of neon couldn't hide the grittiness of Times Square of the late 1960s.

Bright theatre marquis, displaying the names of top shows like *Promises, Promises, The Producers,* and *Hair,* were interspersed with signs for strip joints and XXX-rated movies.

Howard pointed out the prostitutes; some black, some white, most were young, some too young.

"Do you think Bizzy is here anywhere?" Lastun asked, his voice plaintive.

"I don't think so," Howard answered. "This early, she's probably still sleeping. Besides, in this crowd, you could never find her. Hell, If I walked across the street, I could blend in with the crowd and you wouldn't even find me."

Hesitating, Lastun looked around, trying to take in a thousand black and white faces in a glance. He knew Howard was right and after all they did have a plan now. *I'll have to be patient a little longer.*

"Come on, let's go,' Howard said.

Bars and shops loaded with flashy electronics or jewelry stood out between others filled with tourist schlock. Streets were littered with newspapers, plastic cups, and other refuse of so-called civilization. *"I heart New York"* T-shirts, miniature replicas of the Statue of Liberty and the Empire State Building filled other shops. And then there were the sex shops selling magazines, sex toys, posters, and 8mm movies. Strangers approached Lastun, offering to sell diamond rings or Rolex watches at impossibly low prices.

Howard deflected them with a terse, "Not interested," and redirected Lastun, explaining that these were hustlers selling attractive fakes. The whole scene made Howard uncomfortable, but it was something Lastun needed to see.

Lastun thought he'd descended into the bowels of depravity and was thankful that his parents, and his pastor, didn't know where he was.

They walked further up 7th Avenue, glad to leave the most unreal part of New York Lastun had seen thus far. It was five o'clock, but grey clouds from an approaching weather front made it seem later. They reached Central Park South, as office workers began streaming out of buildings for their evening commute.

At Central Park South, Howard directed Lastun's attention north, away from the crowds.

"See the buildings along the side of the park?" That's where the rich people live. Some of the apartments in those buildings are ten times the size of your home in Satartia."

"What?" Lastun said.

"That's right, and the cost of one of those apartments is thousands of times more than your dad will make in his entire lifetime. Many of the people who live here make their money running large companies, or banks. They may be lawyers or doctors. Some make their money buying and selling real estate. Others in ways you wouldn't want to know about."

"Like Mr. Gold?" Lastun asked.

"No, Mr. Gold is a petty criminal. Even he can't afford to live here. But some of those people make money in ways that are just as illegal, just not as obvious," Howard said.

"It's getting late. The subway will be jammed now, and even with this traffic we'll make better time in a taxi."

At seven-fifteen they arrived at Izzy's house. JJ was there and so was Phil, and he looked poised.

Before Izzy could offer Howard and Lastun a beer, Phil got into Howard's face. "What did I tell you guys the other night?" His voice was hard, almost a shout.

"You said not to do anything, and we didn't." Howard didn't move an inch.

"What do you call that stunt you pulled last night?" Phil demanded.

Howard looked at JJ accusingly.

"Don't look at me, man. I didn't say anything."

"He didn't have to. This is my city and I know everything that goes on. I saw you guys on hundred twenty-seventh last night. He didn't give Howard a chance to answer. "Yeah, you didn't know it was me in the cruiser, and the skell that walked by was one of my CI's."

"A snitch," Izzy said, leaning toward Lastun.

"A Confidential Informant," Phil corrected, "And what the hell were you thinking?"

"We didn't DO anything." Howard was defiant. "Just some recon."

Phil sat down. "Izzy, I'll take that beer now."

Howard, Lastun, and JJ didn't move.

Izzy brought beers for all of them.

The four men stood, eyes on Phil, waiting for him to agree to help them.

"Look, I can see that you guys are going to do this no matter what I say."

Lastun didn't need to look at the others. He nodded. Phil saw the resolve in their eyes. But what he didn't understand was that Howard, Izzy and JJ had become emotionally involved. It wasn't just four guys playing GI Joe. It was a mission to help Lastun, whom they'd come to know and respect, recover his wife and child from the clutches of one of the dirtiest lowlifes in The City. To a man, they felt their own sense of self-respect and humanity compelled them to do what had to be done, and Phil knew that.

"Okay then, tell me what you learned from your 'recon' mission," Phil demanded.

JJ described their drive by, the moke out front and a description of the back alleys.

"Not bad," Phil said, grudgingly.

It was the first encouraging thing Lastun had heard.

"We're supposed to get some rain tonight, should start before midnight. That means Gold and the other pimps will be getting the girls off the street early. He'll take them back to the crib." It was a word Howard had to explain to Lastun, "And probably go to his home further uptown." Phil picked up a file folder from the coffee table.

"Lastun." It was the first time Phil called him by name. "You may find this shocking. I have three pictures here, tell me which one you think is Bessie Polk."

Lastun started to reach for the pictures, but stopped when Phil pulled them back.

"She's not going to look the way you remember her. She'd been through a lot by the time this was taken," he said.

Lastun sat on the couch between JJ and Howard. Putting his beer down, he placed his hand on his knees. Phil put the pictures on the table.

The first one was a picture of a black woman with a blond wig.

Lastun shook his head, and Phil put another one on top of it.

The second was a heavy-set light-skinned black woman.

Lastun nervously rubbed his sweaty palms on his pants. The next picture had to be Bizzy. Phil put a third picture on top of the others. The skinny woman in the picture had hair grown out in the Afro style. Her eyes were swollen and bloodshot, and there was a small scar on her forehead above her left eye. Lastun had not seen Bizzy in over a year, but in that picture she looked like she had aged ten years.

Lastun didn't have to say anything. He just put his hands over his eyes and cried. The sight of this picture of the woman he loved—his pretty young wife reduced to this level of degradation—was more than he could bear. After everything he'd been through in combat, no fear of bullets flying around him, no terror as bursting mortars lit the night around him, no shock at the sight of his friends blown to pieces had made him cry before. Now it all came out.

Howard could see the picture Lastun carried bore only a slight resemblance to the girl in the picture on the table. Howard felt his chest ache for his friend, Bizzy and the child they'd never seen.

It took a while for Lastun to begin to regain his composure. He wiped his eyes with his hand. "What's the plan?"

Together, they plotted their mission. As it turned out, the recon was a good idea. They now had a lay of the land. Even though Phil could not be a part of their takedown, he had a strategy to help them from the outside.

When they were done, Lastun asked, "Where are the guns?"

Izzy and JJ looked at Phil.

"No freakin' guns," Phil said in a raised voice.

"What?" Lastun asked.

"Look, this is New York. You're not on the farm anymore. Guns are illegal here. And besides, if you have guns, people are definitely going to die, and some of them might be you. I'm trying to save your feeble asses, not help you get them shot off."

"Won't Mr. Gold's men have guns?" Lastun asked.

"Probably . . . almost certainly."

"And we're gonna break into his house," Lastun continued.

"What part of this aren't you getting? I'm a cop. I'm not going to get you illegal guns," Phil's voice strained to keep from shouting, his expression was as hard as steel.

"So, we're just gonna sneak in and what . . . ugly 'em to death?" Lastun spoke, a hard edge in his voice.

"He's got a point. I'd feel better carrying a piece."

"Damn," Phil exploded. "JJ, you of all people should know better."

"Sorry, man, it's just that this is going to be tough. The whole thing is way outside of what we do," JJ said, ignoring the looks he was getting from Lastun and Howard.

"I know that, and it's exactly why I don't want guns involved. Look, I'm willing to go balls to the wall with you guys on this, but you have to do it my way. No guns." Phil's tone told them this argument was over.

Howard put his hand on Lastun's shoulder. "We fought barehanded in Nam when we had to. We're battle-trained."

"Yeah, but don't underestimate these guys. They're street trained. I know Lastun here doesn't understand that, but you gotta know it," JJ said.

"I couldn't have said it better," Phil added.

"Yeah, I know that, but our advantage is stealth. They don't know we're coming. They don't know who we are. And they don't know we don't have guns," Howard said.

"You should know that's called a tactical advantage. It'll probably help you more than having guns." Phil said, before laying out exactly what part he intended to play in their mission.

When Phil was finished, Lastun locked eyes with him. After a long moment, he nodded.

"Good, then we're set," Phil said, getting up. "And by the way. This is going to be tougher than you think. Stay focused, and for God's sake, don't any one of you think you can play hero. There are no medals for getting killed."

Howard, JJ and Izzy, who'd been silent through the exchange all let out a sigh of relief.

Phil left to begin his eight to four shift.

Izzy got up to make a large pot of coffee. It was going to be a long night.

34

Howard and Lastun knew that no matter how much planning went into a mission, there was always an X factor, some variable that could not be foreseen. For them, it would be like moving through the jungle on a night mission. They had no idea what the inside of Mr. Gold's house was like. It didn't matter. Once Lastun had seen that mug shot, nothing would alter his resolve to rescue Bizzy and his child. The one thing they did have on their side was time. They planned their mission carefully, and it wasn't just to be cliché that they synchronized their watches before Phil left Izzy's house.

Now they drank coffee and waited until it was time to leave.

Howard looked at Lastun. Even though they'd spent many long nights in the jungle talking about home and families, it wasn't until after he'd visited Mississippi and got the shit kicked out of him by some good ol' boys that he began to comprehend the life that his friend had endured, and regarded as normal, growing up in Satartia. Now, in a couple of hours, only a few miles from his home in Brooklyn, he was going to risk all on a mission where there was no arty back up he could call for, and no fighter jets to signal for a napalm drop. He was literally risking his life to help this black man who'd saved his life, and whose life he'd saved. Their debt to each other was square. This was not gratitude. It was a matter of conscience; a matter of humanity. The color of his skin didn't matter. It was a mission to save a family.

Even JJ, a black man who grew up in New York, and endured his share of American racial injustice, had no working knowledge of what life was like for black people in the south. That was just as much an abstraction in his mind, as it was for most northern whites. The only difference was that he was the only one, other than Phil, who appreciated the gravity of their undertaking. He did know what life and death were like in Harlem on a daily basis. He knew that black families trying to survive there were too often the victims of the violence that pervaded that part of The City. But he was driven by a moral imperative, the one that directed many of the things he did these days He had to help the cause of black people trying to break out of the cycle of injustice that subjugated them, even if that injustice was committed by another black man. He and his wife were planning to start a family, and the thought of another black man's wife and baby being trapped in that hellish existence compelled him to action now.

Izzy was another story. As a white man, a journalist and an activist, he spent much of his working time in the black world. He understood both worlds and, in his travels to the south, he'd a first-hand look at the men in white robes burning crosses. This was not an issue he could ignore. Underneath his elfish appearance, when it came to social injustice he was a man of conscience and deep moral conviction. There was no way he could walk away from this.

Lastun sat silently, staring into his mug. He was on edge. It had been over eight months since he received the first troubling letter from his wife. Now he was only a few hours from reuniting with her and the child he'd never seen. During his time in New York, he realized how little he'd really known about Howard. He, too, knew their score was technically even, but could not fathom the depth of emotion that made this white man so invested in helping him. It was less than seven days since he surprised himself in Mr. Kilgore's store by not calling him "sir." Now he was in New York in a white man's home, with another white man and a black man who had no understanding of what he'd been through. He was truly more grateful to all of them than he could ever express. He hoped when it was over and they were safe, he could introduce Bizzy to them and tell her the story of how they all came together to rescue her and their baby. He wouldn't forget to mention Phil or Jeff, either. Once they were safe, he would express his gratitude to each of them.

At oh-one-thirty they left The Village in JJ's car, with Izzy behind the wheel. It had been raining steadily since ten o'clock. Street lights and neon store signs reflected off the shiny pavement. The big car skidded a little on balding tires, as it rounded corners.

They drove past Mr. Gold's house, number 423. The large man they'd seen the night before was in his usual position, cigarette suspended between his lips, eyes scanning the street.

Once past the house, they looked for the first parking space they could find, which was only four houses away. It was now two o'clock.

The four men sat silently, mentally going over the plan.

Lastun saw Howard checking his pocket for the switchblade.

He looked at Howard: "The war never ends, does it?"

Howard shook his head.

At oh-two-ten, a man walked out of one of the houses ahead of them. He walked down the stairs to the street, faced their car and lit a cigarette. It was the GO signal from Phil's CI.

JJ got out of the car, followed by Lastun and Howard. Izzy stayed behind the wheel, the motor running. The three men hurried down the block and ducked into a side alley. They stayed close to the building, avoiding the rats that scurried out of their way, and made it to the alley running behind the buildings. There was enough ambient city light so they didn't need to risk attracting attention with their flashlights.

At oh-two-fifteen, NYPD dispatch received an anonymous call reporting a disturbance at 418 127th Street. "A lot of screaming," the caller said, "and I think I heard a gunshot."

Phil received a radio call at oh-two-sixteen:

We have a 10-52A, possible gunfire, at 418 127th Street, David, are you in the area?

"10-4 dispatch, we are two minutes out." Phil said.

"David, this is Robert. We are on 7th at 126. Will be right behind you, 10-4, out."

The code was for a report of a domestic dispute, violence, and gunfire. Phil's car was designated "D," David for radio clarity. Robert was car "R," available for backup and driven by patrolman Anthony Rizetti, who Phil trusted.

JJ led Howard and Lastun up the rickety fire escape, being careful not to slip on the wet metal rungs. Not sure of how sturdy it was, they climbed one at a time to the rooftop next to 423. They jumped eight feet down to the roof of 423. Still in good physical condition, Howard and Lastun made soft landings, dropping into a roll, and splashing in puddles of rain.

JJ landed hard, uttering a strangled "ugh," as he fell on to his side.

Howard leaned over him. "Are you okay?"

"Hurt my leg," JJ responded. "Not too bad, I can keep going," he said as Howard helped him to a standing position.

The three crept over to the hatch. JJ limped noticeably.

At oh-two-nineteen, they heard the sirens as the police cars raced up 127th street. Seconds later, they could see the flashing red lights reflecting on the side of the buildings.

Howard slowly pulled open the hatch on the roof, revealing a vertical stairway to the landing on the top floor. JJ knew the bad guys always had a clear escape route in case of emergency.

They climbed down the stairs. Lastun gagged on the stench of squalor Howard and JJ had warned him about. The place smelled of shit, vomit and rot.

They had to move fast. The upstairs had three bedrooms, no light showing from under any of the doors. JJ slowly opened each door, inspecting the interiors. The beam of his flashlight revealed moldy wallpaper and broken plaster. A rat scurried along the baseboard, seeking shelter from the intruding light. None of these rooms were occupied. They descended to the third floor, which had three bedrooms and a bathroom.

JJ slowly opened the door to a room that had a light on inside. A bare chested man lay unconscious in a shabby upholstered chair. A needle and a pistol on the table beside him. He was no threat. He was glad Lastun hadn't seen the gun. It was tempting, even for him. He quietly shut the door and went to one of the darkened rooms — only broken furniture and debris. Lastun went in and grabbed a piece of wood that looked like a broken table leg and held it in a ready position.

Howard opened the door to the third bedroom and shined his light in. Two children slept on mattresses on the floor. One was the size of a four year old. The smaller one appeared to be an infant. He signaled for Lastun to look inside.

Lastun shined his light just off the baby's face so as not to wake him or her. Lastun carefully picked up the child and studied its features in the dim light. The baby uttered a weak cry, as Lastun lifted it from the dirty mat. He still could not tell if it was a boy or a girl. It didn't matter. His heart welled with emotion and he clasped his child to his chest, his closed eyes holding back a torrent of tears.

"C'mon man, we have to go. Let's get your baby out'a here." JJ said.

They made their way down to the second level. Lastun followed Howard and JJ. The noise of the police radios out the street was loud enough to mask the occasional creak of the old wooden stairs.

The second level had an open sitting room. A lamp was lit on an end table. The man dozing on the couch had a pistol under his belt. A soft steady hissing sound emanated from the television which showed only a test pattern.

Time was running out. Lastun looked at Howard, who pointed to himself and the sleeping man, indicating his intention to take care of him.

The flashing red lights from the street and the noises from police radios roused the sleeping sentry. Howard rushed him. When the man tried to reach for his gun Howard, blocked his hand with his left. He saw the knife in Howard's other hand and tried to get up but Howard used his weight to hold him down. The man made a grab for it. Howard pulled the knife back and then quickly plunged it down into the man's chest, pushing down on the handle and piercing the heart. It was the same motion he used with his bayonet in Nam.

JJ checked one of the other rooms which had two beds with two girls sleeping in each. Howard checked another room. Finding it empty, he turned back to JJ, while Lastun — baby in his arms — watched the stairs down to the first level.

JJ and Howard shined their lights on the girl's faces and found one who looked like the mug shot of Bizzy.

Howard's heart sank at the sight of the pitiful creature before him. Shining his light, he saw the scars on the inside of one elbow from countless heroin injections. Lastun handed the baby to him before lifting Bizzy off the bed. The other girls were too deep into their heroin induced comas to stir.

When Lastun saw Bizzy open her eyes, he whispered, "Bizzy, I've got you, baby. You gonna be all right now." She seemed almost weightless in his arms. He cradled her tightly. Tears streamed down his face.

JJ touched Lastun's shoulder. "We're running out of time."

Now they had to get out of the building. If anyone else had been downstairs, they too would have been watching the police activity outside. Only the big man outside the front door now blocked their path.

Outside, Phil was watching for them to make their exit, hoping it would be clean and he wouldn't have to get involved. With no real incident to investigate, he had his partner and the backup unit officers questioning residents to buy time, while Howard and his cohorts made their way through the house.

JJ, Howard carrying the baby, Lastun carrying Bizzy, paused just inside the door. The big man's attention was fixed on the police activity across the street.

JJ made a leaping rush for the door, pulled it open and pushed the much larger man so hard he fell down the short flight of stairs, landing on the sidewalk.

Howard ran next. Carrying the baby, he jumped over the big man and took off after JJ, who'd already gotten to the car. Izzy had the motor running and the transmission in gear. He held the brake with his left foot and his right was over the accelerator, ready to mash it to the floor.

Phil watched from beside his car.

Howard jumped into the back seat with the baby and turned to watch Lastun approach.

Carrying the greatest weight, Lastun was slowest.

The guard managed to stand up after Lastun had stepped over him. Ignoring the police cars, he pulled his gun and fired down the street. Lastun staggered. Howard pulled him and Bizzy into the car, pulling the door closed behind them.

Izzy hit the gas hard. The bald tires spun before gaining traction, and the car fishtailed as it rounded the corner. They never saw Phil run from his patrol car and fire two shots, one striking the guard in the neck, killing him instantly.

As the escape car picked up speed, Howard shouted, "Lastun's hit."

"Damn," JJ said, "Izzy head to St. Luke's hospital on hundred fourteenth.

Epilogue

It was Christmas Eve, a time for family gatherings. The Wilson family and friends were in their cozy apartment on the lower East Side of Manhattan. The Christmas tree took up almost a quarter of the room, and its colorful lights added a cheery glow. Presents wrapped in multi-hued paper were piled under and around the tree.

When Solomon Wilson finished telling his story, the room was silent. His wife, Corlene, sat beside him and patted his hand. His son, fifteen-year-old Gideon sat opposite, wide-eyed, trying to take in everything his father had told him.

"And that's how your Uncle Howard and Grandpa Lastun saved Grandma Bizzy and me," Solomon Wilson said.

JJ Wilson and his wife, Kareena, who Solomon Wilson called Mom and Dad, Howard Fishman, and his wife Leah, and Izzy and his wife Willow all joined them for this occasion.

Forty-year-old Solomon saw it as a rite of passage for his son to hear the full story of his father and his grandparents with one of the original participants, Howard Fishman, here to validate it.

"I thought you always said Grandpa Lastun got killed in a mugging," Gideon challenged. His muscled physique looked nothing like his father's gaunt frame.

"That's what I thought, too. That's what Grandpa JJ told me. But when I reached the age you are now," Solomon said, glancing over at Howard, who returned his gaze. "Howard, Izzy, and Grandpa JJ told me what really happened. And now, you know what really happened, too."

"Why didn't you guys tell the truth from the beginning?" Gideon's questioning look encompassed both men.

Howard leaned forward. Age and the sedentary lifestyle of a college professor had added a slight paunch. "Gunshot wounds had to be reported to the police. Still do. We didn't want your grandfather involved in the incident that night at Mr. Gold's building. So when we arrived at the hospital, I took Lastun in separately. After all, he'd been visiting me and we'd been seeing the sights...at least that was our story. I explained that Lastun and I had gotten separated and he'd wandered into an unsafe area where he'd been mugged and shot. I searched for him, found him and rushed him to the hospital."

"Did they ask why you didn't call nine-one-one?"

Howard had forgotten how many things had changed since then, and how young people like Gideon took them all for granted. "No nine-one-one, and no cell phones back then. All I could do was use JJ's car to get him to the hospital as fast as I could. Besides . . ." Howard paused and his eyes teared up. "He was already dead. The bullet pierced his liver and he bled out in the car. There was really nothing anyone could have done."

Gideon looked at his father, who put a consoling hand on his son's shoulder.

"I can't tell you how angry I felt," Howard continued. He faced Solomon. "Lastun fought in Vietnam for a year. Won a bronze star. Then came back to America only to be killed by a drug pusher's gunman.

"I was enraged at Lastun's parents and Bizzy's parents, too, because they wouldn't tell him the truth about what had happened to your grandmother. Lastun was so torn up when he found out she had run away, I had to help him find her. He was only twenty, I was twenty-two, but we felt a lot older. We were just back from combat, full of piss and vinegar. We took a big chance that night and, in his final moment, Lastun did know that we saved Bizzy and his son.

His parents buried him in Satartia. He was still on active duty, so as the only surviving relatives, they received his ten thousand dollar death benefit. That was probably more than the Wicker family had earned in their lifetime before that."

The group sat quietly, while Gideon tried to understand. After a moment, he said to Solomon, "You said Grandma Bizzy ran away because she didn't know if Grandpa Lastun or that Barber guy was your father. They have DNA tests now. Why don't you find out for sure who your father is?"

Solomon plucked at his lower lip. "I thought about it, but decided I didn't need to know. Lastun is the one that came for me. He acted like a father. I don't care what a DNA test might show. As far as I'm concerned, Lastun Wicker is my biological father. Just like JJ and Kareena are my adoptive parents."

Gideon nodded his head in understanding.

"Anyway," Solomon said picking up Howard's story thread, "while Uncle Howard was taking Lastun into the ER, Izzy and JJ took Bizzy and me in separately. Izzy told them that he was out working on a story and ran across this black woman and her baby passed out on the street."

Sleet began falling, the drops making a *tick-tick* sound on the window. The weather forecast predicted it would turn to snow before morning.

"Grandma Bizzy was very sick. We told you that she died of pneumonia," Howard said to Gideon. "That's partially true. She was also severely addicted to heroin and the hospital put her in detox. The combination was too much for her frail body." His expression grew grim.

Howard pulled a handkerchief from his pocket and dabbed at his eyes. "It's ironic. She was a slave, a sex slave, the property of Mr. Gold, a black man. Her life ended no different really, than many of your ancestors of a century-and-a-half ago."

Gideon used his sleeve to dry his eyes, as did Solomon.

JJ stepped in. "You should know that our rescue and Lastun's murder by Gold's guard gave Phil probable cause to conduct a search of the building. He found the babies, the other women, and a substantial drug cache. That was enough to put Gold and his associates in prison for a long time. We know Gold died in prison, knifed by another inmate. That's what I call justice."

"My parents and I arranged to have Bizzy buried in a cemetery in Queens," Howard said. "As far as her parents were concerned, she'd just disappeared. That's the way they saw it when Lastun was in Nam, and we didn't see the need to change that. Just like they thought it was better that Grandpa Lastun not know what happened to her and where she went when she ran away, we—Izzy, JJ, and Phil—thought it best that her parents never know where she went and what happened to her." His voice carried a note of bitterness.

"And now we come to me," Solomon said, with a sad smile. "When I was born, I was just as strung out as my mom was because the drugs Mr. Gold put in her system were in my system, too. And I was undernourished when my rescuers . . ." Solomon paused and gave a look of gratitude to Howard, ". . . found me. I spent several weeks in the hospital's pediatric ICU ward."

Corlene stood. "I'm going to put on a fresh pot of coffee. Gideon, do you want some hot cocoa?"

"Thanks, Mom," Gideon said, not yet able to manage a smile.

Solomon continued his tale. "No birth certificate was issued when I was born. Surprise, surprise. Izzy knew a guy, who knew a guy, who could get one for me...a real, legitimate birth certificate. Reporters are a very resourceful group of people."

"Is that why you became a reporter, Dad?" Gideon asked.

Solomon nodded. "Yes. Izzy encouraged me. Opened doors for me. I was lucky to have men like Izzy, Phil, JJ, and Howard take me under their wings. They each helped me in different ways."

"Corlene," Howard called, "I think I'll have something a little stronger."

"The birth certificate gave my name as Baby Wicker, listed Lastun Wicker as my father and Bessie Polk as my mother," Solomon said. "Grandma Kareena knew somebody at DCF who filed papers giving her and JJ temporary custody of me.

"This was before Grandma Bizzy died. She was still hospitalized and couldn't care for a child. After she died, Grandpa JJ and Grandma Kareena adopted me and named me Solomon Wilson, giving me—and ultimately you—our last name." Solomon held out his hands. "And the rest, as they say, is history."

Gideon thought for a moment, watching the rain through the misty window. "Was that Barber guy really dead?"

Solomon looked at Howard.

"We think so," Howard said. "Izzy made a few inquiries. All he could discover was that Ellis Barber disappeared. It seems he and his buddies were always in trouble. Izzy and I concluded that his gang preferred to dispose of his body rather than report our fight to the sheriff." Howard smiled. "More poetic justice. A white guy killed by a black guy in the south disappears. That would have been hard for them to explain. That's one of many reasons why I haven't gone back there. I don't think anyone remembered my name, except Lastun's family." He cocked an eyebrow toward Solomon. "And we know they were excellent secret-keepers. But if I'd gone there and somebody saw my face, they might have remembered me." He held up a hand. "Plus, they didn't have computers or any kind of national crime database. Even if Barber's death had been reported, it's unlikely anyone would have thought to look for me here."

"Was it really that bad in the south? For blacks, I mean," Gideon asked.

Howard shrugged. "When we were in Nam, Lastun and I sat up late some nights and he would tell me stories of what it was like for black people when he was growing up. When I visited Satartia with your grandpa, I saw it for myself. I saw a black community living in fear of the white community, and the KKK. It was horrible. The civil rights movement was supposed to change things. It changed the laws to give black people legal equality. Changing attitudes takes a lot longer. Now, forty years later, blacks can sit at lunch counters and in the front of the bus, but Confederate flags still fly and statues still commemorate Confederate heroes. While the Civil Rights struggle brought a lot of the racial injustice to light, it also continued a great conflict . . . one that still challenges our national sense of morality and justice."

"Do you remember when I gave you 'the talk'?" Solomon asked, making air quotes with is fingers. "Not the one about the birds and the bees."

"About how to act if a cop stops me?"

"Yes. That's only part of the problem that still exists in this country. That's why I'm going to write a book about Grandpa Lastun and Uncle Howard, and Grandma Bizzy. I'll have to fictionalize it, of course . . . change the names of the people and the places. I'm going to title it, *The War Never Ends*."

Howard shifted in his seat. "That's what Lastun said to me that last night before we went out."

Solomon looked his son in the eyes. He hoped that by the time Gideon had a child old enough to hear this story, the war might have ended. But for now," Solomon added. "It still hasn't."

Ω

About the Authors

Gary Ader was born and raised in New York City, where he received his Bachelor's Degree from Adelphi University. He has had a multi-faceted career, working in government, private industry, and as a business entrepreneur for over twenty years in the travel industry. A Hendersonville, North Carolina resident, he has also lived in Florida and the Washington, DC area. His first novel, *Two-Lane Blacktop* was published in 2019.

Tom Hooker was born and raised in North Mississippi, receiving a degree from the University of Mississippi. He and his family have lived in Hendersonville, North Carolina since 1988. Tom has had short stories and poems published in a number of literary journals across the nation.

Tom taught a creative writing course entitled, "Hooks, Handles, and Men with Funny Hats," through the Blue Ridge Community College continuing education program from 2010 to 2012. He also published a non-fiction work entitled *Calvary's Child: The Life of Amanda Carol Hooker*.

www.ingramcontent.com/pod-product-compliance
Lightning Source LLC
Chambersburg PA
CBHW052022240626
47153CB00006B/1921